WAITING FOR YOU

ANNAPOLIS HARBOR SERIES

LEA COLL

WAITING FOR YOU

How can Ava resist her best friend's brother when she's crushed on him since childhood?

I didn't think Alex could get any hotter, but his time at med school was good to him.

Dirty blond hair. A bit of scruff across his chiseled jawline. And a body beneath those scrubs that makes me think all sorts of naughty things.

Alex seems to be utter perfection… and he barely notices I exist.

Or so I thought. Lately, everywhere I look he's there. Renting a room in my bed and breakfast. Devouring my pastries. Wanting to talk every morning over coffee. Is it possible my lifelong crush finally sees me as more than his little sister's best friend?

Download two free novellas, *Swept Away* and *Worth the Risk*, when you sign up for my newsletter.

Copyright © 2021 by Lea Meyer

Waiting for You

All Rights Reserved.

This book contains material protected under International and Federal Copyright Laws and Treaties. Any unauthorized reprint or use of this material is prohibited. No part of this book may be reproduced or transmitted in any form or by any means, electronic or mechanical, including photocopying, recording, or by an information and retrieval system without express written permission from the author.

All characters and storylines are the property of the author and your support and respect is greatly appreciated.

This is a work of fiction. Names, characters, places and incidents either are the product of the author's imagination or are used fictitiously, and any resemblance to actual persons, living or dead, business establishments, events, or locales is entirely coincidental.

Editing by Olivia Kalb Editing

Editing by The Ryter's Proof

Proofreading by My Brother's Editor

Cover Design by Okay Creations

Photography by Wander Aguiar

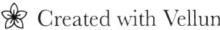 Created with Vellum

BOOKS BY LEA COLL

Annapolis Harbor Series

Hooked on You

Only with You

Lost without You

Perfect for You

Crazy for You

Falling for You

Waiting for You

Second Chance Harbor Series

Fighting Chance

One More Chance

Lucky Chance

Mountain Haven Series

Infamous Love

Adventurous Love

Impulsive Love

All I Want Series

Choose Me

Be with Me

Burn for Me

Trust in Me

Stay with Me

Take a Chance on Me

Download two free novellas, *Swept Away* and *Worth the Risk*, when you sign up for her newsletter.

To learn more about her books, please visit her website.

CHAPTER ONE

AVA

Laila and Charlie led the way down the flower-lined aisle, dropping red rose petals to the lilting notes of "Pachelbel Canon". Nolan stood, his back to the water, in a charcoal suit and a purple tie to match the ribbon in the girls' hair.

I followed at a sedate pace, enjoying the way the music drifted over the water, the twinkling lights that hung in long strands from the trees, and the affection shining in his eyes for Juliana's girls.

Charlie had just reached the last aisle when she dropped her basket and ran the last few feet toward Nolan, her curls flying behind her. She wrapped her arms around Nolan's leg, squeezing him tight.

"You're not supposed to run," Laila admonished as she finished carefully placing her petals on the ground.

The guests around us chuckled softly.

Nolan touched Charlie's head, running his fingers over her hair before dropping down to her level. He whispered something to her that I couldn't hear. Then he lifted her in his arms, holding her on one hip.

Laila picked up Charlie's basket, then took Nolan's outstretched hand to stand next to them.

"I'm so proud of you." Nolan squeezed Laila's hand, then kissed Charlie's cheek.

This time, he spoke loudly enough for everyone to hear.

I sighed. Tears making my throat tight.

I hadn't thought love like Nolan and Juliana's was possible, but they proved me wrong each day, when their love only seemed to deepen.

Nolan nodded slightly at me before his gaze drifted over my head. The music picked up. The guests stood. Juliana must be standing at the end of the aisle. It was my cue to take my place across from Nolan and the girls.

My gaze snagged on the musician. Sitting a few feet away from Nolan and the girls, his head bowed over a wooden cello. His eyes closed, his head and shoulders moved in time with his bow, reminding me so much of Alex, my best friend Savannah's brother. He'd played the cello in high school. But I hadn't seen him in years, and he was supposed to be in med school in New York.

I ignored the pang of disappointment as I focused on Juliana.

Juliana smiled, one hand in the crook of Dad's elbow and a bouquet of red roses in the other as she slowly walked down the aisle, never taking her gaze off of Nolan.

Juliana wore a romantic, off-the-shoulder, lace corset ball gown with floral lace embroidery that cascaded from the bodice down her box-pleated full skirt with multi-layers of silk and sparkle tulle. Her hair had been styled to lie in waves around her shoulders. The look was simple and elegant. She was beautiful. Her happiness radiated from her.

I looked at Nolan to see his reaction to his fiancée at the same time he mouthed, "I love you."

I blinked back tears. Juliana and the girls deserved every bit of happiness, and it was all due to Nolan. He'd come into their lives, easily falling for them. I dabbed at the tear that broke free, not wanting to smear my makeup.

Taking a few deep breaths to clear the urge to cry, I looked up. My gaze caught on the cellist. It was him. Alex St. James. Savannah's older brother.

Suddenly, my dress felt too tight. The air was still. I struggled to draw in a deep breath.

His face and body had filled out since high school. He was more polished. The lines of his body spoke of the confidence he'd gained in college and med school.

Handsome in a gray suit, black tie, and crisp white button-down, his fingers moved over the strings with ease, his head moving slightly with the bow. His gaze, along with the music, sent tingles through my whole body, bringing me back to those moments when I'd sit on the steps in his house after everyone else had gone to bed, listening to him play.

My heart rate picked up, galloping in my chest.

He caught me examining him. He raised a single brow. Blond hair slicked back, his one curl fell over his forehead. Blue eyes seeing me—heating me from the inside out. He was sexy.

And he'd never looked at me like this. His gaze was knowing, like he knew exactly what I was working through in my mind.

His eyes closed for a minute as the notes drifted softly off. I never wanted him to stop playing.

Ripping my gaze from Alex, I focused on Nolan, who had set Charlie on her feet at some point and was now facing Juliana, the girls standing next to them.

Had Alex known I'd be here? Being the bride's sister, I'm sure he guessed. What had he been expecting? The same girl who teased him mercilessly about girls he talked to because I desperately wanted his attention?

I'd been so preoccupied with the opening of the B & B I wasn't involved with the wedding planning. All I knew was that Juliana booked a musician.

I knew Nolan had something planned before the official ceremony with the girls, but I wasn't sure what.

Nolan held his hand out to Charlie, taking a large, white velvet box from his hand. He crouched to their level, opening the box. Two heart necklaces rested against the felt, single diamonds on each reflecting the sun.

"Laila." Nolan looked at her, then at her sister. "Charlie, thank you for letting me into your lives. I love both of you"—he stopped to clear his throat—"so much. I love your mother. I want us to be a family. Laila, will you be mine?"

"Yes, yes, yes." She practically bounced on her toes in excitement as Nolan clasped the necklace on her.

"Charlie, will you be mine?" Nolan asked, his voice thick with emotion.

She nodded.

He kissed her cheek before sliding her necklace around her neck. His voice softened, "I love you."

"We love you, too," Laila said.

I saw a few in the front row dab their eyes with tissues. Tears easily slid down my cheeks. Would I ever find this kind of love with anyone? It seemed so out of reach. So impossible. It was a once-in-a-lifetime thing.

My gaze rested on Alex. His attention was on Nolan and the girls, his cello resting on his shoulder between his widespread legs.

Nolan took both girls' hands, kissing each one on the cheek before standing to kiss Juliana's. I didn't need to see her face to know she was crying.

Nolan and Juliana stood side by side, the girls each holding one of their hands as the preacher went through the traditional wedding vows. It was short and sweet yet so achingly beautiful with the water lapping the shore behind us and the happiness on Nolan, Juliana, Laila, and Charlie's faces. It was perfect.

My heart twinged when I looked at the happy family, then did a flip when I looked at Alex.

When the preacher declared Nolan and Juliana husband and wife, Nolan kissed her before turning them to face the crowd.

Alex picked up his bow to play. The hauntingly beautiful sound of his bow gliding over the strings signaled the end of the formal ceremony.

There didn't seem to be a dry eye between my dad and Nolan's family. I ignored the pang of sadness whenever I thought of my mom not being here. For a long time, a part of me held out hope she'd show up one day—maybe on my sixteenth birthday, high school or college graduation, or Juliana's wedding—to say she'd made a huge mistake. But she never did.

Walking behind Juliana and Nolan, the girls running ahead down the aisle, I knew I was naive to think she ever would.

I waited patiently next to the happy couple while everyone congratulated them, most stopping to say something to Charlie and Laila. Laila loved the attention, but I knew Charlie was feeling a little uncomfortable. Exchanging a look with Juliana when Charlie started edging away, I held my hand out to Charlie. "Want to see what food they're serving?"

With a grateful nod, she placed her smaller hand in mine. Charlie had been diagnosed with selective mutism. It meant she didn't talk until she got comfortable with someone. There was no rhyme or reason for it. Some people she warmed up quickly to, and she'd made a lot of progress in kindergarten, but events like this easily overwhelmed her.

I guided her to one of the tables for the reception. Guests slowly joined us, finding their seats, and talked quietly while Alex continued to play softly in the background.

If he approached me, I wasn't even sure what I'd say. Had we ever said anything to each other back then that wasn't a joke? We'd driven him crazy, teasing him relentlessly when a girl called, and in return, he'd pulled pranks on us by switching out the toothpaste with shaving cream or by placing whipped cream in our shoes. It was lighthearted, but we weren't friends.

"Can I play?" Charlie asked me.

"What do you mean?"

"The man playing the music. Can I play?"

"Oh, you mean Alex. He plays the cello. You want to try it?"

She nodded.

I'd heard how music could be healing to kids who experienced anxiety or speech issues. "I'm not sure how old you have to be to start. The cello's large."

"I'm sure they make ones that are smaller for kids." Nolan crouched down next to Charlie. "You ready to join us at our table?"

Charlie had a special relationship with Nolan. He'd earned her trust. She nodded eagerly. He pulled her into his arms, carrying her to their table.

I moved to sit with Nolan's brother, Cade, his fiancée, and their friends, Avery and Griffin, and Reid and Dylan. It was September, so the weather was still warm even with the wind coming off the water.

I tried not to pay attention to what Alex was doing when he took breaks from playing. When dinner was cleared, Alex resumed playing closer to the dance floor. My gaze kept straying to him. I'd always been mesmerized when he played. Tingles erupted over my skin as if he was playing just for me when I knew he wasn't.

Nolan and Juliana danced to the song they'd chosen, "With or Without You". The familiar notes wrapped around my heart, making me wonder if that crush I had on Alex way back when was more than a little girl crushing on her friend's brother.

After that song, Nolan danced with the girls together. Laila and Charlie took turns stepping on his toes, laughing and giggling when they fell off. Their father didn't have the same easygoing, fun relationship with them, and it was his fault. Nolan was the perfect man for Juliana and her girls.

Then there was the traditional father-daughter dance. My mom was noticeably absent, but Juliana never seemed as affected as I was by that fact. When my mom left us, Juliana was older and was the one to step up to help my father care for me.

As the night went on, the strings of lights Nolan had put up for the occasion flipped on, giving the backyard a romantic feel. I sipped wine, relaxing when I realized Alex would be preoccupied the entire evening. I relaxed more with each sip of wine and song Alex played. I danced with Juliana and the girls, I ate cake, and I enjoyed the evening.

I let the thoughts about my mother fall away and the worries about what I was doing with my life fade. There was nothing more important than the family that was here now. My father, Juliana, Laila and Charlie, and now Nolan.

At some point, the music switched from live to being played over the speakers. I hadn't even noticed Alex packing up to leave. I was relieved, yet oddly sad that I hadn't talked to him. Had he come home just for the wedding, or was he in town to visit his family?

I headed inside the house to go to the bathroom. I went upstairs, leaving the downstairs bathroom for guests. Freshening my makeup and checking to make sure my hair was still styled in the updo the stylist did before the wedding, I headed back downstairs.

Walking back through the kitchen, a man was in the open fridge. He turned, twisting the cap off a water bottle before lifting it to his mouth. He took a long pull of water, his Adam's apple bobbing.

Blond hair, strong, broad back, neatly trimmed nails. He

lowered the bottle, turning to face me.

"Alex?" All of the air rushed out of my lungs.

His lips curled into a smile. "Ava Breslin."

My heart pounded under my rib cage. "That's me."

Silence fell between us. With no cello or music between us, there was nothing to stop his gaze from drifting over me, heating my skin as he went.

"It's good to see you—" he said at the same time I said, "I wasn't expecting to run into you here."

I laughed. "I'm sorry."

"No. Go ahead." He gestured for me to continue.

"I was just saying I was surprised to see you here. I didn't know Juliana hired you to perform." My heart was pounding a steady rhythm in my ears.

He rested the bottle on the counter behind him. "The person she hired backed out at the last second. My mom said she needed someone to fill in, so I volunteered."

"That's nice of you." Should I ask what he was doing in town? I didn't want this moment to end for some reason. I wanted to stretch it out, gaining whatever information I could. "I didn't know you were back in town."

He nodded. "I'm studying to be an emergency room doctor, so I'm doing part of my residency at a hospital in the city."

"Oh. That makes sense." I tried not to cringe at my lame response.

"Once I'm finished, I'll head back to New York."

My heart pinched at the knowledge that he wasn't back for good. Annapolis was a pit stop for him.

He'd be busy with his residency in the city. I'd be busy at the B & B. There'd be no reason for me to see him again. I attempted a polite smile. "It was nice to see you."

I moved past him, wanting to get outside for some fresh air. I couldn't seem to draw in a deep breath around him. He touched me. Looking down, his calloused fingers wrapped around my wrist, holding me loosely in place.

I couldn't bring myself to pull away. We stood close enough I could feel his body heat. He'd filled out since high school. His shoulders were broad, his chest defined under the white button-down shirt, his waist trim.

"Juliana said I could stay at the B & B."

"Yeah, some of the guests are staying there." I hadn't seen his name on the guest list, but Juliana handled the wedding block personally.

"She said you're the manager."

He still held my wrist between us, yet I couldn't break the connection. I didn't want to. When had I ever been this close to him?

"That's right. With two small kids, she couldn't live on site and handle the day-to-day stuff." I was rambling.

Why was he making me so nervous? We weren't kids anymore. Maybe that was the thing that threw me off my axis around him—our dynamic had changed. He wasn't just Savannah's brother anymore. He was a man studying to be a doctor who played his cello at weddings. He seemed like a nice guy. If he were anyone else, I'd consider getting his number. But he wasn't. He was still Savannah's brother. Off-limits in more ways than one.

He winked. "I look forward to catching up."

That one sexy move had me blinking in confusion. He'd winked at me. Was he flirting?

He released my hand, moving away from me in one easy movement. I felt bereft.

"Good seeing you, Ava." He pushed open the door to the backyard, disappearing.

Ava. His deep voice saying my name did funny things to my heart. It was fluttering in my chest. He almost never said my name. Back then, he'd called me a brat.

My breath was raspy, my chest heaved. What just happened?

It was like that crush I felt when we were kids never went away. Instead, it morphed into something else entirely, something that took up every nook and cranny in my chest, threatening to burst free. It felt a lot like hope and happiness.

I shook my head. It had to be the wedding and Nolan and Juliana's obvious love for each other. It made me long for something similar for myself. In the light of day, I'd remember love and relationships weren't for me.

CHAPTER TWO

ALEX

I showered and pulled on jeans and a long-sleeve shirt. My heart rate picked up in anticipation of seeing Ava this morning as I descended the steps of the quaint but luxurious B & B. At the wedding, everyone's gaze was on the little girls dropping petals haphazardly down the aisle, but I'd been transfixed by the bridesmaid in the lavender dress—my sister's best friend—Ava Breslin. Her blonde hair was piled on top of her hair in an intricate updo, but it was her eyes that caught my attention. Soft and full of love as she watched her nieces.

I rounded the corner to find Ava smiling at another guest. The counter was filled with platters of waffles, pancakes, fruit, and pastries.

I never thought I'd enjoy staying at a B & B. Normally I'd prefer the solitude of a hotel until I found a rental, but Juliana had insisted I stay here for the evening for free. I couldn't turn her down. Coming to a stop in front of Ava, I was glad I'd agreed.

"Morning."

Ava lifted her head, meeting my gaze. "Alex. How are you this morning?"

Did her voice waver with nerves, or was that my imagination? "Great."

I'd slept well for the first time in a long while. The pressure of medical school had taken its toll. It was good to be home with familiar places and people.

Her lips curled into a smile. "Are you hungry?"

I rested a hand on my stomach. "I'm starving."

Pleased, she said, "I have anything you could possibly want, and if you don't see it, I can make it."

"When did you become such a great cook?" I asked, sitting on a chair at the counter.

She raised a brow. "You don't know if I can cook yet."

I glanced around the room. The other guests were eating at the large farm table. "I don't see anyone complaining."

"Can I get you something to start?"

I saw the stack of plates, silverware, and napkins. She probably preferred the guests to serve themselves so she could cook and bake without interruptions. "I can get it."

Piling my plate high with a little of everything offered, I poured syrup over it.

"Would you like something to drink? Coffee or tea?"

"Coffee, please. As long as it's not hospital coffee, I'm sure it's great."

"Congratulations on becoming a doctor. Your parents are so proud of you. You're all they talk about."

My heart pinged at her mention of my parents' expectations. "I think they would have preferred me going the surgeon route, but it's not for me."

She poured coffee into a mug that said I heart Annapolis, then pushed it toward me. "Are you pursuing music, too?"

"My parents always said I wouldn't make any money being a classically trained cellist." I smiled to cover the way that made me feel. When my sister found out she was pregnant, she dropped out of college. The pressure to be successful was transferred to me.

She tipped her head to the side. "You played popular music last night."

"I create my own mixes of popular songs. Usually putting two together."

"It was beautiful."

"Thank you." Her praise washed over me in a way no one else's ever had. I knew people enjoyed my music. It was what spurred me to keep performing, but something about Ava's admiration boosted my soul.

She appreciated my music when I was a teenager. I knew she used to sneak out of Savannah's room to listen to me play at night. I never called her out on it because I liked that she enjoyed it. I played for her. Most kids at that age didn't have an appreciation for classical music. It wasn't something the girls were attracted to—not like if I was a drummer or a guitarist.

"I compose my own songs, too."

"I'd love to hear that sometime." Her expression was genuine.

I didn't get the impression she was flirting with me because I was a doctor or had a following on social media for my songs. But I couldn't be sure. I'd dated women before whose endgame was to be a doctor's wife.

"That can be arranged." I smiled at her. Grabbing a pastry from my plate, I took a huge bite. Chewing, I said, "Mmm. This is amazing. Did you make this?"

Her face flushed. "I did."

"You should be selling these."

"That's partly why I took this job. I can practice my concoctions on people without any expectations."

I racked my brain for what I could remember Savannah saying about Ava's life over the last few years. "I thought you were working as a graphic designer?"

"I was. I didn't like the long hours or the competitiveness.

It was sucking the life out of my soul." She laughed. "Sorry, I don't mean to be so dramatic."

"It's good you recognized it wasn't right for you."

She visibly relaxed. "I enjoy running the B & B. For now, anyway. Who knows what the future holds?"

Her positive outlook was attractive. "Are your parents supportive?"

She tensed, looking away from me. "My father supports me no matter what."

I wished I would've paid closer attention to what Savannah said about her over the years. "What about your mother?"

I held my breath, knowing from her uncomfortable posture I wouldn't like her answer.

She finally looked at me. "She left a long time ago. I'm surprised you don't remember."

I reached a hand out to cover hers. "I'm sorry. I'm sure Savannah mentioned it, but I was so caught up in myself, it didn't register."

"It's not something you need to apologize for. At the time, it seemed like everyone around me knew about it, or at least, that's how it felt."

I wanted to know more about her, even though it was none of my business.

"Where are you staying while you're here?"

"That's what I wanted to talk to you about."

She raised a brow while she wiped down the already spotless countertops.

"I wanted to see if I could extend my stay here."

It was in the heart of Annapolis, so I could walk to the bars and restaurants, but more importantly, Ava was here. My heart tripped at the thought of seeing her every morning and evening.

Her nose scrunched. "Aren't you working in the city?"

The commute to the city would be about forty-five

minutes or more, depending on the time of day, but I worked odd shifts. "I don't want to stay in the city. While I'm here, I want to be home."

Home. I'd never thought of New York as home. I thought it would be an adventure to go to college, then med school in New York, but the dirty streets, tiny apartments, and numerous roommates never felt like home. Not like Annapolis. Not like this kitchen, with its aroma of baked goods and fresh-brewed coffee.

"Do you have room?" I wasn't sure what I'd do if she said no. I might have to stay with my parents. I felt too old to be living in my childhood home again.

Ava studied my face as if she wasn't sure I was being completely honest. "I'll have to check the reservations to make sure no one reserved your room in particular."

"I don't mind moving to a different one if that's the case."

She tilted her head. "Are you sure?"

Looking at her, I knew I wasn't making a mistake. I wanted to be in Annapolis. I wanted to reconnect with my friends from home, but more importantly, I wanted to get to know her. "Positive."

"Okay. I'll see what I can do. Will you need breakfast every morning during your stay?"

Was she being formal to depersonalize our conversation? "Are you cooking?"

She smiled faintly. "I'm here every day."

The way her smile faded when I asked about her job made me wonder if she was truly happy here.

"Then I'd love breakfast. Do you provide snacks or dinner, too? Juliana offered me the room, but I didn't research the amenities." Or the beautiful host.

"I try to put out baked goods in the afternoon—cookies or cupcakes. I like to experiment with recipes, and the guests are my guinea pigs." She smiled, easy and carefree. It made her look even younger.

"I don't mind being your guinea pig." I winked at her, and she flushed.

Conversation flowed easily, and I was curious about her, but I couldn't forget I was only in town for a few months. I wanted to get a job in the best hospital, working with the best doctors, so I had to focus on my residency, not how attractive my sister's best friend turned out to be.

"I don't provide dinner because there are so many restaurants within walking distance."

"And it's a bed-and-breakfast." I sipped the coffee she'd handed me. She must have freshly brewed the beans, it was so flavorful.

"That, too. I want to provide the best experience possible for the guests. Have you seen the garden yet?"

I shook my head. "Like I said, I came here because Juliana offered me the room. She said she owned the place, and a few of the wedding guests were staying here. I didn't have a chance to look it up."

"I'd love to show you around after I clean up breakfast."

"I'll be here." I wondered if she offered to show the grounds to every guest. I liked to think it was because she felt something toward me, something more than an obligation to her friend's brother.

She grabbed the pitcher of orange juice and took it to the guests sitting at the farm table. Taking a bite of the blueberry pancakes, I closed my eyes in delight as the berries burst in my mouth. These had to be out of a garden.

I couldn't believe the girl that used to hide in my room and jumped out screaming to scare me was the same woman in front of me today.

My heart skipped a beat when I realized she might be dating someone.

I watched her interact with the guests, pausing to pour orange juice while she answered a guest's question about the best antique store, crab cake, or the best thing to do while they were in town.

She answered each question thoughtfully, never giving away her personal favorite.

She was such an attentive hostess. She probably asked the guests where they were from and why they were visiting when they checked in, then cataloged the information when she was making recommendations on what to see or do.

At the same time, there was this invisible wall between her and the guests—one she didn't let them cross. Would she let me in?

CHAPTER THREE
AVA

My hands shook as I carried the heavy glass pitcher filled with fresh-squeezed orange juice around the table. I asked the two couples how their stay was going and answered their questions about touring Annapolis, but my mind was on Alex.

He sat at the counter, shoveling in my food like someone was going to take it from him at any moment. I took that to mean he liked my cooking. The idea warmed my chest.

While we were talking, he was so attentive, interested in my life and the B & B. It was such a contrast to how he was when we were kids. Back then, he didn't have a second to spare his younger sister or her friend. But now, it was like he was seeing me for the first time.

My mother leaving in middle school was the worst thing that had happened in my life. I assumed she must have left because I was so difficult. I tried to be good to make it easier on my dad. I worried he'd leave me, too, and then where would we be?

As I got older, I realized he'd never do that. But I was never sure how my mother could walk away like we meant nothing. I tried to ask Juliana over the years, but she refused to talk about it or even keep pictures of her on the walls.

Mentally, I shook my head. It must have been Alex popping back into my life and Juliana's wedding that had my mother at the forefront of my mind.

I felt Alex's gaze on me while I replenished the food and drinks until everyone was finished. When we were alone, Alex sipped his coffee at the counter.

"I'll clean up, then we can go." I began carrying the dishes to the dishwasher, rinsing them off, then placing them inside.

"I can help." I turned to find Alex carrying the empty platters of food.

"You're a guest. You don't need to clean."

"I want to help. Besides, I'm not really a guest. I'm an old friend."

"Are you now?" I exchanged a smile with him. We were never friends.

"Or a pest."

I laughed. "That's more like it. We were horrible to you back then. Constantly annoying you, messing with any girls that called or showed up."

He tapped my nose. "You were incorrigible."

The movement should have felt belittling, but instead, it felt intimate, his choice of words sweet. "If you say so."

He stood by my side, drying the dishes I washed by hand. I wiped the table and counters with a dishcloth, taking my time, wondering if he had someplace to be or if he'd back out of my offer. I wasn't sure why I'd offered to show him the grounds other than I was proud of what Juliana built and I managed.

"How about that tour?"

"If you're busy, I can take you later." I wanted to give him an out. Alex had never willingly spent time with me or Savannah.

He leaned against the counter, his arms crossed over his chest. "Do I look busy?"

The way he stood emphasized his broad shoulders and the bulge of his biceps. He looked so incredibly handsome. "Nope."

"Then let's go, shall we?" He pushed off the counter, holding out a hand to me.

I took it, wondering what I was doing. To calm my racing heart, I told myself we were old friends getting reacquainted. Soon, he'd be gone. Then he'd be nothing more than the memory he was before. Except this time, it would be so much more vivid.

The warmth of his hand surrounded mine. He ran his thumb over my wrist. I felt the callouses he'd most likely gotten from playing the cello.

"Are you and Savannah still close?"

"We've always been best friends."

"Huh."

I wasn't sure what that meant. Was he asking because he was interested in me, and being friends with his sister would make things complicated, or was he just being polite in asking about my life? "I go over to your family's house for Sunday dinner a couple of times a month. Whenever my family isn't getting together."

"Are you serious?" He rubbed his free hand over his chin. It drew my attention to the light scruff there that made him even more attractive.

We paused on the patio just outside the French doors. "You didn't know?"

"I don't call home as often as I should. I keep in touch with Savannah and Miles. I'm surprised my mom never said anything."

"Maybe she did, and you weren't paying close attention." I hated the idea that he'd paid zero attention to me when I was a kid and then as an adult. Logically, it made sense even if it still hurt. It reminded me a bit of my mother, even though that was ridiculous. I hated the sensation of being looked over—not important enough to remember.

"You have my undivided attention now."

I loved having his focus. I felt it last night in Juliana's kitchen, and I felt it this morning at breakfast. It was a heady feeling—one I could easily become addicted to. "It was a B & B when Juliana bought it, but she wanted to update it, making the rooms into suites larger and more luxurious than they'd been before. She wanted the guests to feel at home in the living areas. That's how she met Nolan. He was her contractor."

"Did they fall in love at first sight?" he teased.

I laughed. "I think he was annoyed with her plans for this place. He wanted to purchase it himself and flip it, but she outbid him. He had his own ideas about the right way to renovate it."

"Contrary to what she envisioned?"

I nodded. "But owning a B & B was Juliana's dream. She had this vision of a more luxurious destination where couples could go to be pampered on anniversaries, and brides and grooms could stay on their wedding night."

"My room's great."

"We're fairly booked in the summer and fall. A little less so in the winter. Nolan expanded the patio, creating the firepit so that guests could have a drink by the fire. He added plenty of flowers and bushes for privacy from the neighbors and just for the aesthetic appeal." I walked slowly around the property, pointing out his additions.

"Is this your creation?" We stopped at one of the boxes Nolan built.

"I wanted to provide some of the fruits and vegetables for breakfast from our own garden."

Alex considered the layout thoughtfully. "It's a nice thing to offer guests."

"They seem to appreciate those details."

"I bet they do."

Pleasure coursed through me at the intensity in Alex's gaze and his words. The B & B was Juliana's, bearing her name and vision. I'd helped refine it, added on to it here and there, but few people acknowledged my contributions.

I led Alex over the pavers to the white gazebo. "Nolan built this for Juliana. They thought they'd get married here, but then Juliana decided to have the ceremony at their new home. She showed that house to him before they started dating. She's a realtor, too."

We stepped inside, standing in the center. "In the evening, I turn the lights on, and it's magical."

"I believe it." Alex stepped toward me.

The gazebo was surrounded by bushes and flowers; a vine hanging from the ceiling made it feel like we were completely alone. It was a romantic spot—perfect for a proposal.

"This is amazing. You should be proud."

I held my hands out to my sides. "This is all Juliana and Nolan's creation."

"You planned the gardens, the food, and the ambiance. You're part of the welcoming atmosphere here. You take care of the guests, recommend the perfect restaurants and tours."

My heart beat loudly in my ears. "I guess so."

"Juliana's B & B wouldn't be the same without you running it."

"Thank you." My throat tightened with emotion. When I quit my job as a graphic designer, my dad and sister thought it was a rash decision even though they knew I was unhappy with my job. Juliana came around to the idea quicker since she needed someone reliable to run the B & B for her. My dad still worried about me, but that was his job as a parent.

A boyish smile played on his lips. "Will you take me around town and show me the best crab cake?"

I laughed. "First of all, I don't show everyone around. I

make recommendations. And you're from here. You don't need a tour guide."

"I never did any of the touristy stuff as a kid. I took it for granted." His lips turned into a slight pout that I found endearing.

He stepped closer still, brushing a strand of hair out of my face.

It felt like he was saying something more—that he was referring to the idea that he'd taken me for granted, too. "Okay."

"Perfect." He smiled widely, stepping back.

Was he referring to me being perfect, or that I was showing him around? The tingly feeling I usually only got when he played his cello was bouncing around my chest like fireworks exploding.

Walking out of the gazebo, he asked, "Can you tell me more about the inn itself? What was here before, what you changed, and your vision for everything? I'm fascinated."

"Fascinated?" I followed him out of the gazebo and the bubble of intimacy we'd created between us.

"Everything about you intrigues me," he said over his shoulder.

"I'm your sister's best friend." I didn't understand his sudden interest in me and what I was doing.

He slowed until we were side by side, pulling me closer and swinging an arm around my shoulder. "Are you saying I should be giving you a hard time instead?"

The position felt easy, like a hug he'd give an old friend, except we'd never been that. His hard body pressed against my side felt good. I placed a hand on his chest. "No. I like this side of you better."

His expression turned serious. "Me, too. And I want to get to know you better while I'm home."

Maybe he was acting out of some misguided obligation to his sister's friend. He felt bad he'd ignored me all those years, which was ridiculous. He did what any other brother would have done.

We walked toward the French doors to the living room. He didn't drop his arm until I opened the door.

His words *while I'm home* volleyed back and forth in my head. I couldn't forget this arrangement was temporary.

I took him on a tour, telling him the history of the B & B I'd learned and the design elements that Juliana and Nolan added. Alex asked thoughtful questions, always careful to ask what I thought of everything.

Nolan was the expert on the renovations, but Juliana was the expert on design elements since she was a realtor, and I was supposed to run the inn how Juliana wanted. Because Juliana's realty business and her girls kept her occupied, I often made snap decisions, not waiting to ask for her input.

I headed to the staircase, intending to go back downstairs, when Nolan said, "What's this door for?"

He'd paused at the end of the hall by the door to the attic.

"That's mine."

"I wondered if you lived here." He looked almost pleased.

"It just makes more sense. The front desk's number is forwarded to my cell so I can attend to the guests' needs right away."

His eyes darkened on the word *needs*. "That's handy."

His expression and use of the word *handy* sent an image to my brain of his hand gripping his cock, squeezing, then giving it a tug.

I quickly shook my head to clear it. There was no way his mind had gone to the same place mine had.

He'd stepped closer during my daydream. "What are you thinking about?"

My face flushed. Had he guessed? "How much I have to do today."

I couldn't say I was thinking of him touching himself.

"What do you have planned?" Alex brushed past me, the heat of his arm warming me.

"I'm actually having dinner at your parents' house."

Pausing in the foyer, he turned to face me. "You're going to family dinner?"

I smiled. "Remember? I told you I go from time to time."

He nodded. "I remember. I just thought you'd be busy with your family tonight because of the wedding."

I couldn't read his expression to determine whether he was annoyed or indifferent to the fact I'd be there. "Nolan and Juliana are leaving tonight on their honeymoon. Dad's watching the girls, so I'm free."

"I'll have to get used to seeing you all the time. I'm staying here, and you're close with my family." His expression was thoughtful.

"Is that going to be a problem?" My heart thudded loudly in my chest as he stepped closer to me.

"I'm looking forward to it."

"Good." I took a few steps toward the front desk, cataloging what I needed to do before I left for the day.

"Ava?"

Turning in his direction, I asked, "Yeah?"

He raised a brow. "Are you planning on bringing any sweets?"

I shrugged. "Your parents say I don't have to."

He grinned. "Let me guess, my dad loves them."

"He does, so I always bring something."

"Like father like son, I guess. Although, I'm sure everyone loves your creations."

"Thank you."

He smiled so brightly my breath caught. His smile, his words, and his touch were lethal. I needed to be on guard around Alex, or I could easily see myself falling for him.

CHAPTER FOUR

AVA

I showered after work, putting on a sundress and sandals. I wanted to talk to Savannah before going to her house, but there wasn't time, and what would I even say to her —*you didn't tell me your brother had turned into a total hottie?* I mean, why would she? She probably didn't even realize it.

She probably still thought that he was gross and annoying. I thought back to how she used to complain about sharing a bathroom with him. How he refused to clean his dirty clothes off the floor. How he wore too much cologne when he went out with girls. Anything to get the current image of him out of my head.

I faltered when I saw Alex leaning against the wall in the foyer.

Pulling in a deep breath, I continued down the steps. When I reached the bottom, I said, "Hey."

I tried not to wince at my uninspired greeting. I was the manager. Surely I could come up with a better greeting than *hey*.

He pushed off the wall. "I thought you'd want a ride."

I closed my eyes at the image that popped into my head of

me riding him. Spending time with him in enclosed spaces wasn't a good idea. "I can drive."

"We're going to the same place, and we're both sleeping here tonight." He gestured around me.

I cleared my throat in an attempt to clear the images from my brain. We were sleeping in the same house, not the same room or even the same bed. "True."

"It's convenient."

It was. If I'd been thinking rationally about the situation, it made perfect sense. He wasn't fixated on sexy thoughts like I was. "All right."

He smiled, seemingly pleased he'd won the argument. He turned away from me to open the door.

The gray dress pants he wore clung to his ass as if they were made for him. Why did he have to be so gorgeous?

To cover my thoughts, I asked, "Do you always dress up for family dinners?"

"I've missed so many I figured I'd give it the respect it deserves."

"Good answer." He was obviously hardworking if he'd made it through med school, and he was sweet to offer to play his cello at Juliana's wedding at the last minute. Sweet and kind and very, very hot. He was the perfect, irresistible package.

We climbed into his SUV, riding in silence for a few minutes.

As Savannah's brother, he was off-limits. We were disgusted by him when we were kids. She wouldn't understand my attraction to him now. The worst part was that I couldn't even discuss it with her.

Alex shifted in his seat. "Your dad still treat you like a kid when you visit?"

I glanced at his face, surprised by the question. "I don't think so."

I'd never really thought about it, but Juliana did treat me

like I was her kid sister in need of her direction and advice. I got it because she'd stepped into the void my mother left.

"I always feel like I have to prove something. Savannah dropped out of college. There's this added pressure to be successful. I don't know, maybe I'm making it bigger in my head."

"Alex. You're studying to be a doctor. I'm sure your parents are proud of you."

I hadn't been at the last few family dinners. That must have been how I missed the news he was coming home. I was dying to ask Savannah why she hadn't mentioned it.

He tapped his fingers on the steering wheel. "They wouldn't get me private lessons for the cello. They wanted me to focus on my studies."

I remembered he'd played in the orchestra at school. "I didn't realize that. You were always so good, I just assumed you were taking private lessons."

"Self-taught, for the most part. I minored in music in college."

"Your parents didn't approve?"

"They couldn't understand why I just didn't focus on premed. But music feeds my soul, you know? I don't think I'd be the same person if I didn't play." He glanced over at me as if gauging my reaction.

I settled deeper into the leather cushions. "I've never played, but I love to listen to you."

He kept his gaze on the road in front of us, but his tone was soft. "I know."

I was stunned for a second. What was he talking about? Had he seen the look on my face when he was playing at the wedding? "What do you mean?"

"When we were kids, I know you used to sit on the steps to listen to me play. Trust me, I know all the creaky boards in that hallway and the steps. I used to sneak out sometimes. And

I knew it wasn't Savannah. It only happened when you were over."

I shifted in my seat to see his face. "Why didn't you say anything?"

"I liked that you wanted to listen. Most kids made fun of me for playing. I thought if you took the time to sneak out of bed to hear me, then you appreciated it."

"I did." I wasn't sure I should admit how his music made me feel, but I wanted him to know that his music affected people. It wasn't a waste of his time. "I get these tingles when you play. It's so beautiful."

I didn't say that I'd never felt that way about anyone else playing. I never knew if it was the sound of the cello I loved, him, or a combination of both. Seeing him play at the wedding was an added bonus. When we were kids, I could only listen through his door.

"I played the nights you came over." His voice was soft, almost hesitant, as if he wasn't sure if he should tell me.

"You did?" My heart was beating an erratic rhythm. Was he saying what I thought he was—he was playing on purpose?

"I played for you." He accentuated his words by catching my gaze and holding for a second before returning his attention to the road.

I played for you. The words bounced around in my head like a Ping-Pong ball, unable to find a place to rest. My heart swelled in my chest.

He stopped in front of his parents' garage, throwing the vehicle in park. "You ready to go in?"

How could he act like he hadn't said something earth shattering? I had so many questions. What did he mean? Why was he telling me now? It felt huge. My chest was swollen with so many indescribable emotions.

He opened his door before I could figure out what to say. I took a second to compose myself, then joined him on the sidewalk.

Instead of knocking on the front door, he opened it, walking in. "I'm home. I brought Ava with me."

His mom, Lilliane, walked down the hall to greet us, pulling Alex down for a hug. "I'm so happy you're home."

My face felt flush, my head dizzy. I wanted time to process what Alex had said in the car. What if it meant something? What if it was nothing? I was on an emotional roller coaster I couldn't seem to get off.

Lilliane turned her attention to me. "So good to see you, Ava. How was the wedding?"

Grateful for something else to focus on, I said, "It was beautiful. The girls were just adorable in their dresses. Nolan asked them to be his."

His mom rested her hands on her chest. "I love that. I wish I could have seen it. I just love weddings."

Wanting an escape, I asked, "Do you think I could get some water?"

"Of course, dear. Help yourself to whatever…." His mom waved me off before turning her attention to Alex.

I headed to the kitchen, grateful for the reprieve. Their voices followed me down the hall as they followed at a more sedate pace.

"How was your drive?"

"I listened to some audiobooks."

"I worry about you driving all that way. I wish you'd fly."

For the millionth time, I wondered why my mother didn't seem to care about us at all.

"I'd spend so much time at the airport it wouldn't be worth it. I could be here already." His tone was laced with irritation.

Lilliane sighed. "I guess. What did you think of the wedding?"

Opening the fridge, I smiled, knowing a wedding was the last thing Alex would want to talk about.

WAITING FOR YOU

"I was a little preoccupied because I was playing." Alex's tone was dry as he entered the kitchen.

Unscrewing the cap of a water bottle, I took a long pull, coating my dry throat. I wondered if Alex was surprised to see me last night. To know that I wasn't a little girl anymore but was grown up. I liked that idea a lot.

I closed the fridge door, resting the cool bottle against my forehead.

His mom pulled open the oven door. Alex winked at me behind her back.

I raised a brow at him. It was too much. Him admitting to me his issues with his family, his fears about coming home, telling me he played for me. He was revealing parts of himself, his hopes and dreams, but I couldn't figure out why.

Unless he liked me. The realization sent my heart galloping. I rested a hand over my racing heart. The idea that Alex was attracted to me was crazy.

The front door opened, then closed.

"Oh good. Savannah's here." His mom pulled a casserole dish out of the oven, placing it on hot pads on the counter.

Jim, Alex's dad, walked in. "Oh good, you're here. I need you to help me with something."

Lilliane rolled her eyes. "He's trying to fix the lawn mower again. I don't understand why he just won't buy a new one."

Miles ran into the kitchen ahead of his mother, Savannah, whose hair was falling out of her ponytail. "You know Dad. He likes to fix things."

"Pop-Pop!" Miles skidded to a halt in front of Jim, talking a mile a minute about whatever video game he played this morning. It sounded like a building game.

"I'd love to hear about it, but did you even notice your uncle is here?"

"Uncle Alex?" Miles spun around, his gaze landing on him. His face filled with excitement.

Alex's face softened as he lifted him for a hug, even though we'd stopped picking him up a year or so ago.

"Can you help me in the garage?" Jim asked Miles.

"Yes!" Miles touched Alex's cheek. "Are you going to help, too?"

"Sure am." Alex leaned down to place Miles on his feet.

"I know you're going to be a great helper." Jim raised a brow at Lilliane.

Odds were that he wouldn't be, but I loved how Jim and Lilliane were so patient and loving with him.

I watched Alex lead Miles to the garage, my heart flip-flopping at the sight of him with his nephew. Seeing him this way was dangerous for my resolve to treat him as nothing more than Savannah's brother.

I hadn't seen Alex interact with Miles since he was born. Back then, Savannah was reeling from the fact Miles's father had passed. They weren't dating when she found out she was pregnant, or when he died, but she was devastated by his death. Facing motherhood alone was daunting. We'd all rallied to support her.

"I have to go throw in a load of laundry. Be right back," Lilliane said.

As soon as we were alone, I hissed, "I can't believe you didn't tell me your brother was performing at Julianne's wedding."

"I didn't think you'd care." She wrinkled her forehead at my outburst, grabbing an apple from the bowl.

Her reaction made me pause. I wasn't supposed to care. Forcing myself to relax, I said, "I wasn't expecting to see him."

"He's just as annoying as he's always been." She bit into the apple.

I swallowed hard. That was the problem. He wasn't annoying anymore. He was the exact opposite.

She rolled her eyes as she chewed. "Apparently, women throw themselves at him because he's going to be a doctor."

WAITING FOR YOU

Jealousy speared my chest. Even if he wasn't Savannah's brother, he was only here for a short time and had no shortage of available women at his disposal.

She raised a brow. "So, how was the wedding? You meet any hot guys?"

I paused, not sure how to answer. I couldn't say the only hot guy I saw was Alex. "Not really."

"That's too bad. You haven't dated anyone in forever."

Alex chose that moment to walk in from the garage.

Awkward tension filled the room. My face heated. I couldn't believe Savannah had all but admitted my dating life had been stagnant.

Alex pointed upstairs, a slight smirk on his lips that made me think he'd heard every word. "I'm just going to go see if there are any old clothes in my bedroom I can wear."

All I could think was how much I wanted to see his pristine white button-down dirty with grease from working in the garage. He was a doctor, a musician, a caring uncle, and he fixed stuff. He was the total package I couldn't even think about having for myself.

I couldn't even give Savannah a hard time for outing me. I wasn't supposed to care if her brother knew anything about my love life.

"I don't want to talk about dating." Or lack thereof. I'd been so consumed with the B & B I hadn't even bothered. The only people I met were couples staying at the inn. Single guys weren't our usual clientele—until now.

We chitchatted about the shop she'd taken over from her mother. Savannah had been trying to convince her mother for years to switch out the product lines, but she was resistant.

"It's your shop now, isn't it?" I didn't see what the issue was, but then I didn't have a close mother-daughter relationship.

"Technically, but she still gets a cut."

"Have you talked to her about buying her out?"

Before Savannah could answer, I heard Alex's heavy tread on the wooden steps as he came back downstairs. Moving into the room, he wore faded jeans so worn there were actual holes in the knees, not the ones for fashion. He wore a threadbare white T-shirt that left nothing to the imagination.

His chest was defined, his biceps bulging, and his abs might have been a six-pack. There was nothing about him that wasn't attractive.

"I'll just be in the garage." Then he winked at me like he knew exactly what I was thinking.

My mouth was dry, and I would have given anything to be in the garage, too, watching him. Would he take off his shirt if it got too hot? Did he have any tattoos?

Savannah looked from Alex to me. As soon as the door closed behind him, she asked, "Since when did things get awkward between you and Alex?"

Straightening, I shook my head. "It's not awkward. What are you talking about?"

"You're all flushed when he's around. You got embarrassed when I mentioned dating in front of him."

"I wasn't embarrassed."

"You were."

"It's not what you think. It's just…" I ran my fingers through my hair. "He's different, okay? He actually seems nice."

Savannah shuddered. "He's still my brother. He's not dating material. He works long hours, and I know for a fact, he's not looking for anything serious. He's always going on about doctors getting divorced because the job is too demanding. His last girlfriend loved being on his arm for fundraising dinners but complained when he wasn't available for her otherwise."

I shook my head vehemently. "I'm not interested."

"Well…yeah. That would be gross."

An image of Alex whipping off his threadbare shirt and

wiping his grease-stained hand over his hard stomach had my core clenching. Her brother wasn't gross, but I was going to have to pretend he was.

"Your parents must be ecstatic he's home," I said, desperate to divert her attention.

"The prodigal son returns." Her smile didn't reach her eyes.

It made me think Alex wasn't far off the mark when he said there was pressure in the family to be successful.

She sighed. "Speaking of doing what we want to do with our lives… Have you thought any more about selling your pastries?"

I let her change of topic go. "I'm still testing recipes."

She leveled me with a stare. "They're good enough as is."

I shook my head. "I don't know."

"They are. I don't know what you're waiting for, but you could sell something to a local restaurant or even apply to work at the bakery downtown. It's called Treats on Main or something like that."

My heart twinged because my dream was to own a bakery, not work at someone else's. Ever since I quit my job, I'd enjoyed having more leeway to make decisions.

"I know you want to be your own boss, but maybe you should start at the bakery first, get some training, then go out on your own."

That was the other thing. I didn't have any training.

She held up a finger. "And don't even tell me you're waiting to go to culinary school. You have a sense for what should be in the recipe. You don't need to test them out on every one of your guests. You know they're good."

"What are we talking about?" Lilliane asked, coming back into the room.

Savannah waved a hand at me. "How Ava needs to sell her baked goods."

Lilliane nodded in agreement. "I've been telling my

friends about it, and Nora mentioned you should start selling them from the B & B."

Savannah's eyes brightened. "That's a great idea. You could sell them to walk-ins."

I envisioned a display case by the counter. It was a good idea.

"Would Juliana be okay with that? Is there a spot for a pastry case?" Savannah asked, clearly fired up.

"I don't know."

"It wouldn't require much on your part other than maybe a display case, pricing, and getting the word out. I can put flyers up at the stores on Main Street." Savannah pulled out her phone, and her hands flew over the keyboard.

She was probably taking notes. She had to-do lists and notes for everything on her phone.

"I'll need to talk to Juliana first." At the end of the day, the B & B was her vision. I didn't want to take away from her business.

"I think you'd be adding to Juliana's business, not taking away from it," Lilliane said, anticipating my argument.

"It's perfect. I can't believe we didn't think of it before. Thank Nora for us, would you?" Savannah asked.

"Will do. Nora will be happy to know she was right again. That woman always thinks she's right about everything," Lilliane grumbled as she plated the casserole, then carried the dishes into the dining room.

Savannah and I exchanged a look before laughing. Being with the St. Jameses always felt like home.

CHAPTER FIVE
ALEX

I FIXED THE LAWN MOWER FOR DAD. HE CALLED ME AT LEAST once a week with some small thing that needed fixing around the house. I don't think he was as incapable as he led Mom to believe. Maybe it was a way to keep a connection with me while I lived in New York.

"That was so fun," Miles said to Dad.

Dad ruffled his hair. "It was all you, Miles. You're a natural fixer."

"Ya think so? I want to be a tool guy one day," Miles said proudly.

"A tool guy? I thought all six-year-olds wanted to be a fireman or a police officer," Dad said, washing his hands in the utility sink Mom insisted on installing. She didn't like him washing his greasy hands in the kitchen sink.

"Not this one, apparently," I said affectionately. The best thing about this temporary move was getting quality time with Miles.

Dad turned off the water, drying his hands on a towel that didn't look especially clean.

Miles was a shy kid, but he gained confidence when he entered kindergarten. I worried about him because his father died before he was born. Dad stood in for any events at school that required a father, but it wasn't the same.

"Ya think dinner is ready yet?" Dad asked Miles.

"I hope so. I'm staaaarrrving." Miles stretched out the words like he was going to pass out at any second.

I laughed. Savannah already complained he ate nonstop. Growing boys didn't let up in the food department until they moved out.

We filed into the kitchen.

I wondered if the women were still talking about Ava's dating life. I couldn't help but overhear what they were talking about. Ava looked embarrassed that she hadn't dated recently, and I wondered why that was.

"All fixed?" Mom asked Dad as he leaned over to kiss her on the cheek.

"Thanks to Miles. He's a natural."

"Thanks for being a good helper." Savannah ruffled his hair.

"I hope you're hungry. I made lasagna," Mom said.

I rubbed my stomach. "My favorite."

"That's why I made it. It's not every day your son visits."

It was a slight dig that I didn't come home more often. I'd been so busy with school I hadn't come back for extended visits. "I'm here now."

We carried everything into the dining room and sat around the table. Ava sat across from Savannah. I sat in my old seat next to Ava.

She stiffened when I sat next to her. Was she as affected by my proximity as I was to her?

Scooping a huge helping of lasagna onto my plate, I had this burning desire to rile her up like I had when we were kids. Except, unlike when we were kids, this time, my endgame was different. Instead of her running away screaming, I wanted her to scream my name.

"How long are you in town for?" Savannah asked me.

I felt everyone's eyes on me. "I'm here for a few months. Then I'll move back to New York for the last part of my residency."

"Do you know if you'll eventually come back here to work or if you'll stay in New York?" Savannah scooped a smaller amount of lasagna onto Miles's plate.

I grabbed a piece of crusty garlic bread. "It's wherever I'm offered a position. I need to start applying soon if I want to get something at the most sought-after hospitals."

"I wish you'd consider moving home. It would be great for Miles to have his uncle close," Mom said.

Her words pierced my chest. When Savannah quit school after finding out she was pregnant, I felt the pressure to succeed. I wanted to be the best doctor working in the most prestigious hospital. My supervisor turned mentor, Steve Barker, encouraged me, saying my options here were limited compared to New York.

Miles nodded enthusiastically. "Yeah, we can play video games all the time."

Savannah laughed at him. "You have school, and Uncle Alex might have more important things to do than play video games all day with you."

"I'll make time for you, buddy." No matter how busy I was, he'd be a priority.

"See," Miles told his mother.

Savannah shook her head at us.

I sipped my water, glancing at Ava to gauge her reaction. She seemed charmed by the exchange. I wasn't sure what this desire was for her to like me, to see me as something more than her friend's brother. I had this feeling she'd be different than the women in New York. She'd want me for something more than the letters behind my name and the money soon to be in my bank account.

Miles wouldn't be young forever, and I'd already missed so much time with him.

Conversation carried on around me, going from Miles's school to football to the store.

Savannah's shoulders were tense. "I just think we should switch things over. We've been selling cheesy tourist items for years. I want to start adding in classier options."

"Like what?" Mom asked.

"I'd like to showcase local artists. A teacher contacted me wanting to sell her art. She has prints, and she makes some of her designs into stickers. They're really pretty and unique." She scrolled through her phone, tilting the screen to show us her colorful stickers.

Ava leaned over the table to get a closer look. "I love those."

Savannah smiled, seemingly encouraged to continue. "Another artist sews pillows with cute sayings, another that makes wooden signs with the latitude and longitude coordinates for Annapolis. We'd be highlighting local artists and selling items tourists want to buy."

Silence fell over the table as we waited for Mom's reaction.

I thought Savannah's ideas had merit. The last time I'd been in the store, it seemed cluttered, and it could use a fresh coat of paint.

"You don't think the current merchandise is what tourists want?" Mom asked Savannah.

Savannah's shoulders lowered. "I think we need to change with the times. The whole place could use a face-lift. We're trying to sell too much. I worry the customers are overwhelmed when they come in. They do a quick circle and leave without buying anything. It's not inviting."

"What if I don't want to make any changes?" Mom's words were stiff.

"I'm not in a position to buy you out." Savannah chewed her bottom lip.

Savannah was left with so few options since she got pregnant at a young age. Helping Mom run the store made sense at the time, but I could see how she'd eventually want to have some input.

"Do you think we can start with maybe just one of these items? See how they do? Then I can show you the numbers, and we'll know if it's worthwhile," Savannah said.

"That sounds reasonable," Dad said to Mom.

"I don't know." Mom seemed reluctant to give up control.

"It's something we should seriously consider if we want to remain viable. The space next door is vacant, but it won't be forever. Whoever rents it could be competition."

Mom stood. "I'll get more bread."

When she'd disappeared into the kitchen, Dad said, "Don't worry. I'll talk to her."

Savannah leaned back in her chair, her expression defeated. "I'm not sure it's going to make a difference. Maybe I should open my own place."

"Are you in a position to do that?" I asked her, genuinely curious. She rented the space above her shop. It was convenient for work, but it was small. Miles went to a private school a few blocks away. I suspected most of the money she earned went to his education.

Her forehead wrinkled. "No."

"I'd love to help you out, maybe even be a silent investor, but I won't be making money until my residency is over. The hiring process is long."

Savannah shot me a look. "I'm not asking for help."

I wanted Savannah to be happy. I wanted Miles to have a secure future. I'd do anything to give them a boost if I could.

We'd felt for her when she got pregnant in college. My parents encouraged her to continue school, but she wanted to spend as much time with the baby as possible. She thought she'd go back to school later. Instead, she started working at the store.

I liked being close enough to attend family dinners. I liked knowing what Savannah was going through. I wasn't sure what that meant for my career, but for now, I was content to be here.

Conversation turned to dessert when Mom returned with Ava's homemade apple pie.

Getting ready to leave, I found myself alone with Savannah in the living room. "Let me know if you need anything."

"I'm fine."

"I haven't always been here for you. I was gone when everything happened."

She waved me off. "You couldn't have done anything."

Being home made me see how important family was. "I've missed being close, especially spending time with Miles."

"You don't have to live so far away." Her voice was gentle.

It wasn't that simple. I had a better chance of getting a job in New York, where I'd already done most of my residency. "I'm not sure what the future looks like, but I want to be there for you and Miles."

"You're never more than a phone call away. That's enough."

My chest tightened. I was missing out on time I wouldn't get back.

Savannah straightened her spine. "Mom's just being stubborn about the store. I'll convince her."

Savannah was unstoppable when she decided on a plan. Mom didn't stand a chance if Savannah's goal was more control at the store. "Go easy on her, okay?" I teased.

"I've been patient. I didn't want to take over her store, but things are different now. She's essentially retired."

I didn't envy her position. "I'm sure you have a vision for the store, and you're the one working there. It only makes sense you want to implement changes."

"Otherwise, I'm just an employee with no stake in the game." Her face was pinched.

It was rare I ever heard her lament not being able to finish college or pursue her dreams. She'd wanted to get a business degree and open a business, but she had no idea what. She was supposed to have time to figure everything out. Then Miles came, and she had to refocus her attention on him.

"You'll figure it out." I'd be here to support her while I could.

Savannah wrapped her arms around my waist. "Thanks, Alex. I'm so happy you're home. Even if it's only for a few months."

Ava walked into the foyer. "It's a nice surprise to have you home. You're not as annoying as you used to be."

"Hey." I let go of Savannah to try and grab Ava, but she ducked out of my way, giggling.

She crossed her arms over her chest. "I'm used to evading you."

"Don't forget we're staying in the same place tonight, and I know where your room is." The familiar threat tugged on something in my chest.

I waited for a retort, but there was only heat in her eyes.

Miles skidded into the room, interrupting the air, which was thick with tension. "Are we going home now?"

"We are. Put on your shoes, please."

Miles sunk to the floor, pulling his shoes on over his socks.

"We hope to see more of you now that you're here." Mom gave me a hug.

"You will." My words rang true. I planned to spend time with my parents, Savannah and Miles, and find out what I could about Ava. For the first time in a long time, I was excited about what was going on in my personal life. For so long, my life had been school, studying hard so I could have a career one day. My only outlet was playing my cello.

"Don't be a stranger." Dad clapped my shoulder.

"I'm sure I'll be over here fixing things every other day."

"Don't be cheeky." Dad patted my face.

Ava opened the door, and we followed her out.

Miles bounded ahead of us, shouting over his shoulder, "Yeah, don't be cheeky!"

"Want to go to dinner tomorrow night? I can stop by the store, and we can head out from there."

"That would be nice. Miles will love that."

We stopped at Savannah's car.

"What do ya say, Miles? Want to go out for pizza tomorrow?"

"I love pizza."

I'd banked on it, wanting to take them out.

Savannah patted my arm. "See you tomorrow."

The girls said goodbye, then I followed Ava to my SUV.

"You're good with him."

"Miles? I just wish I could see him more often."

We settled into the plush leather seats, the light from the dash illuminating Ava's face. "You're here now. That's all that matters."

Pulling away from the curb, I said, "I want to be a better uncle."

Ava rested her head against the backrest. "Savannah said you guys video chat all the time and play video games online."

"It's not the same. I want to do things with him. Take him out for pizza. Play chess on a real board. Heck, take him trick-or-treating." I'd take advantage of the fact I was home for the holidays this year.

She smiled softly. "Now's your opportunity."

Crossing town to the B & B, I let the feeling of hope and contentment wash over me. Ever since Savannah dropped out of college, I was the one my parents pinned their hopes of success on. It was a lot of pressure. I'd been tunnel-focused on graduating top of my class and getting one of the most coveted positions.

"I think I made the right decision to live in Annapolis during this block of my residency."

"Why *did* you come back?"

"Each month we switch specialties. I had to travel here to do a rotation at the University of Maryland's Shock Trauma Center. I thought I'd extend my stay and complete some of my other blocks."

"What are your blocks?"

"It's the one month we spend in each location, whether it's PEDs ER—which is children—trauma, general surgery, orthopedics, critical care, PEDs critical care, OB-GYN, anesthesia. We do a little of everything. Each month feels like a new thing, a new job, new schedule, new hours, and new expectations. You learn to kind of take things as they come."

"That sounds stressful. It would have to be hard to have a family with that schedule."

"I've never had to worry about it, but I've seen other doctors going through a divorce for that very reason."

"Do you still want to be an emergency room doctor?"

"I like the fast pace of it. The fact that we don't follow up with patients is a blessing and a curse. I leave any issues at the door, but sometimes you really want to know how that person is doing. Especially the kids that come in with more serious issues." I glanced over at Ava, whose gaze was on mine. Seeing her genuine interest, I continued, "Sometimes people are annoyed that they have to wait, some are on drugs or have dementia and might get violent or verbally abusive, others are combative for no reason. Others search their symptoms online and are convinced that they know what the problem is despite the tests saying otherwise."

"I didn't realize you had to deal with so much."

I hadn't discussed much of the realities of my job with my family. I didn't want to sound like I was complaining. So much of my job was interacting with people, not so much the medicine. That was something med school didn't prepare me for.

"I like to relieve stress by playing music. Sometimes I play in the lobby of the hospital, other times I go to the hospital rooms of the patients who are stuck in bed."

"After everything you described, you'd go in on your off-duty time and play?"

The feeling I got playing for other people was indescribable. "Music can really lift someone's mood. I love doing that for others."

It relieved the worry, stress, and tension I felt from the difficult parts of my job. Having a patient die under your care was only trumped by having to tell his or her family the news. If I didn't have an outlet, I'd go crazy.

"I could see that when you were playing at the wedding. It was like you were lost in the music."

"I tend to get carried away and forget where I am." Other times, I was very aware of the reaction of those around me. Not just the ones who dropped change into my cello case, but the ones who stood nearby, their arms wrapped tightly around their body, tears shining in their eyes. I didn't know why they were visiting the hospital, but whatever the reason, they could use the comfort that music provided.

At the wedding, I might have closed my eyes on occasion, but I was very aware of Ava's gaze on me and her appreciation of my music.

I parked at the curb near the B & B, not wanting the night to end.

Ava shifted to face me. "Want a drink?"

Pleased we could spend more time together, I asked, "You got some leftover baked goods in the kitchen?"

We climbed out of the SUV, Ava's laughter ringing out in the darkness. "They say the way to a guy is through his stomach. I never believed it to be true until now."

I rested a hand on my stomach. "I'm going to have to work out more after eating breakfast here every morning."

She opened the door, flipping on lights as we moved to the kitchen. She rummaged through the cupboards, pulling out a sealed container.

"Muffins."

"Perfect."

She opened the lid. "Want tea or coffee? Or maybe something stronger?"

"Tea is fine. Caffeine messes with my sleep. My schedule is so erratic."

"What are your hours?" She filled the kettle with water.

"It's different with each rotation but usually twelve-hour shifts. Some blocks require a twenty-four-hour shift every three days. Ortho and anesthesia have much easier schedules."

"You have to be dedicated to be a doctor. I'm impressed."

"Did I underwhelm you as a teen?"

She gave me a pointed look. "I judged you on your ability to sneak whipped cream into my shoe or toothpaste into my book bag."

"Those things are important."

She tipped her head. "Just not indicative of future success." She was quiet for a few seconds, seeming to assess me. "Why a doctor?"

"I originally wanted to be a full-time musician, but as you know, my parents discouraged me. Said I wouldn't make any money as a musician. They used some example of a friend's son who worked at a paint store with his music degree."

She chuckled. "That's not encouraging."

"I was great at science. I guess what I love about music is the same thing I love about medicine—I just want to help people. Probably the same thing you love about baking."

"Oh. I'm not helping people." Ava's reaction was self-deprecating.

I didn't like it. "You probably enjoy making people happy when they eat your treats. Don't forget, food is comforting in the same way that music is."

"Just not as healthy."

I nodded. "True. But don't lessen what you're doing. It's just as valuable."

A soft smile took over her face. "I like thinking of it that way. It doesn't sound so frivolous."

"You should be proud. You take care of guests at the B & B. You create amazing treats they enjoy while they're on vacation."

When the tea was ready, we sat on the stools at the gourmet island in the kitchen, laughing and joking about the pranks we pulled as kids. I hadn't had so much fun with anyone in a long time. I helped her clean up, walking her to her door.

"Thanks for coming tonight. I had fun."

"I did, too."

I wanted to ask her when the last time was that she'd laughed like she did tonight, with abandon, but I didn't. "Night, Ava."

I walked backward for a couple of feet then turned to open my door. Being so close to her would be nice and difficult at the same time. A few more nights like this one, and I could see myself kissing her, which would be out of bounds for our relationship. I had to remind myself—she was Savannah's friend. I couldn't ruin that relationship or Ava's relationship with my parents. She needed them.

CHAPTER SIX
AVA

The next morning, I was in the kitchen before the sun rose. I was tired from staying up late with Alex, but it was the most fun I'd had in forever.

Since Savannah had Miles, our version of a night out was watching a movie after he went to sleep, or I babysat so she could go on a date. Otherwise, I was tied to the B & B. I didn't mind. I preferred it to the competitive nature of my old graphic design job.

Rolling out the dough for the cinnamon rolls, I wondered if I'd see Alex this morning. I'd set a plate aside for him in case he slept in and missed breakfast.

When I was putting away the last of the dirty dishes, Alex asked, "Am I too late?"

His voice was deeper than when he was a teen. It rumbled through my chest, making my heart beat faster.

Turning to smile at him, my heart skipped a beat at the sight of his hair slicked back from a recent shower and the smell of soap. He wore a white button-down, rolled up at the forearm, a few buttons undone at his neck. He was sexy.

"It smells delicious."

I wanted to say, *you smell delicious*, but that was completely inappropriate. Not only was he a guest, he was an old friend. Not even a friend, the brother of a friend. I shouldn't be thinking about him washing his naked body with soap or what he'd done in the shower.

My face heated at the image that popped into my head—water beating down on golden skin. Alex touching himself.

"Is there anything left?"

I cleared my throat to cover my dirty thoughts. "I saved you some."

I'd counted on being surrounded by people in the morning, but we were alone. It felt intimate.

I pulled a plate out of the oven where I'd kept it warm. Uncovering it, the smell of fresh cinnamon and vanilla wafted out.

"Ava Breslin. You've outdone yourself." He snatched a roll, immediately taking a huge bite.

Pride filled me at his reaction, making it difficult to respond.

Finally, I said, "I made my specialty this morning." For you.

He chewed, then swallowed. "This is amazing. I can't even describe it." He took another bite. "So good," he said over his chewing.

He wasn't just saying that. There was pure enjoyment on his face.

"I'm glad you like it. Want some tea or orange juice?" I asked, remembering he said he didn't like to drink coffee because it messed with his sleep schedule.

Swallowing, he said, "Orange juice, please."

I poured him a large glass, placing it in front of him. He'd sat on the same stool as last night. What would it be like to see him every morning and night? We'd talk about our day over pastries. He'd tell me how good everything tasted. We could go to bed together at night.

Why was I thinking about him like this? He's my best

friend's brother. His family is like my second family. I repeated the words like affirmations in my head, hoping it would sink in.

When it didn't work, I tried to remember how gross he was as a teen. How we'd tease him for the messy bathroom he'd shared with Savannah. Then we teased him for not taking enough showers and being smelly, for wearing too much cologne when he had a date. Looking back, I felt a little ashamed that we were so relentless. Unfortunately, the fresh, clean smell of soap and pure man permeated the air.

Why does he have to be so sexy *and* so nice? A musician. A doctor. He was the complete package. One I could never have.

Gesturing at the cinnamon rolls, he said, "You're living in your genius in the kitchen, Ava. This is what you should be doing."

I was momentarily stunned by his statement. I was living in my genius? "No one's ever said it like that before."

"Well, it's true." He said it with so much conviction I believed him.

"When did you learn to bake like this?"

"Honestly? When my mother died, my father tried to stand in for her, but he didn't know how to cook anything more complicated than grilled cheese. Juliana tried to learn. She was better than him, but it wasn't great, and I wanted to help out. Dad bought me a cookbook, and I started trying recipes. I realized pretty quickly, baking was easier for me. It had the added bonus of being comfort food for us." I paused, worried I'd revealed too much.

He studied my face. "Did she ever come back?"

"No. We never heard from her." It felt like he could see right through me, that he knew how her leaving had left a hole in my chest that could never be filled. I'd never be the full expression of myself because the most important person in my life left without a backward glance. There must be something inherently flawed in me that my mother could do such a thing. It was so glaringly obvious. Surely, he could see it, too.

His face filled with sympathy. "I'm sorry."

"It's not a big deal." I squared my shoulders, placing another cinnamon roll and the leftover blueberry pancakes on a plate for him.

"Isn't it?" His voice was soft.

"Maybe at first. But I'm an adult. I can handle it."

"Have you ever tried to find her?"

My hand trembled as I pushed the plate in front of him. "I searched online a few times. She has a social media account. Last time I looked, she lived in Florida."

"Have you thought about confronting her?"

I shook my head vigorously. "I don't know what that would accomplish. I know she's not coming back." I know she never cared about us.

"It might give you closure."

"I don't know if I need that." Or if it would make a difference. I'd come to terms with what happened, hadn't I?

"It might be nice to have a reason."

"I assumed we were too much for her." I shrugged. A few nights before she left, I overheard Mom and Dad arguing. She'd been complaining that I was too demanding. That was partly why I learned how to cook and bake. I was worried about being so needy my dad would leave, too.

Standing in front of him, the island counter between us, I felt raw. Our family never discussed our mother's leaving. At first, it was because it hurt my father to talk about it. Then it just became something we didn't do. Even if I felt her absence all the time, especially during big life events.

He hummed. "You don't know that."

I threw my hands up in the air, exasperated. "We'll never know since she left without a word, but I don't see how searching her out will change the outcome."

He held up his hands. "It might not change anything, or it might give you the peace to move on."

I was full of energy with nowhere to expend it. "I'm not stuck."

The words felt hollow even to me. I hadn't dated anyone long term. I'd quit my safe job to work for my sister, but I wasn't one-hundred-percent happy here, either. I felt unsettled, restless, but I didn't know what to do about it.

He arched a brow. "I overheard Savannah trying to convince you to sell your baked goods. You don't seem keen on the idea."

"That has nothing to do with my mother."

"I think if it was my mom that left, I'd want to know why." He sat on the stool, taking a long pull of juice.

I deflated at his gentle tone, his admission that he'd thought about my situation. My gaze caught his and held. Something passed between us—an understanding that he got what I was going through. It felt good to share it with someone on the outside.

He took a large bite of the second cinnamon roll, leaving a dollop of icing on his lips. Heat pooled in my belly. I swallowed hard, my fingers curling into fists as I tried to resist going to him. His tongue darted out to lick his lips.

Without thinking, I moved around the counter at the same time he shifted on the stool so that I was standing in between his legs.

His gaze searched my face. "Is there something on my face?"

I removed the icing with my thumb, sucking it into my mouth.

His legs tightened around my hips, his eyes darkening with desire.

I couldn't believe I'd stepped into his space to touch him. My thumb still tingled from the brief contact, the look in his eyes heated me from the inside out.

I should step back. He was a guest. A friend. Not someone I was supposed to be licking icing off of.

Instead, I was mesmerized by the desire I saw in his eyes. I had this overwhelming urge to kiss him, to touch his thighs, to see if the muscles were as hard as they seemed, the soft hair on his neck, the prickly stubble on his face. My core clenched with desire.

"Did you get it?" His voice was low and rumbly.

My throat was so dry. "Get what?"

"Did you get all of the icing?"

My gaze flicked from his eyes to his lips. It was an invitation I couldn't refuse. Resting my hands on his thighs, I went up on tiptoe, kissing the corner of his mouth, then licking the remnants of sweet icing on his lips.

He banded an arm around my waist, hauling me closer until I could feel the hard ridge of his cock on my belly.

Warm everywhere, I felt like a simmering pot of water ready to boil over. My senses were on overdrive from the taste of the icing on his lips, the strength of his hold on me, and the heat I felt through his pants.

I wanted him.

He angled my head, going deeper, plunging his tongue into my mouth. He tasted like the sweetest thing I'd ever eaten.

I wanted to get lost in him, forget whatever it was we were just talking about. He kissed me until the ache in my core was an insistent throb.

I wanted him to slide his hand under my skirt into my panties, to part my folds with his fingers, teasing my entrance, then thrust inside. I wanted to get closer, rubbing my nipples against his chest. I wanted nothing between us.

Groaning, he pulled slightly back. His thumb ghosted over my lips.

I wanted to suck his thumb into my mouth. I wanted him to lift me so I was straddling his hips.

I wanted more.

"What was that?"

It was like ice-cold water had been poured down my back. I covered my mouth with my hand, trying to take a step back, but his thighs pressed harder, keeping me imprisoned. It was the best kind of torture, standing this close to him with his taste lingering in my mouth.

I shook my head, trying to dislodge the dirty thoughts in my head. "I don't know."

He lowered his head until his forehead rested against mine. "I want to do it again."

I flattened a hand on his chest, feeling his heart galloping under my touch. "Alex. We can't. You're Savannah's brother."

I hoped her name would put an end to whatever madness came over us.

He lifted his head from mine. "So?"

"So? She's my best friend. I love your family." I gestured between us. "Nothing can happen between us."

He hummed a noncommittal answer, but he relaxed his legs, allowing me to step back. On shaky legs, I quickly put the counter between us again. Grabbing a dishcloth, I scrubbed the already pristine counters, searching for an errant crumb, anything to distract me from the hunk of deliciousness sitting at my counter.

"What are your plans for the day?"

I glanced up at him. He was eating his pancakes like he hadn't just given me the best kiss of my life. "I take it easy on Mondays."

I realized too late I'd left him an opening.

"I have today off." He let his words dangle in the air.

I knew what he wanted. "You want me to show you around."

His lips twitched. "I wouldn't be opposed."

Once his residency started, he'd be so busy I probably

wouldn't see him at all. It would be easy to keep whatever this was between us on the back burner. "Okay."

"Yeah?" He paused, his fork halfway to his mouth, syrup dripping onto the plate.

Now I was thinking about licking syrup off his bare chest. Why couldn't he be just another guest passing through town? Someone I'd never have to see again. Then I could explore whatever this was between us without guilt.

"Yeah."

He smiled so wide I saw his teeth. He was gorgeous, but when he smiled—it tugged on something inside me, drawing me closer. Being around him was dangerous. I'd show him around, then allow his job to create some much-needed distance. I could avoid his family's dinners and put off Savannah long enough for him to head back to New York.

He'd forget all about me—like everyone else did.

CHAPTER SEVEN
ALEX

Walking away from the B & B, that scene in the kitchen was running through my mind on repeat. It was like there was this invisible thread between us pulling her closer. Removing the icing with her thumb could have been considered friendly until she sucked it into her mouth.

It was so unexpected, all I could think to ask was whether she'd gotten it all. Except the question had come out more suggestive than I anticipated. She didn't waste any time kissing me. She was in my space, between my legs, but I needed her closer.

It was a good thing Ava retreated to her side of the kitchen so I could calm down. I'm sure she felt the evidence of my desire when she was pressed against me.

"What do you want to do?"

I was so lost in my thoughts I hadn't paid attention to where we were going. Looking up, we were at City Dock, Annapolis's harbor, where boats were docked. We stood on a large brick patio lined with benches, a couple of Ping-Pong tables, and potted flowers hanging from the light posts.

Ava gestured at the large boat docked at the corner. "There's a boat ride to see the Naval Academy." She pointed her thumb behind us. "We could do a walking tour of the Naval Academy. There are other buildings we could explore, like the Paca House, St. John's College, or the State House. I'm not sure what you wanted to see."

My goal was to continue what we'd started in the kitchen, but it was too soon to mention that again. I didn't want to get a hard-on in public.

And I didn't care what we did as long as I got to spend the day with her. "Let's start with the boat ride, then we can figure it out."

So much of my life was scheduled or spent on call, it was rare for me to have a day just to be. And to spend that time with Ava was an unexpected bonus.

I'd wanted to argue when she claimed nothing could happen between us. We weren't kids anymore. It shouldn't matter who she was friends with or that she's younger than me. I wish we could focus on what was happening between us now. But I knew she didn't feel the same way. I was looking for something temporary. She seemed like a relationship girl. Plus, my family was important to her, and I had to respect that.

"Lead the way."

She headed toward the kiosk where a young woman stood wearing a captain's hat, white polo, and khaki shorts.

When Ava asked for tickets for the next boat ride that was leaving in fifteen minutes, I pulled out my wallet, shoving my credit card into the woman's hands.

Ava raised a brow.

"This was my idea."

"I'll get ice cream later."

Grabbing the tickets, I said, "Sounds good."

This was starting to feel like a date. I followed her up the short ramp to the boat.

"Want to sit on top?" she asked casually over her shoulder.

I wanted to tell her yes. I'd love to have you on top, riding my cock, your tits bouncing. But I swallowed the words, a strangled, "Sure," coming out instead.

She wore cutoff jean shorts that I just realized barely covered her ass as she made her way up the steps to the top deck. "Where do you want to sit?"

"The front." It was difficult to be around her. Not because she was my sister's friend but because I couldn't stop thinking about getting her naked, her riding my cock, her tongue in my mouth.

I followed her to the front of the boat.

She stood by the railing. Instead of standing next to her, I stood behind her, resting one hand on the railing. She sucked in a sharp breath.

"The view's incredible, isn't it?"

She nodded, not saying anything.

We stood quietly for a few minutes while others boarded, watching the people down below.

"You know, this makes me want to get my cello and play here at night."

She tipped her head back to see my face. "Now and then, they do have live music here."

I preferred to play on a whim. Grab my cello and pick a song for the moment, whatever I was feeling. Right now, I wanted something upbeat to match the rhythm of my heart beating in my chest. She was so close, yet so far away.

The captain made a few announcements, so we sat on one of the benches. I casually wrapped my arm around the back of it, wanting to rest it on her shoulders, but I wasn't sure how she'd react. I knew I needed to act like this morning was an anomaly, not something that would happen again. If I was clear with her about what I wanted, I'd scare her away.

She'd get all in her head about right and wrong, brothers and friends. I needed to keep her guessing, reel her in slowly. I wouldn't think about what it would mean when my residency ended and my time here came to an end. For right now, I was going to enjoy every minute of this unexpected break in my routine.

The breeze rustled her hair; the sun warmed my skin. When a strand of her hair got caught on the scruff on my chin, I brushed it back behind her ear. I shifted closer, my arm lowering to her shoulder.

She smiled gratefully, not mentioning how I'd shifted closer to her.

We listened to the tour guide talk about what we were seeing on each side of the boat. The majority of the tour was a view of the Naval Academy you couldn't see otherwise. "I've never done this before."

"That's what I figured, and it's such a beautiful day."

It was. If we were on a date, I would have said the day was rivaled only by her beauty. But it sounded a little cheesy in my head, and this wasn't a date.

When the boat turned to go back to the dock, the tour guide talked about other tours available on the boat, then was quiet. Ava closed her eyes, resting her head on my shoulder.

It was difficult to breathe with her so close.

Was I attracted to her because she wasn't impressed by my title, or was it something more, something bigger than I'd ever experienced before? Made better because we knew each other. I had a soft spot in my heart for anyone who loved music. That fact that she used to sneak through my house at night to listen to me play was something I'd always treasured.

I tightened my hand on her shoulder.

"This is nice."

I wasn't sure if she was referring to the day, the weather, the tour, or me, but I'd take it.

Unable to stop myself, I leaned closer, kissing her temple. "Thank you for coming with me." Then I decided to make light of the situation so she wouldn't freak out about the kiss. "It would have been awkward coming by myself."

She smiled. "I think you would have been okay. You seem like a confident guy."

"I usually am." She threw me off my game. I had to work harder, especially since she'd pushed me away after that kiss this morning, and we probably wanted different things.

We took our time disembarking. I was in no rush to end my time with Ava. At any point, she could decide she was done playing tour guide and head back to the B & B.

"Where to next?"

My gaze fell on one of the Ping-Pong tables. "How about a game?"

"Okay." Ava smiled mischievously.

"Are you still crazy competitive?"

When we were kids, she'd challenge me to anything, who could skip the most rocks, who could make the most baskets, who could run the fastest. Being younger, she never won, but it didn't stop her from goading me.

She nodded, already heading toward the table. "Yeah, nothing's changed there."

I laughed, feeling carefree. Grabbing a paddle, I said, "I don't remember there being Ping-Pong tables here when we were kids."

"There weren't. This is new. I'm not sure if I like it or not."

I served the first ball. It was an easy lob to get us started.

I enjoyed seeing her eyes light up. "Don't go easy on me, St. James."

"Oh, I'm not." The satisfying sound of the ball pinging off the table, then her paddle, had me focusing on the ball, not her. Ava was a fierce competitor. If I wanted to stay in the game, I couldn't be focused on her eyes, the way her tongue peeked out when she was concentrating, or the way her boobs bounced in that white tank top.

Each time she successfully aimed it back at me, she

cheered, then groaned when she overshot the table. My blood was pumping hard for more reasons than one.

Ava was down-to-earth. She was refreshing.

We went back and forth, keeping score.

She finally settled her hands on her hips, breathing heavily, her chest heaving.

With herculean effort, I kept my gaze on her face.

"Want to call it a tie?" She winced as if the question cost her.

"I wouldn't want there to be any hard feelings when I win."

"When *you* win? Serve."

I chuckled, loving this side of her. As a kid, she'd been annoying. As an adult, she was irresistible. Determined, competitive, sweet, and caring.

A few minutes later, my stomach rumbled. "I'm starving, so next point wins."

Ava focused intently on the ball in my hand. I raised my arm for the serve, sending the ball over the table to her side. She returned it. It was so fast, I barely reacted before it was flying past me.

"I won!" She raised her arms in the air, doing a little dance with her feet.

"Are you for real right now?"

Her eyes widened. "I think that's the first time I ever won."

"I think it is, too." She was finally able to keep up with me. It made me wonder if she would keep up in bed, too. Would she challenge me there as well?

Swiping her hair back from her face, Ava put the paddles and balls away.

"Want to pick up lunch and eat at the circle?" There were plenty of stores and shops near the State House where we could pick something up and eat picnic-style.

"Sure. That sounds great."

Walking side by side toward State Circle, I flexed my fingers, wanting to grab her hand or pull her into my side to feel her curves against me. I restrained myself because I wasn't sure how she'd react.

We walked on Main Street past the fudge and ice cream stores and the novelty shops until it gave way to the trendier stores by the circle, a juice bar, bookstore, coffee shop, and boutiques.

I opened the door to a store that boasted loaded baked potatoes. "This place looks interesting."

"It's good."

We picked out our special baked potatoes, carrying them across the street to the park surrounding the State House. Sitting on an iron bench in the shade, I handed her a potato and a water bottle.

Since it was Monday, it was quiet. Only a few tourists wandered around, touring the grounds.

"This is nice. Thanks for suggesting it. I almost never get out like this anymore."

"I'm glad I convinced you to go then."

"Seriously, I had a lot of fun beating you at Ping-Pong." She smiled wide.

"You're never going to let me live it down, are you?"

She bit her lip, shaking her head. "Nope."

"I'm going to have to challenge you to a rematch."

We ate, talking about what had changed in the downtown area since we were kids. Shops came and went, new restaurants opened up, but some things hadn't changed.

Throwing out our trash, I said, "Let's walk around."

I had nowhere to be until dinnertime, and I wanted every second with Ava. We wandered into every tacky shop. Ava was relaxed, trying on captain's hats, then posing for me. She looked so adorable in them I wanted to kiss her right then and there. But I couldn't.

I settled for tapping her hat. "You should get that and wear it when you're baking at the B & B."

She set the hat back on the rack. "That would look ridiculous."

"Don't you want to give your guests the full Annapolis experience?"

She rolled her eyes, meandering through the shop, picking up one trinket or another. "I'll have you know I'm running a sophisticated B & B."

I picked up a toy pirate periscope. "Miles would love this."

"You should get it for him. Aren't you meeting him tonight for pizza?"

"You should come."

"Don't you want alone time with them?" She held up an earring to her earlobe, checking it out in the small mirror. The blueish-green of the stone brought out her eyes.

"You want the earrings, too."

"I don't need them." She started to put them back, but I grabbed them, placing them on the counter for the clerk.

"We'll take both."

"You don't have to buy me earrings."

"I want to."

Ava bumped my arm with her shoulder. "Thank you."

She was genuinely grateful for the small gesture.

Nodding her head at the price on the register, Ava said, "Whoever made these isn't charging what they're worth. I can't believe the price reflects the time it took to make these and the materials."

"Probably not."

I handed the small bag of earrings to Ava. She placed them in her purse as we headed out.

"I should probably set out cookies and drinks for afternoon tea."

"We can head back."

"You want the cookies, don't you?"

"I do. I can't say I've had this many baked goods since I left home."

Ava tipped her head back, probably to feel the warmth of the sun on her skin. "I can't imagine living in New York City. Was it lonely?"

I almost stumbled on the uneven brick sidewalk. "I was so caught up in exams, studying, and being the best, I never thought about it. Our friends were whoever worked best in a study group."

"I have my sister, my dad, Savannah, and your family. I feel blessed to still live in this small town, doing a job that I love."

"You didn't like working as a graphic designer?" Knowing what I knew now about her, it was surprising she'd worked in that field for so long.

"I worked long hours, commuting to Baltimore. I didn't enjoy it. Not that everyone loves their job."

She said she was happier now, but it didn't seem like she was living up to her potential or doing something that fulfilled her.

An idea popped into my head—a way to have an excuse to see Ava—and possibly help her at the same time. "Can I help you find your mother? Maybe if you had answers, it would help you move past that part of your life."

"Why do you care?"

"I don't know. I just do."

"Let me think about it."

"I have a friend, Sam Ledger, from high school, who used to be a police officer and just opened his own private investigation company. He could help."

"His name is familiar."

"Think about it." I hoped she would. Something was holding her back, and my hunch was the unresolved issues with her mother leaving at a young age.

CHAPTER EIGHT
AVA

"Nothing has changed since I left," Alex said to Savannah, looking around her cluttered shop.

She threw her hands up in the air. "Now you know what I'm dealing with. The space next door is empty. Who knows what will come in next? It might be something fresher. There's no way I'll be able to compete."

"How are sales?" Alex asked, his arms crossed over his chest.

"Slow, honestly. It's hard to compete with some of the trendier shops down the street."

Shelves lined the walls, tables placed in front with items placed haphazardly, and racks in the middle. I couldn't discern what she was trying to sell. Walking around, I felt overwhelmed. I couldn't decide where to look first. Over the years, her mom had added on to her original merchandise, diluting their original brand.

Some of the other shops were open and inviting, drawing you to look closer. Some even offered candles or essential oils that made the smell of the shop pleasing. It was a marked difference from Savannah's store.

With Savannah taking over, it only made sense to take

stock of the store and its continued viability. "I think you should gather pictures of the inventory you want to sell, the renovations you want to make, including costs and expenses, then create a projection of the difference you think the changes will make to the bottom line."

Alex was nodding before I finished speaking. "I agree."

Savannah's forehead wrinkled. "Okay."

Miles came running from the back room, jumping into his arms. "Uncle Alex."

Savannah tipped her head with an affectionate smile. "You spoil him. He's going to want me to start carrying him again."

"I'm the cool uncle. I'm supposed to spoil him." Then he turned his attention to Miles. "You ready for some pizza?"

Miles rubbed his stomach. "I'm sooo hungry."

"I bet you are. They're probably starving you at school, aren't they?" Alex set him down on his feet.

Alex walked with him to the door while Miles talked about what the school cafeteria served at lunch.

"They're so cute together." Who knew a man showing interest in his nephew would do it for me?

Savannah covered her chest with her hand. "It's so good for Miles to have him here, even if it's for a short while."

I couldn't forget that Alex was here temporarily. Once he returned to New York, he'd forget what he loved about small towns. The pull of the hustle and bustle of the city would be too much to resist.

We waited on the sidewalk for Savannah to turn off the lights and lock up.

The adjacent building had a sign in the window for rent. "Do you know if the owner was able to rent the space?"

Her nose scrunched. "I just got notice that he's going to sell the building instead."

Walking leisurely toward the pizza restaurant, Alex asked, "Are you able to buy him out?"

Savannah shook her head. "I need to buy Mom out to do

what I want with this space. I can't afford to buy the building. It's too much right now."

I felt for Savannah. It was a tough situation to be in.

"That's too bad. A new owner might want you to move out," I said, running through the scenarios in my head.

"Or raise the rent," Alex said pointedly.

Savannah grabbed Miles's hand so he wouldn't run ahead of us. "Trust me, I've thought about the possibilities. I just can't worry about it until it happens."

Alex rubbed the back of his neck. "I wish I could help out more."

"This isn't your problem," Savannah said stubbornly.

I loved that Alex wanted to help his sister, it softened part of my heart.

Alex pulled open the door to the pizza restaurant, but Miles stood at the entranceway, looking up at him. "You know they have arcade games here?"

"You're going to play with me, right? It's no fun playing by myself."

Miles's eyes widened. "Can I, Mom? Can I?"

"You may," Savannah agreed as we walked inside. Miles ran to the first open arcade game at the back of the dining room.

"I think he loves the games as much as the pizza," Savannah said.

"Between working at the store and Miles, I feel like I'm always on my feet. I can't catch a break."

There was a hint of vulnerability in Savannah's expression. It wasn't often she admitted that she was overwhelmed being a single mom or just tired.

The waitress asked what we'd like to drink, but we come here so often we already knew what we wanted, so we placed our pizza orders, too.

"Can you imagine if you had more than one kid?" I asked her, watching as Alex put coins into the machine.

"I'm not against the idea of more kids, but next time, I want to be with the father."

Alex stood behind Miles, who sat on the stool, his hand hovering over the joystick to help him play. Seeing that he was occupied, I wanted to talk about what was on my mind. Savannah was the one I'd always confided in about my mom. "Alex mentioned hiring a PI to find my mom."

Savannah shook her head. "Why would you want to find her?"

"Alex thinks I need closure."

"You want to know why she left? I'm not sure you're going to like the reason any more than not knowing."

"Staying in the dark is an attractive idea." But Alex's concern about me being stuck was bothering me.

Savannah's gaze filled with concern. "It wasn't your fault if that's what you're thinking."

My gaze slid from Alex and Miles to Savannah. "Logically, I know that, but there's a small part of me that always thought it was me."

"I'm sure it's a natural feeling, but whatever she had going on, I'm sure it had nothing to do with you."

The server set up the tray of pizza on a stand, handing out plates and slicing it for us.

When she left, Savannah asked, "Have you spoken to your father about it?"

"You know we used to avoid her name in conversation, and nothing's changed." Juliana was pissed at our mother for leaving us. She never forgave her. I took her leaving differently. I blamed myself, and I felt this intense sadness when I thought about it.

"Maybe it's time to talk to your dad on your own. He might know something."

I rolled her idea over in my mind. It had merit.

Alex sat in the seat next to me. "Talk to your dad about what?"

Miles immediately bit into his pizza.

"Careful. It might be hot," Savannah cautioned him.

"Savannah wants me to talk to my dad. See if he remembers anything before I hire a PI to find my mom."

"Did you lose her?" Miles asked.

I thought he'd be too focused on his pizza to pay attention. I didn't want him to worry about losing his mother after he'd already lost his father. "No. I was talking about reaching out to her, maybe visiting her."

He nodded, holding up a piece of pepperoni and dropping it into his mouth. "So good."

"It is good pizza," Alex agreed.

Conversation turned to the video games they were playing. I ate pizza, listening to them talk, enjoying the feel of family. I'd always looked at Savannah's family as mine. If I pursued something with Alex, would that change?

We walked Savannah and Miles home, then to the B & B.

Opening the front door, Alex asked, "Are your duties done for the night?"

I nodded. "Unless someone needs me."

"Want to watch a movie? My vacation is over tomorrow. Then it's back to work."

"Sure." I went to the kitchen, grabbing some snacks and water bottles. "My room or yours?"

"Yours. I want to see what this room in the attic looks like," Alex teased.

"It's really nice." I led the way to the third floor and unlocked my door. The steps opened up to one big room with large, domed windows on each side. Juliana had added a bathroom up here and a small kitchenette for whoever would manage the business. I'd made the rest of the space my own. I'd hung local artwork on the walls and strung twinkle lights around the crown molding. It gave the room a cozy feel. An overstuffed couch and TV stood in one corner, my bed on the other side.

Alex turned in a circle, taking in the space. "This is nice."

"I like it." It was the place I came to get away from everything.

"Let me throw on something cozy, then we can pick a movie."

"Do you have popcorn?"

I pointed to the small microwave in the kitchenette. "The kernels are in the top cupboard, the popcorn maker in the bottom. I like it freshly popped."

I grabbed leggings, fuzzy socks, and an oversized sweatshirt. I told myself I wasn't trying to impress him. I could ignore that kiss we shared this morning. It hadn't meant anything, even if my lips hadn't stopped tingling, and spending the day together only made me feel closer to him.

Changing clothes, I ran a brush through my hair, berating myself for caring what I looked like. Opening the door, I smelled freshly popped popcorn and chocolate.

Alex sat on the couch, a blanket next to him, with two steaming mugs resting on the coffee table. A fire crackled in the fireplace below the TV.

"I found hot chocolate. Hope this was okay."

"Of course." I crossed my leg under me and sat next to him. Grabbing the blanket, I pulled it over our laps, trying not to touch his legs while I arranged it. The movement sent me sliding toward Alex on the couch. Our sides touched from knee to shoulder.

Not moving away, Alex handed me one of the mugs.

Blowing on it, I said, "Thank you. This is perfect."

He lifted the remote toward the TV. "I found a Christmas movie."

Glancing at the menu showing on the screen, I asked, "In October?"

Alex grinned, making him look boyish. "You gotta love streaming."

"Let's do it." I settled deeper into the couch, determined

to enjoy the night, not thinking about what any of it meant. We had one evening before Alex went back to work. Then it would go back to how it was before—my solitary room at the top of the B & B that represented my single life.

Alex clicked on the black and white classic. Then he placed the large bowl of popcorn in his lap. We ate, our hands occasionally bumping as we both went for it at the same time. It should have been awkward, but it wasn't.

I sipped the hot chocolate, hyperaware of the man next to me. Between the movie and our cozy surroundings, I should have been able to relax, but Alex's presence kept me on edge.

I loved *Miracle on 34th Street*. We watched it every Christmas, even if it was only on in the background while we ripped open presents. Even after my mom left, my dad did his best to keep our traditions. Christmas was a good memory. Finishing my hot chocolate, I moved to put the mug on the table in front of us.

Between the warmth of the hot chocolate and the fire, I was getting sleepy. I resisted the urge to rest my head against his shoulder. The mix of popcorn, chocolate, and Alex's aftershave was pulling me deeper. I tried to pry my eyes open, moving restlessly to keep myself awake. Waking with a start, I realized I must have drifted off.

Alex lifted his arm, so I fell into his side. He was so warm, and he smelled good—sweet and salty. I snuggled into him, falling right back to sleep. I never wanted to wake up from this dream.

When I woke again, I was lying down, Alex's hard body pressed to my back. His hand spread over my stomach, anchoring me in place. The fire had died out, but I was very warm. Alex's body was an inferno against my back.

His legs tangled with mine, and my head rested against his chest. I settled deeper into him, never wanting this moment to end.

I wouldn't think about what Savannah would say if she

knew or what his parents would think. My brain was fuzzy, and I easily fell back to sleep. The next time I woke, Alex's fingers were moving in my hair, making my scalp tingle.

"You're awake." His voice rumbled through my body, slowly waking each nerve ending.

I shifted in his arms so I could see his face. I wanted to lift my hand to caress his face and feel the scruff against my palm. "We fell asleep."

My brain felt sluggish. All I could compute was Alex's smell, his warmth, and his strong body surrounding me.

"We did." The look on his face was reverent, his fingers played in my hair, sending delicious tingles through my scalp and down my spine to my core.

I moved my legs restlessly, realizing our legs were intertwined.

I should have moved off the couch, pretending I needed to use the bathroom, but I didn't want to. There was a sense that when we broke apart, we wouldn't get another chance at this.

Something niggled in my brain that what we were doing was wrong, yet it felt so amazingly right. I closed my eyes again, not wanting to move and break the spell.

"Do you need to make breakfast for your guests?" His voice was soft, his fingers caressing the strands of my hair like he was testing the weight of it.

I groaned, squeezing my eyes shut tight. "Don't talk about it."

He kissed my forehead, and I froze.

I didn't turn my head because if I did, his lips would be on mine. I wanted that with everything in my body, but I wouldn't give in to the urge. His bicep flexed under my cheek.

"Ava, open your eyes."

I couldn't resist his quiet insistence.

His blue eyes were tinged with gold flecks up close. "I want to see you again."

My lips twitched even as my heart twinged at his admission. "I didn't know we were seeing each other."

He shifted his leg slightly, and his knee moved between mine, his thigh bumping against my core. I bit my lip to stop the moan that threatened to spill out.

I resisted the urge to rock against him.

"I want to kiss you."

I couldn't say no, even if it was the smart thing to do. He surged over me, his hand angling my face, his mouth meeting mine in a slow seduction, his leg pressed tighter to my core. Everything in my body ached to be closer to him.

I wanted to be naked. I wanted to feel his touch against my bare skin. I wanted his cock to slide between my folds. I wanted everything.

My phone dinged.

He stopped kissing me, resting his forehead against mine.

"That's my alarm."

"I knew we didn't have much time."

Time for what? Had he planned to seduce me this morning, to reduce me to nothing more than a melting pile of goo on the couch, malleable to his manipulation and touch?

"But I still wanted something to remember this night."

I wasn't forgetting it anytime soon, but I clenched my jaw shut, refusing to tell him. I wouldn't let this childhood crush race out of control. We had no future between his family and career, we could never be anything more than friends.

He shifted to move away from me. I wanted to reach for him and pull him back between my legs. My body quickly cooled from the loss of his heat. Alex reached out a hand to help me up. My body ached from the awkward position I slept in.

"Getting too old to sleep on couches?"

I nodded in agreement, not trusting my voice to speak. It was worth every twinge and ache to have experienced that.

"I'd offer to whip you up something or at least brew some

coffee, but I suspect your accommodations are better downstairs."

I smiled. "They are."

He moved to stand in front of me. "I'm going to shower and get changed, then I'll come down for breakfast."

"Yeah, okay." My heart flip-flopped in my chest. Would he kiss me again?

He moved closer, a hand reaching out to cup my cheek. I couldn't resist turning my face into his palm. "See you soon."

Then he was moving toward the door, opening and shutting it behind him. The room was empty like it was every morning. The only difference was the rumpled blanket on the couch, our discarded mugs of hot chocolate, and the popcorn kernels scattered on the floor.

I moved into the bathroom to quickly shower. There was an insistent throb between my legs. I wondered if I had time to ease it before getting to work. I turned on the water, stepping into the warm stream. I lifted my leg onto the bench, my finger traveling down my stomach to between my folds. Circling my clit once, I wondered if Alex would know I'd touched myself in the shower. Was he doing the same thing?

The idea of him gripping his cock in the shower, giving it a tug before stroking it spurred me on. I alternated circling my clit and sliding a finger inside. I tweaked my nipple with my free hand, letting my imagination run wild. If Alex were here, he'd lean over to suck my nipple into his mouth. I'd arch into him, wanting to be as close to him as possible. His strong, capable fingers would take over for mine, thrusting inside, his thumb pressing against my clit.

The image had me teetering on the edge. I wondered what it would feel like to have his cock inside me. He'd lift me into his arms, pressing my back against the cold tile, thrusting inside in one motion. It was too much. I bit back my cry when I crested, spasming around my finger, sagging against the wall.

Tipping my head back against the cool tiles, I didn't feel

satisfied. I felt empty, unfulfilled. I needed him. I groaned in frustration.

Alex St. James was driving me crazy.

CHAPTER NINE

ALEX

Sitting in my spot at Ava's counter, I wondered if she knew I'd jacked off to her in the shower. Her eyes were bright, her cheeks flushed this morning. Had she? I wanted to ask her, to see if she blushed down her neck to her chest, but the other guests sat at the long table, chatting.

"Did you have a nice shower?" I kept my tone soft and light.

Her gaze raised to mine. "I did. Did you?"

"It was very nice."

"I'll tell Juliana you like the accommodations."

The conversation was too formal for what we'd shared last night. For what I'd done in the shower this morning. "The only thing that would have made it better was if you'd joined me."

Ava paused. "Alex. You can't say that. Not here. Not anywhere."

She resumed mixing the batter.

"Why not?"

"Yesterday was nice, but it can't happen again."

"No one has to know if that's what you're worried about."

I didn't particularly care if my family found out, but I respected that she did.

"It's not just that. You're leaving."

I'd gotten caught up in her, but I wasn't sure I wanted anything serious. Not when my life was in New York. "You're looking for a relationship."

She lowered her gaze.

"It's nothing to be ashamed of if that's what you want."

Lifting her gaze, she said, "I think I do. Seeing Juliana with Nolan, I want what they have, even if I'm not sure I'll ever find it."

"Why do you think that?"

She shrugged. "The last guy I dated got a job in Texas."

"You didn't want to go with him?" I wanted this glimpse into her life.

She sighed. "He never asked."

"Did you want him to?" Something about her being hung up on another guy churned in my gut.

"Yes. No. I don't know. I thought we had something serious, or maybe I wanted it so badly I made more out of it than it was. Because clearly, he didn't see me as someone—"

Somewhere along the way, she'd gotten the idea that she wasn't worth holding on to. Anger bubbled in my gut.

"You deserve that and more. You're right to be cautious." Especially when I didn't know what the hell I was doing with her. I liked her. I enjoyed her company. I wanted to feel her skin against mine, but did I want something next month, or the next month after that? Did I want forever with someone? It wasn't fair to get involved with her if I didn't know. Especially if that's what she wanted.

She raised a brow. "Really?"

"Of course."

She ducked her head, smiling softly. "More pancakes?"

"Please."

She checked the ones on the griddle, carefully placing them on a plate before pushing them over to me. Then she handed me the syrup. She knew how I ate my breakfast. She'd had my tea waiting for me when I came down this morning. I liked that.

A relationship was having someone to watch a movie with, pop popcorn with, and snuggle with on the couch. It was knowing their favorite drink and breakfast. I enjoyed that, but was it because it was Ava, or would I have enjoyed last night with anyone?

I ate my pancakes, the blueberries bursting in my mouth, as usual, and watched Ava serve her guests, cooking more pancakes, and cleaning as she went.

She was a good hostess. She was a good person. She deserved so much more than what I had to offer.

The sun spilled through the window, creating this halo effect on her hair, making it look golden. She lifted her gaze to me. "It's back to work today, huh?"

I cleared my throat. "I'm in PEDs, so I hope it will be pretty easy."

Her brow furrowed. "What's PEDs?"

"It's the unit for kids. There's a separate unit for critical PEDs, so it shouldn't be too heavy."

"That's good." There was a wrinkle on her forehead I wanted to smooth out with my thumb.

I finished my breakfast, rinsing off the plate and stacking it in the dishwasher.

She leaned a hip against the counter. "You don't need to do that. You're a guest."

"I don't mind. Especially since you cooked an amazing breakfast."

"It's my job to cook and clean."

"If I can reduce your burden, I'd like to." I couldn't remember the last time I had anyone to consider, much less care about. Maybe that's why my relationships with women went south quickly. I was incredibly busy at work, but I didn't make time for them either.

"Thanks, Alex. Have a good first day at work."

I had the sudden urge to kiss her goodbye. After last night, I felt closer to her. Thanking her and walking away felt like too little after what we'd shared.

Walking up the steps, I thought about how I'd held her in my arms all night. The strands of her hair tickling my nose, how she'd snuggled in with me. I wasn't sure what any of it meant but I liked it.

I'd never worked inpatient PEDs before, so I wasn't sure what to expect. The one thing I was used to was preparing for the unexpected. I never knew before the first day whether I'd get a brief orientation to the floor or if I'd be flying by the seat of my pants.

As soon as I got there, I was told I'd have twelve to fifteen patients at one time. This was one of those rotations where I'd need to figure out where things were as I went. I preferred more of an introduction, but I could do this, too.

I focused on the first file, preparing myself before I walked into the room. I did my rounds, spending extra time with each patient because they were children, and the parents understandably had concerns. I grabbed lunch around three, eating my sandwich at a computer to type my notes. If it was just the current patients, it would have been manageable, but there were more kids being admitted, too.

In the afternoon, I was told to contact a child's pediatrician, school nurse, nutritionist, and whoever needed to be updated with their condition, but I was interrupted by whatever was happening on the floor. By ten, I was beat. My brain felt fractured from being pulled in so many different directions.

I was told to be back by seven the next morning. Driving home, I felt good working with kids. I enjoyed it. I didn't like why they had to be there, but I assured each child and parent they'd get the best care possible, and we'd get them home as quickly as we could.

The lights were dim on the first floor of the B & B. Ava must have already gone up to her room. I'd text her, but I had never gotten her number. Instead, I showered and fell into bed, too tired to think about much else.

THE NEXT MORNING, I STOPPED BY THE KITCHEN AT FIVE A.M. I wasn't sure about traffic to Baltimore, and I didn't want to be late to work.

Ava wasn't in the kitchen yet, but there was a tin of pastries and muffins on the counter that said *help yourself*. I wondered if that was for me. I found a piece of paper and a pen, jotting down a thank you note, telling her I was working at seven each morning, doing twelve-hour shifts. I paused, my pen poised, wondering if I should add something else. But what would that be…I miss you?

We'd reconnected. We'd shared one great night, but we weren't anything more than friends. If we were even that. I signed my name, tucking the note by the coffee maker so hopefully only she'd see it.

I wanted to see her, but I wouldn't be able to swing it. I knew how I got when I worked, I pushed everything out of my mind except for doing my job and sleeping. It didn't leave much room for anything else.

Eating the muffin while I drove, I reminded myself I wanted to be a doctor to help others. What I did was important, and I was told I had a good bedside manner, which was valued by the patients, at least.

The second day was like the first, except I knew more

about what to expect, where things were stored, which attending doctors were the most scrupulous, and which ones were more relaxed. I grew more confident each day and more exhausted.

The only difference with this block was I loved working with the kids. I loved lifting their moods. It was more than practicing medicine, it was connecting with them.

There was one kid who was admitted into the hospital fairly often, but he was so upbeat and cool about it. Braden was an inspiration. I told him if he was still admitted on my next day off, I'd bring the cello in to play for him.

His whole face scrunched up in disgust. "I don't like classical music, Dr. Alex."

"Braden. Be nice." His mother shot me an apologetic look.

"It's a good thing you don't because I don't play classical."

He studied me. "You don't?"

"Nope. I play current music. I mash two songs together." I rattled off a few popular musicians' names and song titles.

His eyes widened. "On a cello?"

"I'm classically trained, but I play everything. Mostly I play whatever anyone wants to hear."

He tipped his head like he was considering it, then nodded. "I'll give it a go."

Smiling, I said, "Oh you will, will you? Thanks for giving me a chance." I winked at his mother over his head.

This kid was great. He was stubborn and not easily swayed.

Despite the long day, these kids energized me in a way other blocks hadn't. They were more optimistic, hopeful, and grateful. It didn't make me think less of adult patients, it made me more appreciative of the kids.

WAITING FOR YOU

That night, I pulled open the door to the B & B, expecting it to be quiet like it had been all week. Walking into the living area, I wasn't expecting to see Ava curled up in a wingback chair in front of the fire.

"Ava?" My voice was rough from using it all day. I wanted nothing more than to snuggle with her in bed. It would be more comfortable than the couch we'd shared, but I wasn't up for conversation or anything else.

She looked up, her soft expression quickly morphing to concern. She stood, moving toward me, her fingers brushing over my cheek and my forehead. "You look exhausted."

"I am."

"Are you hungry?" she whispered.

"I can heat up leftovers." Even though the idea of doing anything seemed impossible at the moment.

"I'll get it." She slipped past me into the kitchen.

Following, I said, "I didn't think you provided dinner."

"Not for guests, but you're a friend," she said over her shoulder.

I lowered my weary body onto my usual stool, watching while she pulled a glass container out of the fridge and plated pork chops, green beans, and mashed potatoes, then heated it in the microwave. Next, she boiled water on the stove, presumably for tea.

"You don't have to do all of this." She had to be tired from getting up early to cook breakfast.

"I don't mind. Besides, you look like you could use some tender care."

Her words and the way she kept shooting me concerned glances made me think she cared for me. The realization made me warm all over.

She filled a glass with ice water, placing it in front of me. When the food was heated, she placed the plate in front of me, along with a fork and knife.

"Tea will be ready in a few minutes."

"Thanks, Ava. I really appreciate this." I gestured at the spread in front of me.

"It's the least I can do. You look like you had a long day."

"It's been a long week, but it's nothing unusual for me." The only difference was I usually came home to an empty apartment with out-of-date food in the fridge. There was no one to express concern about my long hours or to push me to eat.

I cut a generous piece of pork, biting into it.

Ava leaned her elbows on the counter. "I'd ask how it's going, but you probably want a break from thinking about work."

Chewing, then drinking a long pull of cool water, I said, "There's one kid who gives me a hard time."

Smiling, I recounted our conversations over the week. I finished with, "He doesn't think he'll like my music."

She smiled wide. "Are you planning on proving him wrong?"

"I'll take my cello in on my next day off. We'll see." I'd convinced more jaded people than him—there was an elderly gentleman in a critical care unit who grumbled about my playing when I did my rounds, but a nurse said he requested she leave his door open when I played down the hall. I liked to think he enjoyed it even if he refused to admit it.

"I don't know how anyone could hear you play and not love it."

Her words were simple and to the point, but they packed a punch. I reached across the counter, touching her forearm. "You're my biggest cheerleader."

She smiled sweetly. "Your first one, too, if I remember correctly."

"You should come." The words were out of my mouth before I could take them back.

She raised a brow. "To hear you play?"

I nodded, taking a forkful of mashed potatoes. She could bake *and* cook.

"I'd like to see where you work." Then she smiled mischievously. "And I'd love to know if you can impress this kid."

I expected her to ask why he was in the hospital, what he was being treated for, and I couldn't have answered her.

"He sounds like a firecracker." The expression on her face was affectionate.

"He is."

She didn't ask for more, and I appreciated that more than she could ever know. I'd dated women who asked for details about why I'd worked late, and other than *we were busy*, or *there was an accident*, I couldn't disclose private health information.

I finished everything on my plate, then sipped the tea she handed me. "I feel too keyed up to go to sleep."

Ava took my plate. "Want to relax for a bit? We could watch a movie?"

"In my room?"

Ava smiled. "Sure. I can get the full guest experience."

I helped her clean up, then led her upstairs, unlocking my door.

There was a small couch in front of the TV, but I couldn't be upright. I grabbed sweatpants and a T-shirt. "Find a movie. I'll change real quick."

When I came out, the bed was turned down, and she rested against a mound of pillows. "I hope this is okay. I figured you were too tired for the couch."

I climbed in next to her. "You thought right."

She clicked on a superhero action movie. She didn't ask if I wanted to watch it. But I was beyond making decisions. Exhausted, I moved closer to her, breathing in her scent, marveling in her presence.

"Can I hold you?" All I wanted to do was snuggle up to her and fall asleep.

She moved so her back was to my front. I reached around her, pulling her back against me. "Is this okay?"

She nodded against my chest.

I watched for a few minutes until my eyes started to drift shut. Staying here was the best decision. I got to see and talk to her. Best of all, I got to hold her. I was too far gone to think about what it meant. I tucked her closer and fell asleep.

CHAPTER TEN

AVA

Despite those two amazing nights when I'd slept in Alex's arms, I hadn't seen him. I left food out in the morning for him and a note under his door telling him there was a plate in the fridge with his name on it for dinner.

Each morning, the breakfast and dinner items were gone, but he'd leave a note behind. The first one said, *Thanks for thinking of me*, the next one said, *You're beautiful when you smile. I love sleeping next to you.* Each one was sweeter than the last. Yesterday morning, there was a sunflower arrangement, and the note said, *I love to play for you.*

Each time I saw the flowers and read the note, I smiled, my heart pitter-pattering in my chest like I was a teenager with her first crush. Walking softly down the steps, I couldn't wait to see what he'd left for me today.

Rounding the corner to the kitchen, my feet faltered when I saw Alex sitting on what I'd come to think of as his stool. "Alex, what are you doing here? Shouldn't you be at work or asleep?"

This morning, his eyes were bright. "It's my day off."

Happiness spread through me. "I can bake something for you."

He stood, coming to me, placing his hands on my hips. "I asked Juliana to cover the B & B today."

I shook my head. "Why did you ask her to do that?"

His expression was so open. "I wanted to take you to the hospital to hear me play."

I tried to move away from his grasp, but he held tight.

"I can still cook breakfast." I didn't want Juliana to have to cover for me. I was supposed to be easing her burden, not the other way around.

"You deserve a day off." His voice was soft, but insistent.

"That's not for you to decide." My initial irritation was subsiding.

"You've been taking care of me and everyone else the last couple of weeks. Let me take care of you."

"I don't understand—"

He rested his finger against my lips. "I'm taking you out for breakfast then I'll take you to the hospital."

When he removed his finger, I asked, "You're going to play the cello for that child you were telling me about?"

"And anyone else who wants to listen. Want to come with me?"

"I'd love to." There was nowhere else I'd want to be.

Alex moved to fill a travel mug with coffee.

"Are you sure Juliana's okay with covering breakfast?"

He handed me the mug. "She said she'd bring the girls over. They love to help cook and pretend they're running the hotel."

I smiled at the memory of them checking in guests. "They do love it here."

"They sound adorable."

"They are."

"I'll grab my cello while you sit, eat a scone, and drink your coffee." He pushed the container of scones I'd left out for him toward me.

"You're spoiling me."

"I prefer to think of it as taking care of you." He walked out of the room, letting the words sink in.

Warmth spread through my body as I sat on his stool, drinking the coffee I didn't have to make. I took a bite of the scone, I rarely had time to enjoy myself.

He returned to the kitchen with a large instrument case. "Ready? I'm not done feeding you yet."

I slid off the stool, taking his hand. "Can't wait."

We drove to a diner, ordering greasy eggs, bacon, and toast. It was delicious. We talked about his job and how much he enjoyed the fast-paced nature of it and interacting with children.

He didn't know it, but every time he talked about his patients, his eyes softened. He cared about each and every one of them. I'd say he was too caring for the job, but he also seemed to have a spine of steel to deal with everything else he'd described.

He parked in the garage, heading up the elevator to the PEDs floor.

When the elevator door opened to the PEDs floor, the eyes of the nurse at the counter widened. "Dr. St. James, what are you doing here on your day off?"

Alex lifted his case. "I promised a couple of kids some music."

Another nurse, whose name tag said Susie, leaned against the counter. "Braden's been talking about it all week. Good luck. He sounds like a tough one to impress."

Alex smiled, unperturbed by her warning. "He'll love it."

Susie gestured toward a room filled with toys and gaming screens. "When you're done visiting the kids that can't get out of bed, can you play in the activity room? We have a lot of families visiting today, and I think they could use a pick me up."

"Of course. I'll check in with Braden first." Alex reached for me, leading me down the hallway.

I loved seeing Alex in his element.

Alex knocked on the door that said Braden Keiffer, waiting for the voice to say come in before he pushed it open.

"Dr. Alex! You came!" a little boy said from the bed. His eyes looked tired.

A woman, probably his mom, sat next to him in a sweatshirt and leggings. She looked tired.

I bet it was unbelievably stressful to have your child in the hospital—no matter the prognosis. My heart went out to her. I hoped Alex would be able to brighten their day. It was a small thing, but I remembered how much I enjoyed listening to him play, and I wanted that same feeling for them.

"I said I would, didn't I?" Alex sat in one of the visitor's chairs, opening his case.

"Yeah, but you're here every day. I told Braden not to get his hopes up. You deserve a day off," Braden's mom said pointedly.

My chest filled with this indescribable emotion. Was I proud of him, or was it something more?

Alex shot Braden's mom a smile. "This is my day off. Now I get to do what I really love to do." He turned his attention to Braden. "I get to have a seat in your room and visit with you."

Braden's mom ducked her head, and I found tears prickling my eyes as well.

"I don't know if I'm going to like this," Braden said as Alex pulled a black, hollow-looking cello out of his case.

Holding it up, Alex said, "This is an electric cello."

Then he pulled out a small black box. "This is called a looper. It allows me to record myself, then replay it while I'm playing live. It's hard to explain, but you'll understand when I show you."

"Isn't that cheating?" Braden's forehead wrinkled.

Alex chuckled, and I moved to sit in the only other available chair.

"Braden. Don't be rude," his mom chided.

"I guess you could say it's cheating because I'll make it sound like multiple cellos are playing at once, but it sounds so much better that way."

Braden nodded, his expression serious.

Alex settled the cello between his legs. "I learned to play on a wooden cello. It has a richer, fuller sound, but I think you'll find that this one sounds good, too."

"How does it work? There's nowhere for the sound to go," Braden asked.

"Good question. The body of a wooden cello is a sound box that enables the vibration of the strings to resonate for a fuller, louder sound." Alex scrolled through his phone, hitting play. "This is me playing the same song on a wooden cello." He played a few seconds, then stopped it. "Now listen and see if you can appreciate the difference."

Alex's easygoing expression morphed into a more serious one as he picked up his bow, cocking his elbow to play. When the first note rang through the room, I had to place a hand over my heart, which had jumped in my chest at the beautiful sound.

The room was so small and the sound so big it felt like the notes were vibrating through my body. It was a mix of two songs I'd heard on the radio. I was awful at remembering names of artists and songs. I just knew that I loved when Alex played.

I became entranced with watching him move his bow and the way his eyes closed when he became lost in the music. He hit a button on the black box attached to the stem of the cello, and the sound of a second cello complemented him.

When he was done, the last note rang through the room. There was silence for a few seconds.

My ears still rang with the sound. I couldn't say which cello was more appealing—the wooden cello or the electric, but the ability to record himself and play it in the background made for a unique sound.

"That was so cool!"

I smiled at Braden's reaction.

He'd sat up in bed, his whole demeanor different than when I'd walked in. He was no longer withdrawn-looking, but excited.

"Do you think you could teach me how to do that?"

Alex stilled. "You want to learn how to play?"

"Uh-huh." Braden bobbed his head in agreement.

"Braden, he's a doctor, not a music teacher," Mrs. Keiffer said.

"I'd love to," Alex said. "I'll find a three-quarter size cello for you."

"You don't have to do that. We can get him one and hire a teacher."

"I'll respect your wishes, but please know that I'd love to help out in any way I can. My first love is music."

Mrs. Keiffer's shoulders relaxed. "I'd love some help finding a cello, and if you wanted to show him a few basics, we'd be forever grateful."

Alex stayed a little while longer talking to Braden about his favorite video games. When we said our goodbyes and left, Mrs. Keiffer followed us out.

Tears shone in her eyes. "Thank you so much for doing this. I haven't seen him this excited about anything in a long time. He used to love sports, and with his diagnosis, we don't know if he'll ever be able to run and play like he used to. Music is something he can do while he's going through recovery."

"I'm happy I can help. Kids are resilient. Don't be surprised if he works hard at PT after his surgery and is able to play the sports he used to love."

She covered her chest with her hand. "I can't thank you enough for everything. He's only just met you, and every other word out of his mouth is Dr. Alex this and Dr. Alex that."

"I'm just happy that I could brighten his day."

We said our goodbyes, and she went back into Braden's room.

"That was pretty cool."

Alex turned to me as we walked down the hall to the next room, flashing me a wide smile. "Wasn't it?"

I sucked in a breath at the force of his smile. I'd never seen him so happy before. Playing music might have been his first love, but I was positive sharing it was his main one.

"What you offered to do for Braden was really nice." Nice didn't begin to cover it. I had tears in my eyes, and my throat was tight during the entire experience.

He laid a hand over mine. "It was the least I could do. He has a challenging recovery ahead of him."

"You're amazing."

He winked. "You haven't seen anything yet."

It was the same teasing smile he'd given me as kids. Back then, it made us want to protect our stuff so he couldn't put something gross in it. Now it made my insides melt and my blood heat. I wanted to know what would have happened if we hadn't stopped our kisses.

Going into each room, Alex always asked for permission to play and for me to watch. Then he'd explain his instrument, answer any questions, then play. Hushed silence always fell over the room when he did. Whatever these kids were struggling with, the music helped. And I could see the way lifting each kid's mood and outlook, even if only for a short while, fed Alex's soul like he'd described.

Being a doctor was important, but reaching these kids on a different level was something else entirely. We ended up in the activity room where kids who were able to leave their room played. There were families and siblings, too.

They watched him curiously as he got everything ready. One child, who was about six, came up to him, touching the lines of his electric cello.

His father quickly pulled him back, but Alex shook his

head. "It's okay. I don't mind. As long as you're being respectful."

"Why is it missing?" The boy pointed at the hollow part of the cello.

"It's an electric cello." He went on to explain the differences between the wooden and electric cello like he had with Braden. Then he asked the child if he could listen to hear the difference in sounds.

The boy nodded, backing up to sit with his father.

Alex played a few songs, the sound fuller in the larger room. Surprisingly, the kids stopped playing, and several nurses paused to listen. One of the moms taped the impromptu performance.

My chest filled with so much pride for him.

When he was finished, the kids protested.

Alex covered his stomach. "I've been here for a few hours, and I'm starving. I'm going to get some food in the cafeteria, but I can bring my cello back on my next day off."

That seemed to satisfy them because the kids went back to what they'd been doing before.

A few parents came over to thank him. He wasn't just making the kids feel better, but the adults, too.

Observing him made me think that melding music and medicine might be the key to Alex's happiness. He was destined for bigger and greater things than me and our small town.

CHAPTER ELEVEN

ALEX

I was irrationally pleased that Ava was able to come with me today. Picking up my cello case, I asked, "Ready for lunch?"

Ava fell into step next to me, raising a brow. "The cafeteria?"

"I like to show the kids that the food here is good. That they aren't missing anything by being here. It's a small thing, but—" I shrugged.

"That makes sense," she said thoughtfully.

I wondered what she thought of my performance. I saw the way her shoulders relaxed and her eyes softened when I played. At the same time, there was something in her eyes I couldn't quite put my finger on. It almost looked like pride.

It was a treat getting to see her reaction to the music because I couldn't when we were kids.

"You like working with kids," she said matter-of-factly.

"I do." They were so honest in their reactions and questions.

I could reach almost anyone with music, even people who were reluctant at first, but as a doctor, there were some patients who were understandably depressed about their diagnosis. I felt better when I could make a difference in someone's life, even if it was only for a few minutes while I played a favorite song.

After placing our food on a tray, we chose to eat at a table by the window.

"It's nice to see where you work."

"My place of work changes every month."

"That must be tough. Never being able to develop a long-term rapport with a patient."

"That's the nature of the field I'm specializing in. I'll only see a patient for a few minutes or hours. If they're admitted, they'll be passed to a different floor."

"That's true."

"Sometimes I want to know what happens to the patient after we've treated them. Other times, maybe I don't." That was hard to admit. When I first started out, my professors, and later, attending doctors, stressed the importance of detachment. Those who took it to heart had a hard time doing the job. They felt too much.

I still felt it, I just pushed it down deep. Playing music helped ease that ache.

"We have the rest of the day. What do you want to do?"

"This is going to sound silly, but I love fall. I'd like to go to a pumpkin farm."

"A farm it is. You mind if I invite Miles?"

"Not at all." Excitement filled her eyes.

I loved giving her a day off and doing exactly what she'd been longing to do.

I texted Savannah, asking if we could stop by and pick up Miles. She was grateful because he was with her at work.

After picking up Miles and driving to the pumpkin patch, we pulled up to MacCarthy Tree Farm. It was early in the season, but the lot was full. "You went to school with one of the MacCarthy brothers, didn't you?" Ava asked.

"Yeah, Tom, I think it was. Does he work here now?"

"His family runs it. I think most of the brothers are involved in one way or another. In the fall, you can pick apples and pumpkins; in the winter, they sell Christmas trees, wreaths, and decorations; and in the summer, you can pick strawberries, blueberries, and cherries."

"A year-round business." I paid for the tickets, getting in line for the hayride.

"We're going on a hayride?" Ava asked.

"We're here for the full experience. I don't think Miles would let us get away with not getting a pumpkin."

Miles nodded. "We have to have a pumpkin."

We rode the bumpy tractor to the field. When it stopped, Miles ran several steps ahead of us, looking for the perfectly shaped orange pumpkin.

Ava picked up a small orange pumpkin.

"Is that the one?" I asked, moving closer to her.

"I was looking for one to sit on the counter of the B & B. I just have this vision of the perfect white pumpkin that guests will ooh and aah over."

"You should pick something you like for your apartment, too."

I pulled my phone out, holding it up for a selfie of us. Wrapping an arm around her shoulder, I pulled her close. I snapped a few of us smiling. The last one, Ava kissed my cheek. I was a little stunned by her spontaneous kiss but hoped I caught the picture.

Ava stepped away from me as I scrolled quickly through the pictures. "I should take some of Miles. Savannah will want to see."

I turned my attention to my phone. I'd caught the moment she'd kissed my cheek. My eyes were wide with surprise, but I looked happy. Her eyes were closed.

I almost wished she were mine. That Sundays spent at a pumpkin farm were a regular fall outing for us.

"Uncle Alex, look!" I put my phone away and moved toward them.

He'd picked a small, lopsided one.

I told him we needed to pick a large one to carve, too.

"Can you make a jack-o'-lantern with me, Uncle Alex?"

"Of course."

He rolled his eyes. "Mom always messes it up."

I squeezed his shoulder. Savannah was doing her best. "The important thing is that she tried."

"Can we do it tonight?" Miles's face was bright with excitement.

"I don't see why not." I was off tonight, and though I'd hoped to spend time with Ava, I also wanted to spend time with Miles. I couldn't help but wonder if she'd join us.

Ava smiled at me. This day was supposed to be about giving her a day off, inviting her to listen to me play, but it had turned into so much more. She'd gotten a chance to see where I worked, the patients I worked with, and how I used music to brighten their day. But spending time with Miles felt domestic. It made me want to have more in my life than work. It made me long for a connection, someone to come home to.

My heart rate picked up as we picked our way through the pumpkin patch, searching for the perfect pumpkin. Ava picked up one after the other, coming up with some reason why it wouldn't suit from being too dirty to a small imperfection.

"You know it doesn't have to be perfect."

She looked up at me, a sheepish grin on her face. "I know."

"You never know…this one with the slight dimple might give them something to talk about."

"I don't know."

"Sometimes you don't need the perfect thing. You just need to choose something, to start somewhere. You can refine it as you go."

She blinked at me. "We're not talking about the pumpkins, are we?"

"No." My voice was gruff. I wasn't even sure exactly what we were talking about…her family life, selling her baked goods, me?

"I'll take this one. It's the best one I've seen so far, and there's just something about it that called to me."

"See? It's better than perfection. You like its flaws, too." I took the pumpkin from her, put our chosen ones in a bag, marked it with my name, and set it in the wheelbarrow for the workers to move to the store for when we were ready to leave.

"When did you become so wise?" Ava asked, her tone genuinely curious.

"I'm not perfect either. Just trying to figure things out as I go. Just like you."

"It's nice to have someone to share things with. Bounce ideas off of."

"It's nice for someone to have our backs. To encourage us when we're feeling discouraged. To point us down the road we're scared to take."

"Alex." She tugged on my shirt.

Pausing, I looked down at her.

Her gaze was on the ground as she chewed her lip. "I think I want to find my mom."

"What changed your mind?" I hadn't even been thinking about her mom when we were talking about imperfections.

"I'd really like to know why she left, even if it's not what I want to hear, even if it hurts."

"Then you should."

She wrapped a hand around my elbow. "Will you do it with me? I don't think I can face her alone."

"When the time comes, you'll be able to do it, but I'll be right there supporting you every step of the way."

Her shoulders relaxed. "Thank you."

Her gratitude was genuine and heartfelt. It felt better than when she agreed to spend the day with me or listened to me while I played. I wanted to be there for her. I wanted to help her.

"Uncle Alex, come on!" Miles's impatient tone drifted over the field toward us.

Keeping one eye on him, I leaned closer to Ava and asked, "Ready to go race some ducks?"

She smiled and nodded.

When we reached the area set up with games and slides for the kids, Miles ran ahead to the one where you pumped water into a canal for ducks to move back and forth. We joined him, each taking our own water pump to see who could get their ducks moving the fastest.

I pumped it as hard as I could, taunting Miles and Ava. "My ducks swim faster."

"Mine are faster," Miles yelled.

I glanced over at Ava, not really caring if I won. She bit her lip in concentration, pumping as hard as she could. I moved over to her. "Here, let me help."

I wrapped my arms around her. She stilled, sucking in a breath. "What are you doing?"

"Helping you." My words ghosted over the shell of her ear.

She shivered.

My hands closed over hers while I helped her.

"No fair. You're helping her."

"All is fair in love and war."

"Ugh. You sound like Grandpa."

I smiled hugely, not caring how ridiculous I probably looked helping Ava with her ducks. We shouted encouragement at the colorful plastic ducks, and when Miles's last blue duck made it to the finish line, we cheered for him. It was the most fun I'd had in forever.

We followed Miles as he moved from one activity to the other, climbing tractors, going down slides, and trying his hand at the football toss. At the top of the hill, there was a slide built inside the silo.

"Can we do this one?" Miles asked, already taking off before I could answer.

"I guess we're doing the silo slide."

Before I ducked to go inside the building, I noticed Ava stood off to the side. Holding my hand out to her, I said, "Let's go down together."

She glanced uncertainly at the dark tunnel.

I wanted an excuse to touch her, hold her close. "Please?"

She put her hand in mine. "Fine."

I grabbed the piece of burlap, joining Miles in line. When it was his turn, I told him to wait for us at the bottom of the slide. He nodded before I gave him a push.

I arranged the burlap on the white slide.

As soon as Ava sat, I moved behind her, my legs on either side of her body. "Lean back on me."

"Okay." She settled into me, stiff at first, then when I pressed a hand to her belly, she melted into me.

I whispered into her ear before I pushed off. "I've got you."

The slide was fast, whipping around the tight space of the silo. With each turn, I pressed her against me, holding her to me. A sharp drop had my stomach flip-flopping, then we flew out into the bright sunshine.

"That was so fun." Ava's face was flush from the excitement.

I grabbed the burlap, walking with her back up the steep hillside. "Glad you tried it?"

When she smiled at me, I wrapped my hand around her shoulder, pulling her into my side.

Touring Annapolis was fun, but this was more.

"I'm glad you talked me into it."

"Can we go again?" Miles asked when we got to the top.

"Can we?" I asked Ava, giving her my most pleading tone.

"Sure."

I liked to think she enjoyed my touch and being close to me. We went down the silo a few times until Ava complained of being dizzy. Then we grabbed some warm cider and decided to take a chance at the large corn maze.

"I hope we don't get lost," Miles said.

I crouched down to his level. "The way out is to the right. It's not one of the cleared paths, but if you separate the corn stalks, you'll be free."

"That's not so bad." Miles's face lit up with confidence, then he took off running.

Brushing off my pants, I stood. "We're going to have a hard time keeping up with him."

Ava cradled the warm cup. "You're good with him."

We fell in step next to each other, following Miles at a more sedate pace. We could follow him just by hearing the pounding of his feet.

"Kids just want to be seen and heard. They want to trust that when they talk, you're listening." I blew on my apple cider and took a tentative sip. When it didn't burn my tongue, I took a bigger pull.

She looked at me with admiration on her face.

"It's easy enough for me, I'm not handling all of the other tasks that come with raising a child. I don't have to get him to school on time or remind him to brush his teeth." I remembered the times Savannah lamented how difficult making all the decisions was without a partner.

Ava nodded.

"I'm sure Savannah's exhausted doing it all herself. Now she has the store she's worried about. I want to spend time with Miles while I'm here, and if it eases her burden, then even better." Halloween was coming up. I wondered if I'd be off so I could go trick-or-treating with him. I wanted to experience the holidays with him.

"You're a good man." She said it matter-of-factly, like it wasn't a big deal when her words were everything.

"I try to be." I never thought about it that way before, but along with studying and working hard, I wanted to be good. I wanted to be someone others could count on, especially my family and patients.

"It shows. You'll be an amazing father one day." She drank her apple cider, closing her eyes, presumably at the flavor.

The thought of being a dad startled me. "I don't know if I want to be anything other than an uncle."

I tried to imagine myself running after my own child. I'd always thought I'd be so busy with work there'd be no time for a wife and family. Working with doctors, I'd seen many relationships fail due to the demanding job and grueling hours. The ex-wife of my mentor, Steve, couldn't handle the long hours. Now he was embroiled in a bitter custody battle.

She nodded, not saying anything.

"Do you want kids?" I was curious about her dreams. We'd talked so much about mine.

She pursed her lips. "I think I'd worry about whomever I was with leaving me like my mom left my dad."

I wasn't sure what to say to that. There were no absolutes in life. I'd seen enough of my colleagues get divorced.

Miles ran back to us. "Come look!"

Then he took off again.

"I guess we should follow him." Amusement tinged Ava's tone.

"We should." I grabbed her hand, the moment gone.

Ava drank the last drops of her apple cider before handing me the empty cup.

We jogged through the maze, following the sound of Miles's excited voice encouraging us to follow him.

We slowed when we came to a clearing. A tractor stood in what must have been the center of the maze.

"Look at this!" Miles went down the long, twirly slide.

We sat on a nearby bench to watch, the afternoon sun warming us.

Ava's admission that she worried a significant other would leave her bothered me. I wanted to ease her worries, but I wasn't sure how to do that with words.

Checking to make sure Miles was still playing on the tractor, I leaned over to kiss her instead. I meant to just brush my lips over hers, but she tasted like apples and cinnamon, so I angled her chin, taking it deeper. I buried my hands in her hair, running one over her shoulder and back and then cupping her cheek.

Remembering where we were, I slowed the kiss, easing back from her.

She looked dazed.

I shouldn't have done that, not while we were watching Miles, but I'd acted on instinct.

Miles ran up to us. "I have to go potty."

Taking his hand, I said, "Let's find a way out, buddy."

Rushing now, we walked swiftly through the maze, taking the first exit out, which led directly to a couple of port-a-potties.

When he came out, Miles said, "I'm hungry."

"Wash your hands. We'll grab some apple cider donuts. You can eat them on the way home." I gestured at the sinks nearby.

Thankfully, he didn't argue for more time at the farm. I was tired and anxious to have Ava to myself. Something clicked into place when I was kissing her on the bench. My chest swarmed with emotions I couldn't explain and didn't know what to do with. All I knew was that I wanted more.

We dropped off Miles with Savannah, staying to help carve a jack-o'-lantern. She was grateful we'd taken him for the day so she could concentrate on work. But I'm sure she wasn't happy with the two donuts we'd let him consume before dinner.

Miles picked a ghost for his pumpkin. I drew it with the stencil that came with the carving kit Savannah bought. Ava took pictures while we cut into it, scooped out the middle, and then carved it. It was her idea to save the seeds and bake them. I helped Miles place a small plastic candle in the pumpkin, setting it on his dresser. I wished he lived in a home with a porch he could decorate.

We said our goodbyes and headed outside.

"I'm the fun uncle, apparently," I said to Ava when we were alone in the car.

"Apparently." Her voice was full of amusement.

I wasn't ready for it to be over. I tried to think of the perfect way to extend the day, coming back to the last time we'd been truly alone. "Want to watch a movie? Your pick."

I held my breath, hoping she'd say yes.

She glanced at me as if sorting something through in her head. "Okay."

Smiling in relief, I headed back to the B & B that was quickly starting to feel like home. Parking in front of the inn, I tried not to think about what it meant when I'd lived in New York for years and never thought of it that way.

Going inside, we headed to her apartment. I placed a few logs into her fireplace and lit it with the starter she'd left on the mantel and said, "Your place is so cozy and private."

She moved around the kitchen, heating the cider we'd purchased from the farm's store. "I forget I'm over the B & B sometimes. It's so quiet and feels so secluded."

I sat on the couch, opening the kettle corn and popping a few kernels into my mouth. "Nolan did a great job up here."

He gave it a warm, cozy feeling despite the open space.

"I love it." She sat two steaming mugs on the coffee table, then sat next to me.

I tried not to think too much about the inviting bed behind

us. Today wasn't a date, no matter how much it seemed like one. "You pick the movie this time."

She raised a brow as if I'd challenged her. "You won't mind if I watch a Hallmark movie? The pumpkin farm got me in the mood for something romantic."

I shrugged. "Not at all."

I couldn't reveal the day we'd shared had me feeling all melty inside, too. It wasn't something I'd ever felt before, and I wasn't going to admit it just yet.

She turned on a fall movie. After a few minutes, she said, "Don't you think it's funny the guy is the owner of a B & B and the woman is a guest from the city?"

I hummed in acknowledgment even though I hadn't been paying attention to the plot or the characters.

Focusing on the show, I found myself wondering if the woman was really going to leave the guy and go back to the city.

"It's such an impossible situation, isn't it?"

My chest tightened as I watched the woman run through similar thoughts. Her home was in the city, but her job was demanding. Small-town life was less complicated, more relaxing.

I looked over at Ava, who'd finished her cider and popcorn, putting her stockinged feet onto the coffee table, a pillow under her crossed arms.

What would it be like if I worked here? If I dated Ava? Was that something that made sense in my life? Hope filled my chest to the point of bursting and warred with my preconceived notions of what I'd already planned for my future.

My heart raced. I almost never deviated from plans. Could I take a job here? Spend more time with Miles and my family? Maybe even Ava?

Ava gestured at the TV. "You know she's going to go back to New York, realize she screwed up, then do some grand gesture to convince the guy she wants to live in Connecticut."

"Yeah, but where would he work?"

Ava glanced over at me. "I think they said he could commute if he had to."

I couldn't look away from what was happening on the screen. I knew what was coming, but I had to see it play out. When the woman quit her job, she was miraculously offered a job closer to the small town. It all seemed tied up in a neat little bow. That wasn't real life.

Ava got up, cleaning up our trash. "Too bad life doesn't work out that way, huh?"

I leaned forward, my elbows on my thighs, watching her move about the room. She'd changed into leggings that showcased her legs and butt, an oversized sweater, and fuzzy socks. She wasn't wearing anything alluring, but my hands itched to touch her.

I sucked in a breath, desperate for air in my lungs. I could say good night and walk away, or I could do the thing I'd wanted since I saw her walk down that aisle all grown up and unbelievably beautiful.

What would she do if I stepped behind her, grabbed her hips, and pulled her back against me? If I lifted her hair off her neck and ran my tongue over the exposed skin? Would she push me away? Would she tell me we couldn't cross the line from friends to lovers?

CHAPTER TWELVE
AVA

I rinsed out our mugs and placed them in the dishwasher. Alex had been uncharacteristically quiet during the movie.

He sat on the couch, his elbows resting on his thighs, looking contemplative.

I turned, leaning a hip against the counter. "Are you listening?"

He blinked, then focused on me. In one fluid motion, he rose, stalking toward me.

My heart started pounding in my chest. What was he doing? The look in his eyes was almost predatory.

Gripping my hips, he lowered his head.

My breath caught. "Alex? What are you doing?"

His proximity made me breathless.

"Kissing you." He rocked my hips, so that I was pressed against him. Then he kissed me, his lips firm and confident.

He paused every few seconds, his hands and lips everywhere at once. "I'm going to kiss you until you push me away."

He lifted my shirt, running his hands underneath until they rested on my ribs. "I'm going to touch you until you tell me this is a bad idea. The worst I've ever had."

He nibbled on my neck. "Until you remind me of all the reasons we can't do this."

He's my best friend's brother. A friend. This was going to change everything.

He paused, pulling back. "I'm going to tell you right now that I don't care about any of them. All I can think about is how soft your skin is." He ran his fingers up until they teased the edge of my bra. I arched, begging him for more.

"How you'll feel with nothing between us."

Visions of his naked skin filled my head. My soft against his hard. I had to bite my lip to contain the moan that threatened to erupt from deep down.

"I. Want. You." He punctuated each word, so I felt it in my soul.

"Yes," was all I could manage. None of the reasons mattered. Not when he'd palmed my breasts, his thumbs strumming my nipples through the lace. Then his mouth was back on mine, and I lost all coherent thought.

He backed me up to the bed until the back of my knees hit the mattress. Then I was falling, my legs spread wide. Alex stepped between them, looking down at me.

He was amazingly sweet, but in the bedroom, he barely restrained himself. His fingers curled into fists at his side, his chest heaving with his breath.

"Tell me this is crazy. Tell me to stop." His eyes were dark, his words pleading.

I could put the brakes on this right now. We were stepping over the invisible line in the sand I'd drawn. Nothing would be the same if we continued, but I couldn't bring myself to care. "I can't."

He placed one knee on the bed, his hands going to my thighs. The heat of his strong hands radiated through the thin material of my leggings.

"Alex. I need you." My words unleashed an inferno between us.

He ripped my leggings down my legs, taking my panties with them. Kneeling on the rug, he caressed the arch of my foot, kissing my knees. He was sweet and gentle, yet at the same time, confident and sure.

He spread my legs with his shoulders.

"Take off your shirt."

I ripped it off, unclasping my bra and letting it fall down my shoulders. Flinging it to the side, I leaned forward, cupping Alex's cheek. He kissed my palm. The movement was slow and sensual, his eyes dark with desire.

"I want to taste you."

No one had ever asked for oral, much less demanded it quite like that. I was dripping from his words alone.

"Yes," I hissed, unable to look away from him as he lowered his head, separating my folds and licking me from opening to clit.

"Fuck." I fell back on my elbows, wanting to watch him.

I couldn't believe Alex was going down on me—no, he was devouring me with his mouth, his tongue, and his fingers. The act was so intimate. I felt open and vulnerable, yet I wanted to be closer to him. I wanted to give him everything.

The combination of seeing him on his knees between my thighs and his determination to make me come had me sliding over the edge before I knew it. Spasming around his finger, I reached out to him, wanting him on top of me.

Alex stood, shedding his clothes and grabbing a condom from his wallet. He ripped it with his teeth, my pussy clenching hard in reaction to the sexy move. He sheathed his cock, kneeling on the bed between my legs.

His cock perched at my entrance, I tensed, every muscle in my body waiting for the sensation of his cock entering me for the first time.

"Are you sure?"

"I've never been more positive."

He surged inside me in one thrust.

The sensation of being full stole my breath.

He paused, resting on his elbows, his mouth hovering above mine. "Are you okay?"

I nodded, overwhelmed with emotion, but not wanting him to stop.

Regardless of whatever happened after this moment, I'd never forget being with Alex. I widened my legs farther, welcoming him deeper.

He groaned, his forehead dropping down to mine. "You feel so good."

Then he moved in long, slow strokes, kissing me while building me up again. Sitting up, his thighs under mine, he repositioned me, hitting a spot I'd never felt before.

"That's it. Don't stop." I hung on to his bulging biceps, meeting his thrusts with my hips. I could barely talk over the rising sensation, my muscles tensing right before I exploded in an orgasm so big I didn't think I'd ever come down from it.

I chanted nonsensical words, feeling out of control as my pussy clenched hard around his cock.

He reared up, holding my legs wide, quickening his pace.

I didn't want it to end. *He made me want more.*

With a final thrust, he went deeper than before. Spilling inside me, he rested his weight on me, his face buried in my neck. My heart still racing, I stroked his back, holding him tight. His muscles flexed under my touch.

Was he having any regrets? I was afraid to know.

He kissed my shoulder, slowly pulling out. I felt empty when he stood next to me.

"Let me take care of this."

I watched his ass flex as he walked to the bathroom. He had a nice ass, an amazing cock, and the perfect tongue. I was ruined forever, and he was Savannah's brother. If he decided we were one and done, I'd still see him across the table at their family dinners or holiday meals.

The decision that seemed so easy a few minutes ago now seemed rash and irresponsible.

I was contemplating the possible outcomes when he opened the bathroom door, sauntering over to me.

My gaze moved slowly up his muscled thighs, his ridged stomach, defined pecs, and finally paused on his growing smirk.

"You like what you see." It wasn't a question.

I couldn't stop my lips from quirking. "I didn't have much of a chance to look earlier. You kind of pounced."

His smirk spread into a confident smile, losing the arrogance entirely. "I couldn't hold myself back anymore."

"No regrets?" Then I winced at my question. Why had I brought it up?

He slid into the bed, wrapping an arm around me. "None."

His tone was so confident I believed him. I tried to let that feeling soak in, but it didn't stick. He didn't regret it today, but would he tomorrow?

"Stop thinking so hard. Just enjoy the moment."

I pushed out any thoughts that his time in Annapolis was temporary. I soaked up the feel-good endorphins he'd released, letting myself drift. I was suddenly exhausted from the day.

Just before I drifted off, I swore I felt Alex's lips brush against my forehead.

The next morning, I woke early, a heavy arm banded right around my middle, a leg between mine. Closing my eyes, I wanted to bask in this moment. I wasn't ready to face Alex—how everything was different this morning.

I couldn't go back to him being my friend's brother. He was so much more—childhood crush, an adult fling—or was it something more? Something that wouldn't ever be realized because he was leaving at the end of his residency.

Alex groaned. "No thinking."

I rolled to my back, his arm loosening. "How do you know I'm thinking?"

"You tensed as soon as you woke." A wolfish smile broke over his face. "I know a good way to loosen you up."

I smiled in spite of myself. "You do, do you?"

He hummed in response, kissing my shoulder, pulling the sheet down to expose my nipples that pebbled in the cool morning air. I arched into his mouth as he took the first one in his mouth, then the other. He tugged the sheet down my body, settling between my legs.

"So beautiful."

With his words and actions, he erased the doubts and worries that had crept in overnight. He was erasing them one at a time, replacing them with new memories.

"Alex." I was needy and aching for him. "Please."

He used his mouth, tongue, and fingers to wake me up. When I was still coming down from my orgasm, he grabbed a condom from his wallet, quickly rolling it down his cock, then entering me. I twisted my fingers in the sheets, my eyes closing. It felt even better than last night—an irresistible combination of new and familiar.

"Look at me." His voice was rough.

I opened my eyes. The morning light allowed me to see every groove of his hard body and the intense pleasure on his face.

I felt powerful, knowing I affected him this way, realizing it wasn't just a one-time thing.

He guided me onto my knees. Pulling me up with an arm banded around my stomach, he entered me again. I felt more vulnerable in this position, open to him, knowing he could see every imperfection.

He reached around, tweaking my nipples before circling my clit. I bit my lip when the orgasm rushed through me, harder and quicker than the last. He gripped my hips, pulling all the way out, then thrusting inside. He felt huge in this position, deeper than before.

It felt amazing. With one final thrust, he emptied himself into the condom, then rested over my body, running his hands over my back.

He murmured words in my ear about how amazing we were together, how gorgeous I was. I'd never felt more beautiful, more desired. He finally pulled out, going to the bathroom to take care of the condom.

I sagged into the mattress, wanting to stay in bed the rest of the day.

Returning, Alex sat next to me. "Do you have to go to work?"

For the first time since taking over the B & B, I wanted to play hooky. I wanted to stay in bed with him all day, exploring his body and the amazing connection we had.

Glancing at the clock, I realized I had only a few minutes to shower if I wanted to bake before the guests stirred. "Yeah."

He kissed me. "I wish we could stay in bed."

"Me, too."

"I have to work later." His tone was regretful.

The urge to care for him took over. "Stay in bed for a while. I'll save you breakfast."

He kissed me again. "Thank you for thinking of me."

I ran my fingers through his hair, sifting the strands. "You're not used to someone doing that."

Sadness filtered into his expression. "Not since I moved away from home, and it's different with you."

I smiled, trying to lighten the mood. "I would hope so. I'm not your mother."

He smiled, losing that boyish expression and giving him an almost rakish look, making his face appear so much younger. "Definitely not."

He cupped my breasts, brushing his thumb over my nipples, igniting a zinging fire with a direct path to my core.

I arched into his touch. "You can't do that. I have to take a shower."

He lowered his mouth to my nipples. I moved to pull him away but held him to me instead.

"I'll join you." He stood, tugging me up with him.

"That sounds like the best idea I've heard all day," I teased, following him to the shower.

He turned on the water, holding his hand under the stream to test the temperature. "And it's so early."

Hope and happiness surged through me when he stepped into the shower. Joining him, he moved me so I was in front of him, hogging most of the warm water. I tipped my head back, soaking my hair while he poured shampoo into his hands.

Turning me, he gathered my thick, wet hair in his hands, and he lathered it, his hands massaging my scalp.

"This feels so good."

"Better than sex in the morning." His tone was amused.

"It's close." My eyes closed of their own volition. I was lost in his touch, his hard body surrounding me. "I want to wake up every morning just like this."

He kissed my shoulder, then my neck. I arched my head, giving him better access. "That can be arranged."

He lathered his hands with body wash, spreading it over my shoulders, spending extra time on my breasts, holding them in his hands as if weighing them. His expression was almost reverent as his hands traveled down my stomach and between my legs. My knees weak, I leaned against him.

"How much time do you have?" he whispered into my ear, spreading my folds.

"Not much." But it would be so worth it to be late.

He turned me to face him and kneeled. The sight of this man on his knees in front of me made my heart flutter in my chest like a butterfly testing its wings.

He nudged my feet apart. "You're very, very dirty."

"Can you help?" My voice was huskier than I'd ever heard it.

"Happy to." With a gleam in his eye, he licked me, working me up again.

I didn't think it was possible to experience so many highs in one morning. He was ruining me, but I was going to enjoy every second. By the time he lifted me in his arms, pressing my back against the cold tiles, I was positive I was going to be very late.

But nothing mattered except the flex of his muscles as he surged inside me, his hard body claiming me, making me his.

Afterward, we quickly showered, dried off, and got dressed. We parted ways at my door.

"I'll be down soon."

I nodded, not able to respond from the emotions filling me. Things I'd never felt before—pure light and happiness and the scariest one of all, hope. Hope that what we had was real. That he'd want to see me again. That he'd stay.

CHAPTER THIRTEEN
ALEX

After I was with Ava, work felt lighter and flew by quicker than it ever had before. That first night, I knocked on her door, and the next day there was a key with a note under my door. She said she loved waking up with me and to use it whenever I wanted.

I refused to think too hard about what that meant. I was going to enjoy whatever was between us, not thinking about the future or the repercussions.

She seemed happy to live in the fantasy, too. Each night, I slid into her bed, waking her slowly with my mouth, then my fingers.

By the time I entered her, her eyes were bright with desire. I couldn't get enough of her. I wanted to bury myself inside her each night.

I was usually too tired to wake when she did in the morning, but I'd grab breakfast to go before heading into work. The stolen moments when I was able to eat breakfast with her or when I fell into bed with her at the end of a shift were the best I'd had ever spent.

She was an indulgence—one I usually wouldn't allow. My practical side said it was ridiculous to get involved when I would most likely have to leave in a few months. My other side wanted to enjoy every second we had.

Being with her made everything better—the stress of my job, the worries about the future. Having her to look forward to at the end of each night was addicting.

On my next day off, I'd made an appointment to meet with my friend and PI, Sam, at a local diner. I'd told Ava I wanted to make the introductions, even though he might recognize her from school. In reality, I wanted to be there to support her.

Each day, she seemed more and more tense about it. We arrived and sat on the same side of the booth to wait for him.

"We're just going to talk to him. You don't have to hire him." I turned over my coffee cup, nodding at the waitress walking around with a carafe of coffee.

After the waitress poured our coffees, Ava said, "I'm afraid of what he'll find."

"You don't have to do anything with the information he gathers. If he tells you where she's living and what she's doing, it can end there."

She breathed deeply before answering. "I know myself, Alex. I'll want to confront her."

I wrapped my fingers around my mug. "Have you talked to your sister or your dad about it yet?"

"I know they won't like me talking to Sam."

"You should tell them what you're doing—what *we're* doing." I wanted her to know I was in this every step of the way with her.

The door to the diner opened, and cool fall air followed Sam inside. He wore dark jeans, a black T-shirt, and heavy boots.

I waved him over, standing when he approached to shake his hand.

Gesturing to her, I said, "This is Ava."

Ava half stood to shake his hand. "I remember you from

high school."

"You looked different back then." Sam glanced at me then sat across from us.

He'd asked me why I was calling on her behalf to make the appointment. I'd told him she was a friend of my sister's, and I was just helping her out. He accepted it then, now I wondered if he realized there was more going on.

He placed a notebook and white manilla folder on the table between us.

"Thanks for meeting with us," I said.

The waitress came by to get our orders. Sam ordered a coffee.

"I hear you're trying to find someone," Sam said to Ava, cutting to the chase.

I covered her hand with mine on her leg.

"That's right. My mother left us when I was thirteen."

"Did she write a note, say if she'd be back?"

Ava's forehead scrunched. "She sent us off to school that morning like any other day. She didn't tell us she was leaving. As far as a note, I never saw anything, but it's possible she gave something to my dad he didn't share with us."

Sam took a few notes on his pad. "Have you spoken with your father about it?"

She shook her head. "I can if you think it would help."

I knew she was reluctant, but if Sam thought it was necessary, I hoped she would.

"In situations like this, it's very possible your dad had an idea of what was happening, but wouldn't share it with you. Would you like me to interview him separately?"

She shook her head. "Let me talk to him first."

"Anything else you can share? Even if you don't think it's significant, it might help me."

Ava went through the usual details: her mother's birth date, family, places she liked to spend time, and hobbies. Her mother quitting her job to become a stay-at-home mom…

Ava pulled out her phone, scrolling until she found her mother's social media account. She turned it to face Sam. "This is her. I've read through her posts. There's not much. At some point, she lived in Florida. She looks like she could be a drug addict."

Sam's face grew concerned when he looked through her photos. "She doesn't look healthy."

He pushed the phone back to us. Her mother had blonde hair, but it hung in strings; her eyes were lined with heavy makeup, but there were dark circles under her eyes. Her face was gaunt now that he'd mentioned it. Beatrice looked older than her years.

"That's why I thought she was doing drugs. I haven't confirmed it or anything. I can barely remember what she looked like back then. We have pictures, but Juliana never liked them out. Not after she left."

I squeezed her hand. I couldn't imagine losing my mother at such a young age. Then not being able to mention her name or look at her pictures.

"Your father ever mention drug use?"

"Not that I can remember. I should have talked to him before we met with you."

"It's fine. I'll get it later. Had she ever been injured, been in an accident?"

Ava paused as if she was thinking. "I think she was. A few months or so before she left."

"Was she admitted to the hospital?"

"No. But I remember her being in pain and sleeping a lot. Does that mean anything to you?"

"She might have become addicted to the pain pills and jumped to something more serious."

"You think she left because she was doing drugs?" Ava's body was stiff.

"I'm just gathering information."

Ava was strung tight, like she was barely holding on. I

knew this would be difficult, but I was starting to wonder if this was a bad idea all around.

"You mind if I speak to your sister?"

Ava shook her head. "Let me talk to her first."

"I have to be honest with you. The more information I have to go on, the better. I can do it without speaking to the rest of the family, but since Juliana is older, she might remember something you don't. Same with your dad."

"I understand. I just want to warn them before you talk to them."

"Fair enough. That's all I need for now. I'll do some electronic searching while I wait to hear from you." Sam gathered up his things.

Ava reached a hand out to stop him. "Wait. We didn't talk about cost."

Sam looked at me for confirmation.

I'd discussed this with him over the phone. "I've got it."

From her expression, Ava didn't like it, but she didn't argue.

I stood, shaking Sam's hand. "Thanks for helping us."

"Not a problem."

Sam nodded at Ava before leaving.

Sitting next to her, I asked, "Are you okay?"

Her expression serious, she said, "It's my mother. I want to pay for it."

"Let me do this for you," I pleaded.

She bit her lip, finally nodding. "All right."

I stood. "Ready to get out of here?"

She slid out of the booth.

We walked out the door and toward the B & B for a few seconds, not talking.

She rubbed her arms like she was cold. "I'll need to talk to Juliana and my dad."

"I can do it with you." I wanted to be there for her if she needed me.

"That's okay. I don't think they'll want anyone there. It's so personal, you know?"

I nodded. I understood even if I didn't like it.

I wanted to ask her if she was regretting her decision to locate her mother, but I needed to take her mind off it.

Ava tilted her head to the side. "Will you play for me?"

"Of course." I had the day off and wanted to spend it with her.

Ava paused by the door to the B & B. "I love the idea of others hearing your music. Would you want to play at the harbor, or is that too public?"

"I've played in Times Square, the subway, the hospital. I don't mind."

"I'll grab my case." I headed up to my room, grabbing my cello. When I met her outside on the porch, I offered, "If you want me all to yourself, that's okay, too."

"I kind of want to be out enjoying the day, sharing your music with others."

I stroked her face. "Whatever you want."

She tilted her face up to mine. It was filled with hurt—from what I assume was our conversation with Sam—and something else—hope?

In that moment, I wanted to give her everything. I wanted to make her happy.

I kissed her softly. I vowed to myself to always try and make her happy, however long I was with her. I wouldn't think about what it would feel like to walk away. I knew that was getting harder to contemplate with each day that passed. We had today, and I was going to enjoy every minute.

When we got to the harbor, I opened the case, sitting away from the water so it didn't spray my instrument.

"It's not awkward to just get out your cello and start playing in public?" Ava asked, looking around. It was a weekend morning, so there were quite a few people wandering the area, admiring the boats, and waiting for the tour to begin.

"Maybe the first time I did it. But I've recorded my public performances and put it online, so I've gotten used to it."

"I didn't realize you sold your music online."

"I use the money to donate to whatever hospital I'm working with at the time." I nodded at the case. "People throw money in there when I play, too. It's not much, but it adds up over time."

"Are you serious?" Her expression was a mix of awe and admiration.

I played a few chords to warm up. "Yeah, I never wanted to profit off my music."

"Is that because of your parents saying you'll never make money from it?"

I'd never thought of it that way. "I like how it feels to give back."

Her shoulders relaxed. "It's a nice thing to do."

Warmth filled my chest. "Any special requests?"

She tipped her head as if thinking. Then she asked softly, "Can you play the song you played at the wedding for the first dance?"

I played a few notes. "Ah, the most requested wedding song."

She shrugged, smiling softly. "It's probably cliché, but I love it."

"Whatever the lady wants, she gets." I wanted to collect all of her favorite songs and play them for her. When the urge to say forever popped in my head, I quickly shoved it away. We weren't forever, we were right now.

"Sit down." I nodded at the space on the bench next to me.

"So bossy," she murmured, settling next to me.

"You asked me if it felt awkward to play in public, and I said no, but I sure like you sitting next to me." It felt natural to have her here.

Then I played the beginning notes of the song she'd requested. She settled back on the bench, relaxing.

I liked to see her relaxed and happy. It was tearing me up inside to see her so upset at the diner.

When I looked around, people had stopped to listen. A few walked by, dropping money in the case. I nodded in thanks at them, but kept playing.

When the final notes of her song faded over the water, I said to those gathered, "This beautiful woman requested I play for you. I hope you enjoy it."

A few people were recording on their phones. I didn't mind. I hoped word got around. Maybe I'd play a few more times before I left Maryland. The thought of leaving was always in the back of my mind, no matter how many times I tried to ignore it. It swirled in my gut like something bad I ate. It would have to be dealt with at some point. I just didn't want it to be now.

After several songs, I'd drawn a crowd. "Thanks for listening. I'm going to take a break."

"Will you play again?" a little boy asked.

"I'll be back." The familiar surge of energy I only got from performing was thrumming in my veins.

When the crowd dissipated, I asked Ava, "Do you want to visit the bakery?"

"Are you hungry? I can bake you something."

"I thought you might like to talk to them about helping out or selling some of your stuff."

"I don't know."

"It's scary to put yourself out there."

Ava smiled. "But you just did."

"It wasn't easy the first time. I was sweating bullets. I was a small-town kid in New York. What did I know about performing on the streets? I thought people would laugh at me or, worse, ignore me."

"You're amazing. How could you possibly think that?"

I gave her a pointed look. "I could say the same about you."

She chewed her lip. "What happened the first time you played?"

"My microphone had horrible feedback. The crowd cringed. I gave up on introducing myself and just played."

"I love that. Your music speaks for itself."

"I have a feeling you're my biggest supporter."

"I love it, even though I've never played anything myself."

I squeezed her shoulder. "What do you say about checking out the bakery?"

"It doesn't hurt to check it out."

"That's my girl." I tugged her to standing, holding on to her hand while I placed the cello in the case.

Carrying it, we headed away from the harbor, past the marketplace, and toward the Main Street shops.

She laid a hand on my chest. "You're very persuasive."

I winked at her. "I can be."

"I don't know what I'm doing with you. You've turned my world a little upside down. You have me talking to PIs and thinking about starting a business."

"I hope you don't think I'm meddling."

She was thoughtful for a minute as we walked. "You're encouraging me to take that first step."

Happiness surged through me. It wasn't just about helping her. She made me happy.

We stopped in front of the bakery storefront, blue and white letters over the large windows read Sweets on Main.

Ava walked inside ahead of me, the smell of sugar and dough hitting our noses.

I swear, Ava sighed in contentment as she looked around.

"It's amazing." Her eyes filled with wonder.

This was what she wanted to do. I hoped there was some way she could live her dream.

CHAPTER FOURTEEN
AVA

Standing in the bakery, a vision of a similar display case at the B & B popped into my brain. I could cook for the guests and anyone who walked by. It would be a sneak peek of the inn. Maybe they'd want to stay another time.

It would bring in foot traffic from the tourists. It would be something unique we could offer.

"Can I help you?" A blonde woman asked.

Stepping forward, I said, "Hi, I'm Ava. I run the B & B on Admiral Street by the Naval Academy."

"I've heard your baked goods are to die for," the woman gushed.

"You have?"

"Your guests come here thinking I make the pastries at the B & B."

My heart pounded in my chest. "Are you serious?"

Her smile was friendly. "Wouldn't lie about that."

"That's amazing."

"I've been telling her to sell her stuff," Alex said.

"You should."

"I don't want you to think I'm encroaching on your business."

WAITING FOR YOU

"There's plenty to go around. Some days I can't keep up because there are so many tourists. We're not on the same side of town, either."

"That's true." Could I do it? Would Juliana be okay with the addition of a bakery? "I'll think about it."

I was so grateful Alex mentioned stopping in. I never would have known how much guests appreciated my wares.

"We'll take six of those." I went through the display case, asking for a little of everything. I wanted to support her.

Alex pulled out his card to pay.

"I'm sorry, I didn't get your name."

"It's Sophie. Here's my card. My cell number's on the back. A bunch of the local business owners get together once a month; we share ideas and talk about issues with the town. Would you like to join us?"

I pocketed the card. "I'd love to. Thank you."

She smiled widely as she took Alex's credit card and rang us up.

"It was so nice to meet you," I said as we were leaving.

"You as well. Come back soon."

On the sidewalk, I said, "Sophie was so friendly. She wasn't concerned about competition."

It was surprising. I'd expected a different response.

"She's right. You're technically on opposite sides of town if you consider that most people are walking. You can handle the Naval Academy and waterfront restaurant side, and she has more than enough traffic on Main Street."

Main Street ran through the heart of Annapolis, ending at the harbor, and it was lined with shops selling tourist items, fudge, ice cream, sandwiches, and coffee.

On the back of Sophie's card, she'd written, *Shops on Main meet the first Monday evening of the month.* Next to it was her cell.

"Call her. Meet with the other shop owners. At the very least, you'll make new friends. You might get some more ideas for how to sell your baked goods to local restaurants."

I held the card to my chest as we headed back to the B & B. "I'm so excited. For the first time in forever, I'm excited about the future. I don't feel like I'm just existing. Does that make sense?"

"Perfectly."

Alex already had his future mapped out—he had a following on social media of people who loved and listened to his music, he would be a full-fledged doctor in a few months. He had everything. Soon he'd be gone, living his life in New York. I needed to pursue what I wanted, too.

"Thanks for encouraging me."

"You would have gotten there eventually."

"I can't believe guests go to the bakery looking for my pastries."

"Why? Your stuff is amazing. Why wouldn't the guests want to take some baked goods home to share with friends and loved ones?"

"I never imagined things would take off like this. I thought managing the B & B would give me time to experiment with recipes. Honestly, I thought it wouldn't pan out. That my baked goods would just be ordinary. I didn't go to school for it."

"It's raw talent."

Hope soared through me. I'd finally found something I was good at. My whole life I lived in Juliana's shadow. Everything she touched turned to gold. She was amazing in school, in her realty business, her design business, she attracted sponsors on social media, she married young and had beautiful twin girls. Even though it ended in divorce, she met and fell in love with Nolan. She had everything. I wasn't jealous. I just wished I could have something like that, too. Something of my own.

"You're going to do amazing things."

His voice dropped off at the end. Was he thinking what I was? He probably wouldn't be around to see what I did. I couldn't ask him to stay. I wouldn't be the person asking him to give up his dreams. He'd resent me in the end.

"I'll talk to Juliana about it tonight. We're getting together for dinner."

His face pinched. "Do you want me to come?"

"I should talk to them on my own, but thank you for offering."

"If you change your mind, I'll be there."

"Is it weird I've been dropping into your family dinners forever?"

"You are a pest like that." He squeezed me tighter to him, running his knuckle over my head like he did as kids.

"Hey! Stop that!" I twisted away from his grip, opening the door to the B & B.

He had a mischievous grin on his face.

I knew he wasn't done teasing me. I dropped the box on the counter by the door, running up the steps to my room, and unlocking it with him hot on my heels. I heard the door slam closed behind me, Alex following me inside. When we reached the open expanse of my room, he wrapped an arm around my waist. Then I was twisting in the air as we fell onto the bed.

His weight settled over me. "You know you weren't really running away from me."

Out of breath, I said, "I didn't want to."

I wanted to run toward him. A vision popped into my head of me chasing him while he ran faster away from me. I closed my eyes against the endless loop of images running through my head.

"Hey, where'd you go?"

"I was just thinking about something I had no business worrying about."

He brushed a strand of hair off my forehead. "You worried about your mom?"

I didn't answer, not wanting to admit it was him I was longing for.

"We don't have to find her. I can tell Sam to forget it."

"It's fine."

"I'll be with you every step of the way."

Would he be, though?

"There's nowhere else I'd rather be."

I let his words sink deep, forgetting that I should have added *for now* to the end of his sentence. I wanted him to stay, to get a job here. I wanted him to be a part of my life and Savannah's and Miles's. I wanted it more than I'd ever wanted anything.

"I want you," he whispered across my lips, kissing the underside of my chin and neck. His hands ghosted under my shirt.

The sentiment to his words was slightly different than what I was thinking, yet I kidded myself into thinking it was the same.

I knew I was delaying the inevitable. I was getting in so deep I'd never find my way out, but I couldn't seem to stop myself. I wanted him, however I could have him.

He took his time, removing our clothes, exploring, stroking, and sucking every inch of my skin until I was beyond ready to have him inside me.

Flipping our positions, I hovered over his cock. "I want you now."

He raised a brow. "I think I like when you're demanding."

I sank over his cock, feeling every ridge as I took him inside.

Alex groaned. "I'm not wearing a condom."

I paused. "Do you want me to stop?"

"I get tested. You?"

"Same. I'm on birth control."

"There's no need unless you want it?" Alex's voice was strained, his muscles tensed under me.

I knew he wanted me to move. When I thought he

couldn't take it anymore, I slowly moved up, then back down. "I want you like this."

His grip on my hips tightened. "You're so beautiful."

I expected his expression to be feral, full of want and desire. Instead, he gentled his touch, cupping my breasts, his eyes full of tenderness.

I leaned down to kiss him. "You make me feel beautiful."

"You're perfect." His words washed over me, making me feel like I could do and be anything I wanted. A feeling came over me, it was so large and big, I could barely contain it.

He surged up, sucking a nipple into his mouth, disturbing my rhythm, scattering my thoughts. My need grew out of control. Gripping my hips, he surged into me from below, sending me over the edge. Spasming around him, I whimpered.

I'd never felt anything like I did when he was inside me. Was it chemistry, or was it something more?

He flipped me onto my back, holding my thighs apart, his gaze on his cock entering my pussy. It was erotic and raw. I watched his face contort as he went over. It was primal and real.

As his body sank into mine, I wondered if he'd felt what I had or if he was able to keep his emotions separate.

He thrust deep, stilling inside me. His face contorted in pleasure as his fingers gripped me tighter.

He rolled to the side, moving me to his chest. "I'll clean up in a minute. I just can't right now."

I chuckled. "I killed you, huh?"

One eye opened, he said, "Something like that."

Was he as overwhelmed as I was? Was he questioning what we were doing? Or was this just a fling for him? A way to spend the time while he was in town.

I drew in a breath; the pain was so sharp, it pierced through my torso as if I'd been stabbed with a knife.

He kissed my forehead. "I think I'll take a nap."

"Yeah, okay." I knew I'd never be able to sleep—not with the thoughts that were running through my head.

I didn't want to be needy. I didn't want to ask him what we were doing. I tried to relax as his breathing evened out, but I couldn't sleep. I carefully moved out of his embrace without waking him, cleaned up in the bathroom, then got dressed.

I needed something to calm my mind. I headed downstairs to the large kitchen, needing to bake. I sent a message to Sophia, asking if she wanted to meet for coffee sometime before the next business meeting in a couple of weeks. She readily agreed.

I had to move forward with my life as if Alex wouldn't be here. I needed to think about my future.

A couple of hours later, Alex walked into the kitchen. His shirt was wrinkled and his hair in disarray. "Where'd you go?"

"I decided to test some recipes."

He cocked a brow.

Every spare inch of the counter was covered with ingredients. I'd made cookies, cakes, pies, and brownies. "I don't have enough space upstairs."

"Or enough ovens. Who's going to eat all of this?"

"I can drop some off for my family. The girls and Nolan eat a lot." My cheeks felt hot.

"This can't all be for them." He popped a still-warm chocolate chip cookie into his mouth.

"I'm testing out what I should sell in the display case."

He stopped chewing. "You're going to do it?"

"I'm going to talk to Juliana and ask her what she thinks. It's her business."

"What are you going to do if she says no?"

"I'll figure something out. I want to do more than cook for the few couples who stay at the inn. I can sell to restaurants or other hotels in the area who need breakfast provided to their guests."

He moved around the counter to stand in front of me. "I'm so proud of you."

Resting my hands on his chest, I said, "I haven't done anything yet."

"Once you've made the decision to act, it's a done deal."

"How do you know me so well after a few weeks?"

"You forget I've known you since we were kids. I remember you being stubborn and tenacious."

"Was it all those pranks we pulled?" I teased.

His expression remained serious. "It was how you picked yourself up and moved on after your mom left. I can't imagine going through anything more difficult than that."

Sobering, I said, "I never thought it made me strong. I always felt weak for needing her to be in my life."

"That doesn't make you weak. It makes you human."

I closed my eyes, reveling in his kind words. "You say the sweetest things."

He smiled, popping another cookie into his mouth. "Not as sweet as this."

I laughed. "I don't think there will be any left if you keep eating everything."

He shot me an incredulous look. "Trust me. There's enough for an army here."

Looking around the kitchen, I said, "Maybe I'll take some to the restaurants as samples of my work."

He glanced at his phone. "Want to do it now?"

Nerves fluttered in my stomach. "Let's do it."

We packed everything up, separating what I was taking to my family from what we'd take to the restaurants. Alex drove me from one place to the next. I took a small box into each place with a note stating my name and what I was hoping to do. At some places, I was able to speak to a manager, but most I left with a hostess.

After the last one, I dropped into his passenger seat, exhausted. "I need to get some kind of business card."

"You don't have to be perfect to get started, you just have to do it."

I let his words give me confidence. "You have a good business sense for someone who's studying to be a doctor."

He winked. "I'm very smart."

"Or very cocky," I said wryly.

He placed a hand over his heart, pretending to be wounded.

Rolling my eyes, I said, "You know you are. I bet the women fall over themselves to be with a doctor."

He sobered. "Is it cocky if I said you're right?"

Wincing, I hated that I was.

He reached over to take my hand in his. "I like being with someone who doesn't care about that, though."

"You do?" I loved when he said sweet things about me. I'd never get tired of hearing them.

"I want to be with someone who smells like sugar and dough. You make everything sweeter."

My heart contracted at his words, his actions, and his loving support. I was falling in love with him. Overcome with emotion, I looked out the side window, hoping he hadn't noticed my reaction.

I had to be careful. I was getting used to his steady support, but he wouldn't always be here. I had to remember that.

CHAPTER FIFTEEN
ALEX

After my shift Friday night, I showered quickly, anxious to meet Savannah, Ava, and Miles at his school for movie night. I parked on the street because the lot was full by the time I got there. Rounding the building, I bypassed the line for pizza, popcorn, and candy. I stood on the hill, unsure how I'd find them with the sun quickly setting. The movie was already playing on a blow-up screen in the field; a spotlight was on the playground next to it where kids were playing.

"Uncle Alex!" Miles yelled as he ran up to me. "You made it."

"I wouldn't miss it." Thankfully it was a quiet night at the hospital so I was able to leave on time.

He grabbed my hand, pulling me over to where Savannah and Ava already sat on camping chairs, a blanket in front of them with an open pizza box.

"Do you want any pizza?" Savannah asked.

My gaze caught on Ava's. Savannah and Miles didn't know we were together, but I really wanted to kiss her hello. "I ate earlier."

"Can you get me popcorn and candy?" Miles asked.

"He just got here. I don't think he wants to stand in the popcorn line," Savannah said.

"I don't mind."

Ava stood. "I'll go with you."

The air was cooling as the sun went down. We walked side by side up the hill to the concessions, not talking.

When we reached the line, I looked back to check if I could see their blanket. There were too many people between us.

I leaned down, whispering in Ava's ear, "Can I kiss you?"

A slow smile stole over her face, which I took as a yes.

I tilted her chin, giving her a soft kiss, then murmured, "I missed you today."

She smiled wide. "I missed you, too."

I felt almost giddy to be here with her, knowing Miles and Savannah were waiting for me.

I pulled her in front of me to protect her from the jostling crowd and as an excuse to be close to her.

She tipped her head to see my face. "I'm glad you could make it."

"Me, too." I couldn't help but think working nearby would allow me to do more events like this.

I was happy the line was long so we could have some time for ourselves. When we reached the front, I grabbed several bags of the freshly popped popcorn and candy, and then we made our way back to the blanket.

Finding Savannah by herself, I asked, "Where's Miles?"

"He's playing with friends at the playground."

I handed her a bag. "Might as well eat this while it's warm."

I sat on one of the chairs with Ava next to me. It was some animated Halloween movie I'd never seen before, and I could barely hear over the kids running back and forth through the crowd, playing with their friends.

WAITING FOR YOU

After a few minutes, Savannah stood. "I should probably check on Miles."

I handed my popcorn to Ava, wiping my buttery hands on a napkin. "Stay. I'll go."

I was here to spend time with Miles and to give Savannah a reprieve. Unlike the other families, she came to most of these events alone.

Savannah offered me a soft smile as I stood, heading toward the playground. Being there for Savannah and Miles felt good.

Once I found Miles on the playground, I stood back with the other parents to keep an eye out. It was completely dark now; if one of the kids ran away from the playground, it would be hard to spot them.

A few minutes later, Ava approached. "It's a little crazy, isn't it?"

A parent standing close to us said, "I feel like I came to watch a movie I don't care about, while the kids don't watch the movie so they can play with their friends—"

I laughed with him.

Ava nodded toward the kids screaming and running around on the playground. "But they're having so much fun."

Miles spotted me. "Uncle Alex, watch me swing on the monkey bars."

I kept an eye on him, smiling and nodding when he hopped off. "That's awesome, buddy."

Miles's eyes filled with excitement. "I can jump from the rock wall to the monkey bars. Watch me?"

"I have to see this." Then I asked Ava, "Is this safe?"

She smiled indulgently. "He's literally a monkey on the bars. He's done it a million times before."

I bumped her shoulder with mine. "If you're sure. I don't want him to get hurt on my watch."

"He won't." Ava's face was soft.

When Miles jumped, grabbing onto the bars, I let out a

breath in relief. Watching Miles together felt natural. Being here, close enough to spend time with my family, with Ava, was nice. It eased an ache in my chest.

Until now, I hadn't realized how lonely I was in New York. My family and friends were my coworkers. I could see those were empty relationships compared to what I had here.

Savannah came up to stand next to us. "It's so nice to see him playing with friends. In preschool, he'd stand off to the side."

"He's growing up," I said to her.

"Thanks for coming tonight. Miles was so excited. He told all his friends you'd be here." Savannah shot me a meaningful look before she took a few steps toward Miles. She held a hand out to him. "Let's go eat your popcorn before it gets cold."

Miles took her hand while we followed them back to our seats.

Instead of sitting on the blanket, Miles curled up on my lap with his bag of popcorn. He felt so warm and cuddly in my arms. "Will you go trick-or-treating with me?"

His voice was soft. It made me wonder what it would feel like to hold my own child, to have him fall asleep in my arms. I couldn't imagine anything better.

"I'd love to." Glancing over at Savannah, I asked, "When is it?"

"When it gets dark on Halloween."

Halloween was Sunday night. I usually got off around six or seven. I hugged him tighter to me. "I wouldn't miss it."

"Cool. I'm going to be a ninja."

"You're going to be the best ninja."

Ava smiled, and I wanted her to keep smiling like that at me—like I was a good guy, not the one who'd be leaving soon.

In New York, I rarely had the time or energy to go out. I certainly never thought I'd be content going to a movie night at my nephew's school, but I was. I wanted more evenings like this.

WAITING FOR YOU

Halloween night, I texted Savannah that I was on my way before getting in the car to go straight to their house. I promised Miles I'd be there, and I refused to let him down.

When traffic stopped due to an accident, my heart rate kicked up. All I could think about was the disappointment on Miles's face if I couldn't be there. When I maneuvered past the accident, the highway opened up, and I drove as fast as the speed limit allowed and parked as close as I could get to their apartment. People probably traveled to downtown Annapolis to trick-or-treat. I walked quickly toward their apartment, texting as I went.

Alex: Walking to you now.

Savannah: We started, but we're only a few buildings down from our apartment.

I weaved through the groups of trick-or-treaters, looking for a familiar boy in a ninja costume.

Seeing him standing between Ava and Savannah, waiting in line at a store handing out candy, I tapped his shoulder from behind. When he dropped their hands and turned to me, I lifted him up. I didn't want to think about the day when he didn't want me to greet him this way.

He wrapped his arms around my neck. "You made it."

"I told you I wouldn't miss it." I kissed his cheek, then put him down to see his costume.

I cocked my head, tapping my chin with my finger. "Are you sure you're Miles? You look like a ninja."

Miles puffed out his chest with pride. "I am Miles."

I shook my head in disbelief. "If you're sure."

Ava smiled at us while Savannah shook her head at our antics. We slowly moved forward in line.

Savannah leaned over to whisper, "He was so worried you wouldn't make it."

"I made it." I didn't want them to worry or question

whether I could be somewhere, even though it was the nature of my job. I saw how it tore other doctors' relationships apart. I didn't want that for my family, but if I lived here, I wasn't sure how I'd avoid it. Not having connections in New York made that aspect of my job easier, but infinitely emptier.

We walked with Miles, Savannah and I holding one of his hands until his pumpkin bucket was too heavy to carry, and he was tired.

I was grateful that Savannah had Ava to accompany her to events like this. My heart pinched when I thought of not being here next year.

When Miles slowed, his eyes getting droopy, Savannah said, "Let's go home so we can count how much candy you got."

Miles perked up, talking a mile a minute about his favorite candy, how much he got of each kind, and what he'd eat first.

Ava and I walked behind them. She leaned over to say, "Savannah will confiscate most of it by tomorrow."

I held a hand over my chest. "Seriously?" At her nod, I said, "Poor guy."

Ava rolled her eyes. "He'll survive."

He didn't need all the candy. It was the experience of going door to door and seemingly getting tons of candy for free that was the thrill. I liked that he'd look back on this night and remember I was here. I wanted to be part of his life growing up, not on the periphery, with occasional calls and visits.

This evening, combined with movie night and the pumpkin patch, made me want something like this—a family of my own—with Ava.

The last realization had my heart pounding under my ribs. Ava fit so easily into my family already. Was staying here a possibility even if it didn't fit into my carefully constructed plans?

CHAPTER SIXTEEN
AVA

Halloween was fun. I usually attended everything I could with Savannah and Miles. I felt bad when it was just us because I worried he missed out on having a father, but with Alex there, we felt complete. I still hoped Savannah could find someone who loved her and Miles, but having Alex there made Miles's day.

I parked in Juliana's driveway. I'd asked for a family dinner tonight so I could tell them about Sam, his investigation, and hopefully ask a few questions.

Alex had asked if I wanted him to come for support, but I needed to do this on my own. I wanted to have this conversation in private. It was past time for me to ask for answers.

Checking my phone before I got out, I noticed a new message from Alex.

Alex: I'm thinking of you. Remember, you didn't do anything wrong. It was your mother who left these loose ends. All you want is closure. There's nothing wrong with that.

Ava: I don't think they'll see it that way.

I was nervous about my sister's reaction. As a teen, she'd blow up when Mom's name came up. I learned quickly to avoid any mention of her. I knew it was because she was hurting and dealing with it in a different way than me. I wanted to talk about it; she wanted to clam up.

He must have been near his phone because I saw the bubbles indicating he was typing a response.

Alex: I'm here for you—no matter what.

Gratitude flowed through me.

Knowing I needed to have this conversation, I put my phone away and grabbed the boxes of pastries I'd brought.

When I opened the door, Laila came running. "Auntie Ava!"

I crouched down to her level, balancing the boxes in one hand. "How are you, sweet girl?"

"Did you bring cupcakes?" Laila's eyes were round as she took in my box.

"I did."

Laila's responding squeal was so loud I wished I could cover my ears.

"Sorry. You'll be deaf if you hang around with us too long," Nolan said, taking the boxes from my hands as I stood.

Following him into the kitchen, Charlie stood next to Dad.

I gave her a hug and a kiss.

"What did you bring?" Juliana asked, opening one of the boxes.

"Cupcakes!" Laila exclaimed.

"Cookies and pies, too," I said.

Juliana's eyes widened. "What's the special occasion?"

"I took samples of my baked goods to restaurants, and I had some left over."

Juliana's brow arched.

It was the perfect time to broach the subject of what I really wanted.

"I was thinking it might be a good idea to add a bakery display case at the B & B. We could offer baked goods to tourists coming off the street, and the guests could buy some to take home."

Juliana looked uncertain. "I don't want to mess with the current vibe. We're a quiet B & B with relatively few guests due to the number of rooms."

"It could bring more people in." But that's not what Juliana wanted.

Juliana tipped her head to the side. "I kind of like that we're off the beaten path. Selling something might bring in too much traffic."

My confidence slipped. I hadn't thought that Juliana wouldn't want to increase traffic. "We visited the bakery, Sweets on Main. The owner, Sophie, mentioned our guests go there asking to buy my baked goods."

There was a gleam in Juliana's eyes. "Have you talked to her about selling your stuff there?"

I shook my head. My excitement about my idea dissipated. "It's her bakery. I don't know if she'd want an assistant."

Nolan opened the cupcake box.

Laila placed her hands on her hips. "Ooh. Can I have a cupcake?"

"Not before dinner," Juliana said.

"I want you to eat the spaghetti and meatballs I made," my stepmom, Sheila, said.

"Nolan had one," Laila pouted.

"It's not fair," Charlie added.

Nolan unwrapped two more.

Juliana pointed at Nolan. "You're spoiling their dinner."

Nolan lifted the quieter twin, Charlie, into his arms, handing her a cupcake. "But they're so good. We couldn't resist. Right, Charlie?"

She nodded happily, taking a huge bite.

Juliana shook her head. "You're impossible with them."

I knew my moment to discuss my idea was lost in the

chaos of the girls and dinner. I hoped one of the restaurants we'd dropped baked goods off to would call me.

Dinner was loud and messy. There was spaghetti on the girls' faces, the table, and the floor. Even the curtains behind them were splashed with sauce.

After dinner, Nolan took the girls into the living room to play with dolls.

I helped carry the dishes into the kitchen where Sheila was stacking the dirty dishes in the dishwasher, and Dad was placing the leftover food into containers.

When things were mostly cleaned up, I decided it was the best time to talk to them. Taking a deep breath, I said, "I wanted to talk to you about something."

"What about?" Dad asked, placing the last container of spaghetti in the fridge.

Sheila put the last dish into the machine, wiping her hands on a towel before turning to face me.

Juliana leaned a hip against the counter.

I decided not to sugarcoat it. "I talked to someone about Mom."

Sheila moved to stand next to Dad.

Juliana sucked in a breath.

Our father braced his hands on the island. "Why would you do that?"

"I have a lot of questions, and I was curious."

Juliana covered her chest with her hand. "She was the one who left us."

I'd expected Juliana would be upset. "I'd like to know why."

"She clearly didn't care about us." Juliana crossed her arms over her chest.

I turned my attention to Dad, hoping he'd be more reasonable. "Do you know something that could be helpful?"

He shifted on his feet.

"I blamed myself for her leaving," I confessed.

I heard the girls in the living room playing and Nolan's high-pitched voice as he role-played a game for the girls. Usually, I would have found that endearing, but my stomach was in knots.

Juliana moved around the island, wrapping an arm around me. "Why would you think that? It had nothing to do with you. She was selfish."

"Dad?"

He'd been silent this whole time. He looked conflicted as if he wasn't sure what to say.

Finally, he said, "There are things you don't know."

Juliana straightened. "What do you mean?"

My heart thrummed in my ears. "You know your mother was in an accident a few months before she left."

Juliana placed her hands on her hips. "What does that have to do with anything?"

My stomach sunk. Is that how she got into drugs?

"She became addicted to the painkillers. I didn't realize it. Not at first. I just thought she was more tired than usual. She was still recovering from the accident. Until there was a message from her doctor saying he couldn't refill her prescription because she'd refilled it too many times."

I shared a disbelieving look with Juliana.

"I didn't want you to know. There really wasn't a need."

"Is that why she left?"

"She claimed she didn't have a problem. She was in pain, and she'd find another doctor who'd fill her prescription for her."

"So she just left?" Juliana's voice raised in pitch.

"I encouraged her to go to rehab. I even reserved her a spot. We had a horrible fight the day she left. I gave her an ultimatum. Rehab or leave." Guilt marred his face.

"Oh, Dad," Juliana said, moving over to him, covering his hand with hers.

"It's not your fault she left," I said.

"And it's certainly not yours," Juliana said to me.

"I pushed her too hard."

Juliana patted his arm. "You did what you needed to. You cared about her. You were worried about her."

He shook his head, dropping it below his shoulders. "I failed you girls. I pushed your mother away."

Juliana shook her head. "We don't blame you."

I tried to think of questions Sam would want me to ask. "Did she ever contact you?"

"I'd get an occasional call late at night. Her voice was slurred. She said she was sorry. She missed you girls."

I expected that admission to affect me, but I felt numb.

"She must not have if she never came back. Never sent a birthday card. Nothing." Juliana's lips set into a straight line.

"She wasn't in the frame of mind to be a mother to you, so I never said anything about the phone calls."

"We understand." Juliana stroked his arm soothingly.

"The pills changed her. She was a good mother before."

I sensed Dad did everything he could. I wasn't sorry I'd brought it up. It was good to get the truth out in the open. No more tiptoeing around the past.

Dad approached me. "If you want answers, then you should try and get them."

I nodded, my throat tight.

"Just know, it wasn't your fault."

"I know that now." I hugged him tightly, breathing in his familiar scent, the one I always associated with home.

When Dad pulled away, I asked Juliana, "You're not upset with me?"

"I hate to dredge up the past, but if you thought it was your fault, then I think you need to get whatever closure you can get from talking to Dad and Mom."

"Thank you."

She hugged me. "Let's go see what the girls are up to."

I sensed Dad wanted to talk to Sheila alone.

In the family room, Nolan had a purple boa wrapped around his neck, a tiara perched on his head, and a small teacup in his hands. "Everything okay?"

"Daddy, you're supposed to speak like Harriett." She pointed at one of her dolls.

"I'm sorry, darling," Nolan said in a high-pitched voice.

I had to cover my mouth to contain my laugh.

Turning to us, he repeated in a falsetto, "Everything okay?"

I smiled at Juliana. Finding out that Mom hadn't left because of me eased the tightness in my chest. "We're good."

"Yeah, we're okay," Juliana agreed.

I sat on the couch next to Juliana, watching Nolan interact with Charlie and Laila. They were so sweet together. It reminded me there was a lot of good in my life. My family, Savannah and Miles, her parents, and Alex.

I wasn't going to worry about the what-ifs anymore. I wanted to enjoy what I had now.

CHAPTER SEVENTEEN
ALEX

Over the last few weeks, we'd fallen into a nice routine. I ate breakfast with Ava when I could and spent time with her when I came home. After her talk with her dad and Juliana, she'd been more at peace.

Only one of the restaurants she'd dropped off samples to wanted to serve them on the menu, but it gave Ava hope. She looked into renting a booth at the marketplace at the end of Main Street by the harbor. It was a great location. She'd gotten Juliana's permission to use the kitchen at the B & B to bake her goods, she took a class on food safety, and perfected her recipes so she could submit her food labels to the health department for approval. There would be minimal startup costs. The biggest being the cost of ingredients and rent for the booth at the marketplace.

We celebrated Thanksgiving the day before because I worked the actual holiday. Walking into my family's house had always been loud and boisterous, but it was even more so with the addition of Miles.

"Uncle Alex," he cried as soon as we kicked off our shoes and hung up our jackets.

I caught him in my arms. "What have you been up to?"

"I'm building a hospital. Want to see?" Miles asked as we walked into the kitchen.

Mom stirred something on the stove, and Savannah was pulling dishes out of the cabinet. "He got this Lego book from the library. He's trying to make everything in it."

Football played on the TV in the family room.

Ava set the apple and pumpkin pies she'd made on the counter, then asked if there was anything she could do to help.

"Can you warm the dinner rolls?" Mom asked her.

I loved that they were so close. Knowing I was leaving soon, I didn't want to do anything to damage their relationship.

"Where's this hospital?" I followed him into the living room where Legos were scattered all over the floor and pushed out any melancholy thoughts.

There was a large green Lego base plate on the floor with the beginnings of a red and white structure.

He pointed at the book propped against the coffee table. "Can you help me?"

"I'd love to," I said, sitting cross-legged next to him.

Helping consisted of finding whatever pieces Miles needed. I was not permitted to add any of the pieces to his building. It was amazing to watch him construct it based on the picture without any instructions.

Dad gestured at what he'd constructed so far. "It's pretty impressive, isn't it?"

"Makes you think he'll be an engineer or something."

"Building Legos is a job," Miles insisted.

"I don't know about that," I said, exchanging an amused look with Dad.

"You might make more money if you turn your skill into building real buildings," Dad said.

Miles's eyes widened. "I could do that?"

"I don't see why not," Dad said. "You seem to have a knack for it."

"That would be so cool." Miles refocused on his Legos, asking me here and there to find a specific piece for him.

"How's the job going?" Dad asked.

"I finished the pediatric block. Now I'm in orthopedics. The hours aren't too bad." I wasn't dealing with critical patients in this rotation. The worst injury was chronic pain we couldn't heal with surgery or physical therapy, but we referred those patients to a pain management doctor.

"What are you doing next month?"

"Shock trauma." It was the reason I'd transferred here for part of my residency.

Dad whistled. "I bet that'll be tough."

"It's more serious injuries." I didn't mention the specifics in front of Miles, but I anticipated critical gunshot wounds and accidents that may require life flights.

"I guess we won't see much of you that month."

"Probably not." That's why I was enjoying every second I had with Ava and my family now.

"You leaving after that block?" Dad drank his beer.

"It ends before Christmas." I needed to get back to New York right after the holiday to work my next block.

"Too bad you can't finish your residency up here. It's been nice having you around more. You think you'll look for a job here?"

"I hadn't thought about it." It wasn't entirely true. Some nights when Ava fell asleep before me, I watched her, wishing I had a choice in where I finished my residency, but I didn't. Extending my stay in Baltimore for two months was unusual.

My mentor, Steve, advised waiting until I was more established in my career to get serious about anyone. When he'd given me that advice, it had seemed like a good idea. I was focused on my job, I didn't need the distraction of a relationship. Now I wasn't so sure. Was I prepared to let Ava go? To see her date someone else?

Jealousy shot through me, hot and jagged, scaling everything it touched, leaving open wounds in its wake.

"You dating someone in New York?" Dad asked.

I shook my head, feeling the raw pain from my thoughts. "Nope."

Dad studied me. "Thought maybe that was why you were so keen on getting back."

"Didn't leave anyone behind." Instead, I'd be leaving Ava here. But I couldn't talk to my father about her.

Ava and Savannah walked in carrying wineglasses.

Savannah touched my shoulder as she passed. "I wish you could stay. Miles loves having you here."

A lump formed in my throat, making it difficult to swallow.

Miles glanced at me, focusing on our conversation. "You can live with us."

The sheer simplicity and innocence in his words ripped the gaping wound wider.

Reaching over to ruffle his hair, I said, "I wish I could. I don't get a choice in where I live during my residency."

Savannah smiled at Miles. "And our place is too small."

"He can sleep with me—I have room under my bed."

Everyone chuckled at that. Miles had a loft bed with a slide. So, there *was* room underneath where he kept a sleeping bag and pillow.

"Sweetie, I don't think Uncle Alex wants to sleep on the floor."

At Miles's crestfallen expression, I quickly added, "Maybe we can have a sleepover before I leave."

"That would be so cool!" Miles flashed me a huge smile.

"I have an air mattress I can blow up for you," Savannah offered.

I wanted to keep that smile on his face. I wanted him to be happy. I tried not to think about how he'd feel when I left.

Video calls weren't the same thing as being physically present in his life.

"Are you still looking for a job in New York?" Savannah asked.

"That's what Dad just asked me. I have to send out applications in a couple of months, a few months before graduation." I'd need to decide soon. Would Ava date me long distance through graduation in June? Would she be willing to wait for me?

Mom walked in, sitting next to Dad. "Any luck selling your desserts, Ava?"

Ava smiled. "One restaurant is carrying them so far. Another was interested, but they already have a contract with a different supplier."

Savannah sighed. "It's too bad Juliana wasn't open to you selling out of the B & B. It would be the perfect solution. Minimal start-up costs. Built-in clientele."

I knew she was thinking of her own issues with Mom still making most of the business decisions. She longed to be running things on her own.

"Sophie, from Sweets on Main, mentioned a local shop owners' meeting once a month. I thought I'd go and network. See if it sparked any ideas," Ava said.

Savannah's face fell. "I've always wanted to go, but it's after Miles's bedtime."

"If I'm not working that night, I can watch him." I wanted more time with him anyway.

"You can sleep over," Miles said.

He wasn't going to let that go. "We'll see."

"You know, *we're* getting used to having you around. It's going to be hard when you leave." Savannah tipped her head toward Miles.

Ava looked away.

I didn't want to hurt him or Ava.

"I'm getting used to being here, too." It wasn't just seeing my family, it was Ava. Any time I thought about leaving, it felt like there was a weight crushing my chest.

Dad watched us carefully. I wondered if he guessed that my relationship with Ava was more than friendly. If he did, I hoped he wouldn't say anything.

"Dinner should be ready." Mom stood, walking into the kitchen.

The smell of turkey and stuffing made my stomach rumble. Sitting at the table, I said, "Smells amazing."

I'd come to appreciate home-cooked meals. At home in the city, I was always on the go, eating whatever I could grab. Here, Ava took care of breakfast and dinner, I grabbed whatever lunch I could scrounge from the cafeteria, then I had these family meals to look forward to. When was the last time I'd been home for Thanksgiving?

An odd sensation rolled around in my chest. I was happy here.

The decision about my future loomed like a huge gray cloud on a perfect day at the park. It was large and imposing—my chest filled with foreboding. I didn't know what the future would bring, but I knew I wouldn't like it. Something had to come to an end, either my life in New York or the one I'd built here during my short time back in town.

Dad carved the turkey as we ribbed him on his skills. It felt good to be back home for a holiday even if we were celebrating a day early. Mom brought in the platter of dinner rolls, which we grabbed until there were nothing but crumbs remaining.

"You eat like savages," Mom grumbled.

"I wouldn't go that far," Savannah said.

"You love it," I said.

Mom loved having us all home. I'd distanced myself over the years to do what I needed to do with medical school, but being home, I realized how much I'd missed. How much I was going to continue to miss out on if I went back.

I wasn't sure the cost was worth it anymore. What was there in New York for me? A prestigious hospital—the best job—long hours and an empty apartment.

"We'll miss you when you go back," Mom said.

I couldn't answer because my throat was tight with emotion. I felt Ava's gaze on me.

The talk turned to the holidays and a play at Miles's school.

"Do you go?" I asked Ava.

"I wouldn't miss it." Ava smiled affectionately at Miles.

I wanted to be here for all of Miles's big events, not just holidays. I wanted to experience everything I could until my next block took over my life. Maybe it would be good. I'd have a month to get back into the swing of things, where the hospital was my life. It would be a good transition back to life in New York.

"One of my customers mentioned she'd heard someone play the cello at the harbor front," Savannah said.

"I asked him to play for me," Ava offered.

"People are wondering if there will be another performance," Savannah said pointedly.

"I'm happy to oblige." I never felt better than when I was playing for others.

"I thought you'd stopped playing because you didn't have time," Dad said.

I paused, setting my fork on my plate. I couldn't say what I was thinking. Mom and Dad thought it interfered with my studies and work, but I was bereft when I didn't play.

"He played for the kids in the hospital. It really lifted their spirits. One even wanted him to teach him to play." Ava's voice was full of admiration.

Mom's lips set in a straight line. "You're not going to give up medicine to teach music lessons, are you?"

Ava's eyes widened at Mom's comment, and the age-old tension crept into my shoulders. "I enjoy playing."

WAITING FOR YOU

Why did I have to choose between being a doctor and a musician? Why couldn't I do both?

In New York, I freely played the cello, made videos that I posted online, hosted fundraisers for patients and the hospitals I worked at. It was fulfilling. It motivated me to keep going when work at the hospital was tough. "It's a great outlet for my work."

Ava shot an uncertain look at me before speaking. "I searched online. I saw the fundraisers you do for whatever hospital you're working at, at the time. I think it's great. I enjoy listening to you play."

"Thanks, Ava." It felt good to have her support in front of my parents, people she looked up to as well.

"Don't you want your boss to take you seriously?" Mom asked.

"I like to think I'm having a positive effect on the patients and visitors in other ways. It fulfills me in a way that being a doctor doesn't. Sometimes I can't fix whatever the problem is, but music can lift someone's mood, making them forget about their diagnosis or their family member's diagnosis."

"If you play to help patients, why do it at the harbor?" Dad asked, genuinely perplexed.

Playing at the hospital was an easier sell. "I like making people feel better. You never know what people are going through."

"Hmmph," Mom said, while chewing her food.

I felt unsettled, like I always did after this conversation with my parents. Why couldn't they just accept that music was a part of me? Meeting Ava's encouraging smile across the table, I said, "You don't have to like it."

Silence spread over the table. I'd never said that before. I always tried to prove that my hobby had value. It made me feel good. It made others feel good. That's all that mattered. If my parents couldn't see that, then it wasn't my issue anymore.

Picking up my fork to spear a piece of turkey, I realized

that heeding my feelings is what kept me falling into Ava's bed each night.

Conversation turned to events happening around Annapolis, with Christmas coming up.

"There's a new event coming up where you get out a fancy dress, like for prom or being a bridesmaid, and wear them."

"What's the point of that?" Mom asked.

"It drives customers to Main Street," Savannah said.

"Events like that don't attract as many people as they think. People drink and eat, but they don't necessarily shop."

Savannah's eyes narrowed. "I like to think it brings people to the area, makes them notice shops they hadn't before, and maybe they'll come back to visit."

Mom's mouth was pinched. "It's a long shot."

"Isn't any publicity good publicity in business?" I asked, breaking off a chunk of crispy bread.

"I think so," Savannah agreed.

"Can I go play Legos now?" Miles asked.

He said it so sweetly that I would have said yes, but Savannah chided, "How do you ask?"

His nose wrinkled. "May I please be excused?"

"Much better. Wash your hands before you play."

"Ugh. Fine." Miles scrambled down from the chair, running to the powder room.

"You're a good mom."

Savannah's eyes softened. "It's nice to hear. I have to be both parents, and sometimes that's hard."

I wanted to say I'd be the father figure he was missing, but I couldn't promise that, not when so much was up in the air.

CHAPTER EIGHTEEN
AVA

I was incredibly nervous waiting outside Max's Bar & Grill for the Shops on Main meeting.

Savannah walked around the corner in a sundress and heels, looking effortless as usual. Seeing me, she smiled and hooked her arm through mine. "Are you ready for this?"

I sucked in a shaky breath. "I think so."

Alex was able to watch Miles so she could come.

"It'll be fine. You already know Sophie."

"You've probably met everyone."

"Most, but just in passing. I'm either working at the store or taking care of Miles. It doesn't leave much time to socialize with the other shop owners."

"It would be nice if Alex could watch Miles every month so you could go."

A shadow passed over her face. "The last few weeks have been amazing. Miles loves having him here, but I know there's an end date."

I nodded grimly. It made each minute I spent with Alex that much more meaningful. Every time we made love, I held on tighter.

We opened the door and walked inside. A restaurant filled

the space to the left, and a bar with TVs playing sports was on the right. I registered dark wood paneling and brass fixtures before heading up the steps to the second-floor space where we'd be meeting.

After reaching the second floor and stepping inside the room, Savannah said, "There's Sophie."

An empty bar lined the wall to my left and a long table ran perpendicular to it.

"I'm so glad you could make it." Sophie stood, hugging me, then Savannah.

I relaxed at her friendliness. "Me, too."

Sophie introduced us to everyone. There was Remi, who owned Remi's Juice Shop; Easton, who owned Resails and sold bags made out of sails; Isla, owner of By Design, the artisan shop; Hailey, who owned Spice & Tea Shoppe; and Brooke, who owned Java Books.

"We meet here so Max can attend. He works most nights."

"Oh, there she is." Sophie moved to greet a woman who'd just arrived.

"How come your mom never came to this?" I asked Savannah when we'd met everyone and sat down.

"She thinks networking with the newer shop owners is a waste of time. Her store's been here longer than most of theirs."

"You need to change with the times." Excitement flowed through me that I was with people who could help me with my business aspirations.

Sophie stood at the end of the table. "Usually, we'll discuss any issues we're having and troubleshoot business problems, but today, we have a very special guest." She clasped her hands together, her smile representative of her happiness at who she'd invited.

"We have downtown's newest event coordinator, Naomi Thatcher. She's going to talk about some of the events coming up and how we can take advantage of the increase in traffic."

The woman who'd been standing off to the side and held a Java Books cup moved next to Sophie.

"Thank you so much for coming." Sophie hugged her before taking a seat to her right.

Naomi wore a tailored black suit in contrast to the other shop owners, who dressed more casually.

"Thank you so much for inviting me to talk this evening. I'm the new event coordinator. The town council would like to add to the reasons why both locals and tourists come downtown. We have a number of art festivals, and of course, the boat festivals, but we'd like to draw in a different crowd."

Easton raised a finger to get her attention. "When are you scheduling things? During tourist season we're pretty busy."

"These events would be spread throughout the year, but right now, we're focusing on fall and the holiday season."

A man in a black T-shirt that read Max's Bar & Grill came into the meeting space, scanning the room before leaning against the bar. He crossed his arms over his chest, displaying his tattoos. He must be the owner, Max.

"Do you think things will change once the election for mayor happens next November?" Isla asked.

"Honestly, I don't know what will happen if a new mayor is elected. I've been brought on temporarily to see if I can liven things up a bit. That's what I plan to do for the next year." Naomi waited for more questions. When none came, she handed a stack of papers to Sophie.

"What's coming around is a tentative schedule of dates, starting with Midnight Madness when the shops stay open late for bargain hunters, the Chocolate Binge Festival and the Holiday Lights Festival in December, the Craft Beer Festival in January, and the new Bubbles & Tulle Festival, yet to be scheduled.

"What's the Bubbles & Tulle Festival?" Remi asked.

"That's brand new for this year. The idea is to grab that dress in the back of your closet, the wedding dress, prom dress, or bridesmaid dress, and come downtown for wine and dancing."

Remi smiled. "That sounds so fun! I have so many old bridesmaid dresses that would be perfect to wear."

Naomi smiled, pleased with Remi's reaction. "The street will be closed for the festival. Tickets will be limited. Shuttles required."

Easton folded his hands. "When Main Street is closed, the focus tends to be on the event, not on shopping at the stores. It precludes actual shoppers from coming downtown."

"The idea is to draw more people downtown with the idea that they'll eat at the restaurants, grab dessert at one of the many ice cream and fudge shops, and hopefully linger to shop in the stores."

Easton's jaw clenched, but he didn't counter her argument.

Naomi went through the tentative schedule for the spring. It sounded like a mix of new events sprinkled with the old.

When she was finished, I said, "As the manager of Juliana's B & B, I think it will be nice to have something else to recommend to the guests looking for something to do on a weekend. I realize the B & B's needs are different than the stores', though."

I didn't want to offend the other store owners before I had a chance to befriend them. I had a feeling people coming downtown for a festival might want something sweet to eat.

Naomi finished her presentation, giving us her business card, telling us we could contact her with any questions.

After she walked Naomi out, Sophie returned to say, "I think we're going to have to wait and see. If there are any issues, we can certainly bring them up to Naomi and the town council."

When Easton nodded in agreement, Sophie turned to me. "Ava, would you like to introduce yourself and tell us why you're here?"

Standing, I said, "Like I said earlier, I manage Juliana's B & B. I cook and bake for the guests. I'd like to sell my baked goods to local restaurants, maybe even open a stand in the marketplace. I realize we already have a bakery. I don't want to step on any toes, but I think there's enough demand to have bakeries on both the south and north end of Main Street."

Sophie had been great so far, but I wasn't sure if she'd appreciate the competition.

Sophie waved off my concerns. "There's numerous ice cream, fudge, and candy shops. We can coexist with the amount of traffic we get downtown."

"I'd look into the marketplace. I think that could be great for you," Hailey offered.

"The only issue is that it's been closed several times and renovated because the owners haven't been satisfied with the amount of foot traffic they're getting. Make sure you read your contract carefully to see if they can close you down anytime they want to," Easton said.

"It's worth looking into. It's a way to dip your toes in the water without renovating a larger space. The display cases are already in place. You'd just need a menu, your goods, and prices," Sophie said.

"Thank you so much for your advice. I'll look into it."

Savannah stood to speak next. "I have a small child, so I can't make it to a lot of the meetings, but I'd like to be more involved if you have an email chain or some other way of communication."

"Absolutely. We understand not everyone can make it," Sophie said.

"I took over the shop from my mother, and I'd like to freshen our offerings."

"Oh, I'd love to discuss ideas with you," Isla offered.

I thought Sophie said she was the owner of the artisan shop, but I wasn't positive.

They exchanged numbers, and the group broke apart.

"What did you think?" Savannah asked as we walked toward her apartment.

"It's so nice to talk to other business owners who have the same motivations and ambitions. To work for yourself, to create something." I appreciated that the group discussed ideas with you. Not having owned a business before, I liked the perspective."

"I agree. I loved their energy."

I made a face. "Maybe not Easton's. He seemed skeptical of a lot of the ideas."

"I wonder if it's because his business is unique. There aren't multiple sail bag shops. He doesn't need the increased traffic."

"I've seen the bags. They're pretty cool."

"I'd love one, but they're so expensive."

I wish Savannah didn't always have to worry about money and raising Miles on her own. She deserved someone to look after her and not just her family. I wanted to broach the subject of her dating, but I didn't want her to ask what I was doing. I couldn't exactly say her brother.

Going inside her apartment, we found Miles asleep, his head against Alex's shoulder.

"Why isn't he in bed?" Savannah whispered.

"He wanted more time with me. I couldn't say no."

Savannah scooped up Miles, carrying him to his bedroom.

I sat next to Alex. "You're a big softy."

He scrubbed a hand over his face. "When it comes to Miles, I am."

He'd do anything for his family. It was me who'd only ever get this small piece of him. A moment of his time.

A few minutes later, Savannah came back out. "He didn't even move when I put him down."

Alex stood. "We'll get out of your hair so you can get some sleep."

"Thanks for helping out." Savannah plopped down on the couch.

"Was the meeting worthwhile?" Alex asked us.

"I thought so," I said.

"It was nice to get to know the other shop owners."

We chatted a bit about the events Naomi mentioned before leaving.

Alex was quiet on the drive back to the B & B. After arriving home and going inside, he grabbed my hand, pulling me up the steps to my room.

"What's the rush?" I hurried to keep up with him.

Normally, we'd stop in the kitchen to grab some pastries or tea.

"I need to be with you."

I noticed he'd said *need* not *want*. "Okay."

I watched him; he looked exhausted with lines under his eyes. He seemed stressed.

He stepped closer, his hand on my cheek, his thumb brushing my temple. It was a sweet gesture that squeezed my heart.

"I wish we had more time. I wish we had forever."

Tears swam in my eyes. I wanted to say we *could* have forever. There was nothing stopping him from looking for a job here. I couldn't form the words. It was clear he'd made up his mind. We were temporary.

"Will you be with me while I'm here?" He stepped into my space, his body pressed against mine. His familiar masculine scent wrapped around me.

"You already have me." I'd already fallen in love with him. There was no turning back. I was already gone for him.

Then his lips were on mine, his hand on my neck, holding me to him. His kiss was possessive. He owned me, body and soul. I'd give him anything he wanted.

Still kissing me, his free hand touched my knee, then traveled slowly up, moving my dress higher. He tugged my panties down. I helped him, kicking them off to the side. Then he broke his lips from mine, pulling my dress over my head until I was naked in front of him.

I unleashed every emotion I felt for him. Did he know I already fell for him? That I'd never be the same if he left?

My heart ached, contracting in time with my thoughts. I always loved and lost. This was no different. My mom left. He'd leave, too. There was never an option for me to keep him.

He was destined for greater things.

I helped him remove his clothes, my hands shaky, desperate to see him bare.

I poured everything I was feeling into our kisses. He lowered me onto the bed, covering me with his heat, his protection, and his love.

I wouldn't delude myself into thinking we had a future. We didn't.

I lost myself in the sensation of his lips on mine, his hands memorizing my body. When he pushed inside, I'd never felt so raw.

Did he feel it, too? Or was he so stuck in his mind, he couldn't see past whatever plan he'd made in med school? The one I didn't factor into.

I forced any errant thoughts out, enjoying his body moving over mine. The grace, the simplicity, the beauty of coming together.

When we climaxed at the same time, tears filled my eyes that I willed not to spill over. I wouldn't let on how hard I'd fallen for him.

He kissed my forehead, rolling to the side. "That was intense."

He had felt it.

I couldn't speak because my throat was thick with emotion. He wrapped me up in his arms, holding me tight to his chest. He felt it and intended to leave anyway.

Nothing I could do or say would ever change his mind.

His breathing evened out. He relaxed in sleep, his grip on me loosening. It was a foreshadowing of things to come. He'd loosen his hold on me and let me go, it was just a matter of time.

Unless I left before he could.

Resolved not to get hurt, I rolled away from him, wrapping myself tightly in the sheets, trying to replicate the feel of his arms around me. I had to get used to being alone again.

CHAPTER NINETEEN

ALEX

My time in the orthopedic block came to an end, and I moved on to shock trauma. I was so focused on the change in position and the pressure of my new block, I didn't realize Ava had been drifting away from me for a few weeks.

She still left food for me for breakfast and dinner, but she was asleep when I got home.

I didn't feel right waking her up, not when I was so exhausted anyway.

Any moment I had to think of her was fleeting, because there was always another emergency to deal with—a patient to treat. Here, everything was serious. Otherwise, the patient wouldn't have been routed here.

I had to be on all the time. There was no room for error, no room for daydreams. There was barely any time to think of what came after or where I'd work.

I was exhausted, barely able to manage a quick shower before falling into bed with Ava.

One morning, Ava's moving out of bed woke me. I reached for her, startling her when my hand wrapped around her wrist.

Glancing back at me, dark circles lined her eyes.

"Hey." My voice was gravelly from exhaustion.

She leaned over, kissing me. "Go back to sleep."

My eyes closed despite my desire to speak to her, to tell her I missed her. I heard her move away, but I couldn't manage to rouse myself.

We had time to figure things out. I just needed to get through this rotation. Then we'd have Christmas. I tried not to think about what would come after.

The stress from the job weighed more on me each day. I loved the fast-paced nature of the emergency room, but this was on another level entirely.

Every family member arrived in tears, expecting the worst. When we had some good news to tell them, it helped, but we were the first line of defense, getting their loved one stable before we moved them to another hospital.

I was doing the best I could—working hard, giving my best to each patient and family member.

I tried not to think about how I was neglecting Ava and my family.

I'd told them to expect this, but it still sucked. I longed to be with them, to spend quality time with them, but what I was doing was important and necessary. I kept telling myself it was only for another week.

Then I'd have time to figure everything out.

I wanted to spend time with Ava before I needed to go back to New York. I wanted to drink hot chocolate and eat popcorn while watching a movie.

That night, my boss sent me home after a particularly difficult stream of patients had come in from a pileup on the beltway.

Weary and exhausted, I headed inside the B & B, not expecting to see anyone. Ava was reading on one of the chairs in front of the fire.

She rose when I came inside. "Alex, what are you doing home?"

I walked toward her, wanting to touch her, be near her. When I was close, I pulled her into my arms. I reveled in the feel of her in my arms, and her familiar smell of cinnamon and vanilla wrapped around me.

"I need a shower." I probably smelled like hospital and blood. I couldn't seem to escape those smells lately.

"Would you like company?" She tipped her head to the side, considering me.

My shoulders were tight, my feet sore from being on my feet.

"Come on. I'll take care of you." She angled me toward the stairs, guiding me up.

I went with her to my room willingly, wanting her to take care of me. She turned on the shower, took off my clothes, and checked the temperature before telling me to get inside.

"Join me?" I reached for her, wanting her near me.

I couldn't think, all I could do was feel.

"Of course." She made quick work of her clothes, stepping in front of me. She pumped body wash into her hands, working up a lather before spreading the soap over my chest.

Despite my exhaustion, blood pooled in my dick.

"Someone's happy to see me," she murmured, getting my shoulders and arms, moving down my torso to my ass, then to the backs of my thighs, the sensitive spot behind my knees, my calves, and finally, to my feet.

"Ava, I need you." I needed to be inside her. I needed her with me. I never wanted to let go. I wanted a life here, with her.

I couldn't say any of that because I wasn't sure I could make it happen.

On her knees, her hands on my thighs, she looked up at me. "You've got me."

The question was for how long.

She sucked me into her mouth, and every thought dissipated into thin air. There was nothing but the feel of her hot, wet mouth surrounding me and her hands on my ass, pulling me deeper into her mouth.

She was exactly what I needed after a long day. I gave myself over to the feel of the hot water pounding down, her fingers digging into my skin, and her expert mouth working me over.

I erupted into her mouth with a roar. My legs weak, I touched her hair, tugging her up. My mouth was on her, tasting myself, pushing her against the cold tile. With a hand braced next to her head, I palmed her breasts, brushing over her nipples until they were hard, aching peaks.

"I want to drive you crazy like you just did to me."

Her head fell back against the wet tile with a soft thud, her mouth opened in an O.

Using my mouth on one nipple then the other, my fingers separated her folds, finding the spot that needed my attention the most. She widened her legs, inviting me inside. Thrusting into her, I was lost in her reaction to me.

The way her body sagged against the wall, her legs widened, her hand tangled in my hair, I knew I'd never get enough of her.

When she peaked, I covered her cries with my mouth, lifting her in my arms, and sliding inside.

We didn't speak. There were no words for this. It was all feelings, emotions, and sensations.

"Alex," she murmured, kissing me.

I thrust harder, driving deeper, wanting to show her she was mine. That I needed her to get through this.

Frustration filled my chest that I couldn't be with her the way I wanted to be. I couldn't go to every fall festival, family event, or even have a quiet night at home. That was my life.

Frustrated, I thrust once more, shuddering as the orgasm tore through me.

Lowering her feet to the floor, I moved her in front of the stream. "Now, let me take care of you."

I couldn't tell her everything running through my head. It was too soon, too intense for how long we'd been together. Instead, I worked shampoo into her hair. She leaned her head back, closing her eyes in ecstasy.

"Does that feel good?"

Her eyelids fluttered open. "So good."

I massaged her scalp for a few seconds before turning her so her hair was in the stream. I lifted and separated the strands until no more bubbles appeared.

Then I kissed her, my hands buried in her hair. I'd never get enough. "I get lost in you so easily."

I turned the knob, the steady stream of water slowing to a drip. Grabbing blindly for a towel, I wrapped the thickness around her and stepped out of the shower.

Drying off quickly, I followed her into the bedroom. She'd grabbed the spare brush she'd left on my countertop a few weeks ago and sat on the edge of the bed.

I held my hand out to her. "Let me."

I moved behind her.

"I thought I was supposed to be taking care of you," she said over her shoulder.

"It goes both ways."

I ran the brush through her hair, working through the tangles. Would it be like this every time I came home from work? Ava waiting on me while reading a book in front of the fire, a warm plate saved in the oven or wrapped in the fridge? Would she always be this happy, or would she grow to resent the long hours, the stress, the phone calls in the middle of the night?

I couldn't forget what Steve had said: Women liked the money and material things it afforded them as a doctor's wife, but it never lasted. They eventually wanted to be with someone who had time for them.

As much as I wanted to think Ava was different, no one

wanted to be with someone who could only give small pieces of themselves. She deserved everything.

"What are you thinking about?" she asked when the brush ran smoothly through her hair. I set the brush on the nightstand, laying back on the bed.

"How much I enjoy spending time with you, even when we're doing little things like showers, watching TV, or sharing a snack." It wasn't lost on me that our relationship was mainly stolen moments.

She shifted on the bed until she was straddling my lap. I pushed the towel away so I could see her naked. "I want you however I can have you."

Searching her face, I wanted to ask how that was fair, but I didn't. I wanted the same. Kissing me, she pushed me back on the bed, her pussy gliding over my cock. I palmed her breasts, wanting her again, wanting her forever.

I closed my eyes as she took me inside her again. I'd never get enough of this. No matter how much time I had.

Afterward, I fell into a restless sleep, where I dreamed of trying to grab on to something but wasn't able to. That elusive feeling stayed with me all night.

Up earlier than usual, I quickly showered, got dressed, and headed down to have breakfast with Ava.

When I walked into the kitchen, she looked up, surprised to see me. "What are you doing down here so early?"

"Didn't sleep well."

She poured some tea into a cup, placing it in front of me. "Sit. I'll get you something to eat."

Bustling around, she put some eggs into a pan. "An omelet okay?"

"Yours are perfect."

"You look like you're going to fall over. Has it been rough?"

"Not all nights are like yesterday but more often than not, yes."

She shook her head. "I don't know how you do it."

Was this the beginning of her telling me she couldn't handle my job? Was it too much?

"Someone has to." My tone came out testier than I meant it to.

She placed a hand over mine. "I know what you do is so important. I'm so proud of you."

I nodded, and she moved back to the stovetop.

"What are you up to?"

"I signed the lease for the booth at the marketplace."

"Yeah? That's great."

"I'm really excited."

"Will you be able to work both places?"

"I think Juliana felt bad about not letting me open something here, so she's looking for part-time help. If not, I can open the bakery after breakfast, take a break to put out tea and dessert here, then run back over for a few hours. As long as I'm on call here, it should be fine."

"What about check-ins?"

"Juliana can help, too. It'll be difficult, but I have to try, you know?"

I felt terrible that I hadn't been a part of the process. "I feel like I'm missing out."

Savannah told me Miles had a talent show at school, and I couldn't make it.

"You didn't miss anything. I handled it."

It wasn't anything I could help her with, but it sucked I wasn't around to even have a conversation about it. "Things will get better soon. One more week left."

She raised a brow. "Then what?"

"Enjoy the holiday with you. Go back to New York, start applying for jobs."

Something flashed in her eyes when I mentioned New York, but she didn't say anything.

I couldn't reassure her because I didn't know where I'd be

working. I wanted to be with her, I just couldn't guarantee I'd get a job in Maryland. Even if I did, I still had to finish my residency. We'd be apart from January to June.

I wanted a life with my family and her. But I wasn't sure if it made sense to live somewhere I'd constantly be letting people down.

I wanted to change the subject. "What are your plans today?"

"I'm going to check out the spot I'm renting at the marketplace. I'm sure it could use a good cleaning. I'll plan what I'm going to sell and how much I have room for. I'll have to adjust depending on how many customers I get there."

"You'll probably need more than you can make."

She smiled, but it didn't quite reach her eyes. Was something else going on with her?

I just had to make it through the next week, then I could enjoy Christmas with her.

CHAPTER TWENTY
AVA

Alex offered to meet Sam with me, but he was so busy at shock trauma, I couldn't ask him to take off. I wasn't even sure he could.

I sat in one of the booths, ordering coffee.

I could see how much his work drained him, not just physically, but emotionally. It made me see how he used music as an escape, not just from his patients, but from his work.

I wish he'd let me in. All I could do for him was make sure he had something to eat when he got home and before he left for work again.

I wanted to do more. I wanted to be there for him, emotionally and physically, like last night. He hadn't talked much about his evening, but I was able to soothe him with my body.

I'd never felt closer to him.

The bell over the door rang, and Sam walked in—all in black—his blond hair slicked back.

Dread filled my stomach. I had a feeling I wasn't going to like what he had to say.

Seeing me, he headed straight over, sliding into the booth

across from where I was sitting. He set a manilla folder in front of me.

I knew that folder held answers. I just wasn't sure if I wanted to know anymore.

The waitress stopped by our table, holding a carafe, and asked, "Coffee?"

"Please." Sam waited until the waitress was finished before speaking to me. "I know where she lives."

I huffed out a laugh. "You don't waste time, do you?"

"You asked me for information. I like to get to the point."

"Of course." I waved for him to continue.

He slid her address and phone number to me on a card. "Would you like me to tell you what else I found, or would you rather read it in the file?"

I licked my lips. On one hand, he'd tell me everything I wanted to know now, or I could wait until I had the courage to open it. That might be today, or I might never open it. The idea of taking the folder home and tucking it deep into a drawer where I'd forget about it was strong.

"It's up to you."

I sighed, squaring my shoulders. I wanted to get it over with. "Tell me."

I held my body rigid as he spoke.

"You already know your mother ended up in Florida. She moved around quite a bit once she got there, but she's never left the state."

Pain hit my chest. She'd never tried to come back for us.

"She's worked several odd jobs over the years—waitressing, receptionist, administrative assistant. Nothing stuck."

When she'd lived with us, she'd stayed home. Had she been unhappy doing that?

"She was arrested here and there for minor drug possession. She never had enough on her for it to be considered distribution. About five years after she moved there, she got pregnant."

Spots danced in my vision. "She has a kid?"

"She *had* a kid."

I have a brother or sister. The shock froze my body. I couldn't think straight. "Wait, what? What do you mean *had*?"

"The baby was immediately taken from her by child protective services because he was born an addict."

My heart raced, I felt light-headed. "Taken away?"

"The boy was adopted by another family. It was a closed adoption. I don't have his legal name. Before he was adopted, he was listed as a John Doe."

"She never had a chance to name him." My brother. He was born when I was eighteen; he'd be about ten now. Did he look like me, Juliana, or his father?

Sam leveled with me. "She was still an addict after she had him."

I swallowed, realizing his implication. He was better off without his mother—*my* mother.

"Do you want me to continue?"

Waves of despair washed over me. "There's more?"

"That was the worst of it."

"Yeah, okay." Between the shock and disbelief, a strange numbness was settling in my chest, making me feel cold. I sipped my still-warm coffee, hoping to warm up.

"She seemed to clean up her act about three years ago."

If she'd truly cleaned up her act, why hadn't she done anything to contact her children?

"She's held a steady waitressing job since. Boyfriends have come and gone. At some point in the last few months, she got pregnant again. Now she has a girlfriend."

I couldn't process the last few pieces of information. It was too much. Everyone was right. I didn't want to know. I thought I did, but I was wrong. So, so wrong.

I slid from the booth, not able to get away fast enough. Wiping my sweaty hands on my jeans, I said, "Alex paid you for your time?"

Sam considered me thoughtfully. "He did."

"Thank you. I appreciate you finding her for me."

"I'm sorry it's not what you were looking for."

I shook my head, tears stinging my eyes. "I don't know what I was looking for."

But it was this hollow cavern in my chest. This numbing sensation that felt like it was spreading down my arms into my fingers.

"This is yours." He pushed the folder to the end of the table.

I looked at it, not wanting to touch it.

"Take it. Feel free to call me. You might have questions later."

I tucked it into my purse, then pulled out a few bills to cover the bill for my coffee. "Thank you."

I moved past him, not wanting to talk to him or anyone. I felt too exposed. Raw. My mother had a child with one on the way. I had a sibling besides Juliana. Did I want to meet him? Was it even possible?

She hadn't just left us, she'd let down her son. A part of me worried she'd moved on, had a second family with someone else. That she was happy. That would have hurt, but this was worse. She'd become a drug addict.

Tears built behind my lids, threatening to spill over.

She'd brought another child into this world that couldn't depend on her. I pushed open the door to the outside. The air was cool despite the bright sun.

I swiped angrily at one offending tear that tracked down my cheek.

She was pregnant. Would the state take that child, too?

I stood on the sidewalk, blinking from the bright sun. I couldn't talk to Juliana, she'd say I told you so, and I couldn't go to Alex. He was in Baltimore, working.

Needing to be alone, I headed to my apartment, desperate for the solitude it usually afforded me. Climbing the steps to the attic, my footsteps felt heavy, the air thin. Closing the door behind me, the tears spilled over.

Wiping them away, I curled up on the bed into a fetal position, pulling myself into a tight ball. I squeezed my eyes shut, hoping to block out Sam's words that tumbled around in my head like tumbleweeds—drug addict, arrest, baby, adoption.

Despite the tight ball I'd curled myself into, my body trembled. It was too much. Why had I thought I could handle the truth?

Why had I thought I could talk to her? She was too far gone. She probably wasn't even the same person I remembered. She'd changed, or the drugs had altered her.

I was deluding myself if I thought we could ever have a relationship. She was too weak to overcome the addiction—if she'd ever tried.

Sam never mentioned her checking into a program.

She was my mom. My history. A drug addict. Someone who'd leave her children. Who'd get pregnant knowing she'd left two children and lost another.

Was I so unlovable? Alex flashed into my head. He'd been upfront that he had to finish his residency in New York. He'd leave, too.

Did I put myself in these situations knowing there was no possibility of commitment on purpose?

I lay there unseeing, not able to sleep, and not able to get up. At some point, I heard the door click open. I pretended to be asleep so I wouldn't have to talk to him. I only relaxed when his arm banded around my waist, and his breath was hot on my neck.

CHAPTER TWENTY-ONE
ALEX

I woke with a start. The sheets beside me were cool to the touch.

Checking the time, I had to hurry if I wanted to talk to Ava before I went to work. I quickly showered, throwing on a fresh pair of scrubs I left in her room for the mornings I stayed with her. These days it was almost every night.

Jogging down the stairs, there was an urgency running through my veins. I felt unsettled.

Walking into the kitchen, she glanced at me. For the first time, she didn't smile. Ignoring the guests seated at the table, I headed straight for her, turning her so she faced me.

"How are you?"

She sighed, looking down. "Tired. I didn't sleep well last night."

"No matter what happens when I go back to New York, I care for you." *I love you.*

Her shoulders stiffened as she plated the omelet, checking the clock above the stove. "You'd better eat."

I lifted her chin, her eyes questioning what I was doing, kissing her softly on the lips. "Thank you."

I wasn't sure if I was thanking her for breakfast, the last

few months, or being in my life. Being home was nice, but it was Ava that made everything better.

I ate quickly, starving from not eating dinner last night.

"Sorry for not leaving dinner last night," she said when she noticed me shoveling in food.

I grabbed her wrist, stopping her from moving away. "You don't have to make me breakfast and dinner every day. You need to take care of yourself, too."

She nodded, and I let her go.

It eased the ache in my chest telling her I wanted to be there for her, take care of her, that I appreciated her doing the same for me. It made something bloom in my chest, it felt a little like hope. That maybe this thing between us could be something more.

Would she be open to a long-distance relationship while I finished my residency?

At lunch, I was able to steal a few moments in the cafeteria. Relaxing for the first time all day, I took a bite of my club sandwich. When my phone buzzed, indicating Steve was calling, I swallowed, drinking a sip of water before swiping the accept call button. He didn't usually call to make small talk.

"Hey. How are you?"

"Just wanted to check in. See how things are in Baltimore."

I fiddled with the empty wrapper for my straw. "It's tough but challenging. Just like you said."

"When you get back, you'll need to start sending out applications. Have you thought about where you'd like to be? I can send some feelers out."

I paused. When I started out, I was hopeful I'd make a few connections so that when the time came, they'd pass on a good word for me. Now that Steve was offering, I wasn't sure what I wanted.

"What's with the hesitation? You seeing a lot of your family?"

"I have. It's been nice."

"It's tough having family at home waiting for you. You can never make promises in our line of work."

We'd had this conversation dozens of times before, and I'd always agreed. It was best to remain unattached and focused on my career. An image of Ava sleeping in bed this morning popped into my brain, and I wasn't positive about anything anymore. "It's a bit more than that. I met someone."

Steve groaned. "I thought I could have it all at one point, too. A wife and kids, a homelife. Sylvia assured me the hours didn't matter. Then when we had kids, understandably, everything changed. She complained she was doing everything on her own. I couldn't blame her because she was right."

I remained silent. I knew it pained Steve that he couldn't be there like he wanted to be. That he'd hardened his heart to ever being in a relationship again.

"Now she's using my job against me in court for custody. She's telling the judge I'm never home, or when I am, I'm on call. She wants to limit my visitation."

"I'm sorry." I knew how much he wanted to spend time with the kids.

He sighed, and I could picture him running his hand through his hair in frustration. "Take it from me. It's not worth it. Focus on your career. Be real sure before you get involved with someone."

Regret settled like a rock in my gut. Steve had a good point. Ava said she was okay with my long hours, but would she feel the same after a few months, a year? Was it worth risking my plans for the future?

My phone buzzed with a text from my department: **We**

need you. Seven vehicle pileup involving two tractor-trailers on 95.

"I gotta go," I said into the phone while I stood, dropping my food in the garbage.

"Remember what I said," Steve said.

"I will." I hung up, a chill running down my spine as I stood, steeling myself for whatever I'd find. Hurrying back to my department, I reminded myself how important my job was to those who needed me. Not my family or a significant other, but those who needed medical care from a dedicated, focused doctor, not one that was distracted with whatever was going on in their personal life.

On the drive home, I felt exhausted yet accomplished. What I did had an impact on people's lives. I wasn't sure I was ready for the distraction that Ava would provide. Maybe it was better to pull back a little before we got in any deeper.

When I arrived home, I decided to take a night off from going to Ava's room. I was off center about what happened at work and my conversation with Steve.

Needing a few minutes to myself, I showered, letting the hot water beat on my aching muscles. It didn't alleviate the stress of the day, but it helped.

CHAPTER TWENTY-TWO
AVA

EVER SINCE MY CONVERSATION WITH SAM, I'D BEEN ON EDGE. I had this feeling that whatever was going on with Alex was tenuous. When I saw his car parked out front but he didn't come to my room, the feeling intensified.

I hoped being with him would ease the worries I was having about us. We had keys to each other's rooms, so when I heard the water running in his bathroom, I unlocked the door and waited on the bed for him to come out.

A few minutes later, the water shut off. He came out of the bathroom with a towel tied at his waist, rubbing his wet hair with a second towel.

"What are you doing here?" His voice was gruff.

Maybe he wanted to be alone. I stood, wiping my sweaty hands on my leggings. "When you didn't come up to my room, I thought maybe you had a rough day. I wanted to make sure you were okay."

"I'm fine." His tone was terse.

I got the impression he didn't want to talk about what happened.

I didn't want him to have to relive his day, but I wanted to be a soft place to land. "You don't seem fine."

Alex sat on the bed. "There was a bad accident. I had to deliver news to the family."

I sat next to him, touching the tense muscles of his forearm as understanding filled me.

Alex moved to rest his elbows on his thighs, dropping his head slightly. "Steve called to check in. He wanted to know where I was thinking of applying for jobs in the next few months. He wants to put in a good word for me."

My heart skipped a beat. "For a job in New York?"

"That was the plan."

"Right." I removed my hand from his arm. I wasn't sure if it was the best time to talk about his future after what he'd been through today. I'd been unsettled since my conversation with Sam. Talking about Alex going back to New York intensified my uneasiness.

I stood, making my way to the door. "You need some time. I probably shouldn't have barged in—"

"You met with Sam." His voice paused my forward motion.

I turned to face him, wrapping my arms around myself. The emotions Sam churned up mixed with what I was feeling now. If I didn't hold on tight, I might fall into pieces. "He told me where my mom's been, what she's been up to."

"Yeah?"

"She never came back. She had another kid, and the thing is, I don't understand why. Not when she left the ones she had and never looked back."

"Ava." His voice broke on my name.

Moving closer, he tugged my arms to my side, then pulled me into his body.

"I'm okay." I rubbed a cheek against his bare chest.

He tipped my chin, so I had to look at him. "You don't think it's your fault, do you?"

I steeled my expression. "She's responsible for her actions. She has an addiction. She's the only one who can beat it."

He pulled back, gripping my shoulders. "Do you know that for sure?"

"She never checked into rehab."

"Rehab is expensive. Maybe she couldn't afford it."

"If she'd stayed, Dad would have helped her." Dad would have done anything for us to have a mother in our lives.

He moved me until we were sitting on the edge of the bed again. "What do you mean she had another kid?"

"I don't know if she was trying to replace us or regain what she had, but she had another child that child protective services took when he was born, and she's pregnant again."

"He was born addicted."

I sucked in a shaky breath. "Yes."

"Where's he now?"

"He was adopted. Sam said it's a closed adoption."

"I'm sure he's with a family that adores him and takes good care of him."

I blinked away tears. "He's my brother, Alex."

Alex cupped my cheek. "I know."

Frustration climbed up my spine. "Why was she so irresponsible?"

"You'll never know, but assuming the worst isn't good for you. You can choose to believe he's with a good family and overcoming any challenges he's had. That he's in a better place."

It felt better to believe that, and what choice did I have?

"Did he say how she's doing now?"

"Sam said it looks like she's cleaned up her act. She's held a job for a while. She's going to prenatal appointments. Something she didn't do last time."

"Maybe this time will be different."

A disbelieving laugh escaped. "Until she leaves him like she did us."

"You don't know that."

"I should have left it alone." It was a bad idea to investigate my mom while I was falling for Alex. I'd stirred up these old feelings of abandonment.

He shook his head. "Maybe I shouldn't have encouraged you to hire Sam."

I stood, pacing the room. "Ignorance is bliss, isn't that the saying?"

"You would have always wondered what happened."

"Now I know. She was a drug addict."

"She couldn't have been there for you. I see a lot of addiction in the ER. It's tough to kick even when the family is involved."

"I know some of it was out of her control."

He tugged me into his lap. "You have to let go of what you can't control. What your mother did had nothing to do with you."

"Why didn't she try for us? Why didn't she come back?"

"You won't know the answers to that without talking to her."

"I don't know if I want to."

"You don't have to. But if you want me to, I'll go with you."

I didn't say what I was thinking—soon he'd be in New York. He wouldn't have time for me, much less time to accompany me to confront my mom in Florida. I was on my own.

"Listen, we don't have to figure out anything tonight. Want to watch a movie and cuddle?"

At my nod, he pulled on a pair of sweats and a T-shirt, then pulled down the blankets in an open invitation for me to join him.

I chewed my lip while he surfed channels. "Why did you come to your room first?"

"I needed a few minutes to decompress. Sometimes what happens—it's too much. I don't want it touching you."

I touched his cheek. "If it helps you, I want to hear about

it. I know you can't give me details, but I still want to be here for you, even if it's just to be here."

He turned his head, kissing my palm. "Thank you."

I snuggled into his side. I fit perfectly. Being with him felt right. Like I was exactly where I was supposed to be. Unfortunately, he thought he was supposed to be in New York.

I wanted to avoid the future for as long as I could.

CHAPTER TWENTY-THREE
AVA

TODAY WAS MY FIRST DAY WORKING MY BOOTH AT THE marketplace. The owner was motivated to fill the empty booths and get me up and running before Christmas. He'd been really helpful. The building itself was enclosed with glass windows, a brown pitched roof, and located in the heart of the historic downtown area by the harbor, the restaurants, and shops. Restaurants faced the building on three sides, and a road ran around the building itself.

The other booths sold fudge, gelato, crab cakes, and deli sandwiches. The surrounding restaurants sold primarily seafood dishes.

Making sure the glass case was shown, I set the small chalkboard I'd written prices on with colorful chalk on top of the case. I'd gone with scones, cookies, small pies, and donuts. I figured I'd get people coming in for a quick snack after walking around all day.

I wondered if I should sell something to drink since there was no booth in the marketplace for coffee, tea, or smoothies.

"Can I get some of these cookies?"

The voice broke through my musings on adding beverages

to my offerings. Seeing Savannah, I said, "What are you doing here?"

She placed a finger on her chin. "I heard there was this amazing new bakery in the marketplace. I just had to stop by."

"You want Miles's favorites?"

"Of course."

"You know I'd bring the leftovers over at the end of the day for free," I said, using a piece of wax paper to transfer chocolate chip cookies to a small box.

"I have a feeling you're not going to have leftovers." She glanced pointedly at the line forming behind her.

Nerves kicked in. I hadn't expected a line this early. I figured it would take some time for people to realize I was here.

"How do you think people knew about it?"

"Several of the shop owners might have made a flyer and posted it in our stores."

I handed her the box. "Thank you."

"How much do I owe you?"

I rang her up only because I didn't want the other customers to think I was giving cookies away for free.

"Stop by tonight for dinner," she said, taking her credit card and bakery box out.

I nodded.

I was busy the next few hours, boxing what I had for the customers. The response was overwhelming, but amazing at the same time.

I couldn't believe it worked.

In the middle of the afternoon, there was a lull. One of the other vendors placed a wrapped sub on the top of the case.

"What can I get you?"

"I actually got an order for you."

"What do you mean?"

He looked at a slip of paper. "An Alex asked that I make a sandwich and bring it over to you. Don't worry, he paid and tipped me."

I took the sub from him. There was even a bottle of water and chips. "Thank you. I'm starving."

"Thank this Alex. Sounds like he really cares about you."

I wondered if he'd asked how business was for me and realized I'd be too busy to leave for a minute to grab lunch.

"I'm Ava Breslin."

"Derek Chambers. I work at the deli shop." He pointed at his booth.

"I figured."

"Well, enjoy. I'm getting a line again."

There were two people staring at the menu hanging from the top of his booth.

I unwrapped the sub, took a huge bite, and drank water before I dialed Alex, expecting his voice mail.

When he answered, "Hey, you," I was surprised.

"Thank you for lunch."

"I was worried you wouldn't have time to eat."

"You thought right. It's been crazy here."

"You had a lot of customers?"

"So many. Savannah was my first, then it was nonstop until now. I have a feeling, once the school lets out at three, it will pick up again."

"I'm sure it will."

My baked goods were halfway gone. "I'm going to have to bake more tomorrow."

"You're going to need help."

"That's a good thing."

"I'm so proud of you."

"It's a great feeling." I was tired from making extra baked goods this morning but exhilarated at the same time. I was proud of myself. Instead of waiting for the perfect opportunity,

I'd made it happen. I found I liked figuring out what to sell, how much to sell it for, and how much I needed to make to cover the cost of the booth. I liked being my own boss. If I had an idea, I could turn it into reality without a discussion with someone else.

The afternoon sun came through the window, warming me.

"I have to get back to it. I just wanted to make sure you ate."

"No one's ever done something so thoughtful for me before." No boyfriend had worried about whether I'd found time to eat. Especially not one with a demanding job like Alex's.

"You deserve it."

"See you tonight?" Even if we didn't talk or I wasn't awake, I'd gotten used to him sliding into bed at some point.

"Looking forward to it."

I heard a smile in his voice. I liked that he'd thought of me at work. He'd worried about me, then ordered lunch and had it delivered. Between Alex and the bakery sales, I floated through the rest of the day.

With each customer, I planned what I'd need to make more of the next day. I had to be careful to meet demand but not exceed it.

Walking toward Savannah's shop, an idea popped into my head. One I couldn't help but get excited about. I turned toward Remi's Juice Shop, which was located toward State Circle on the north end of Main Street.

Pulling open the door, it was brightly colored with white counters and rainbow-colored signs. They reminded me of Remi's personality.

"Hey! What are you doing here?" Remi asked, pleased to see me.

I stopped at the counter, sitting on the high barstool. "I have an idea."

"I'd love to hear it." She put down the dishcloth she'd been using to clean the counters and focused on me.

"I'm selling baked goods at the marketplace, but I'm not selling anything to drink. I was really busy today, and people wanted something with their pastries. I noticed they were eating it right away." They'd go outside to enjoy the beautiful late fall weather and eat at one of the small tables.

Her eyes widened. "Go on."

"What do you think about joining forces? I could sell some of your juices, we'd share in the cost of the booth, and I'd get a small percentage of your sales." I'd never propositioned anyone other than Juliana for a business idea.

Going into this, I wouldn't have said I was business-minded, but I was growing more confident.

I held up my hand before she could respond. "It would give you customers down by the harbor, not just the ones wandering around by the statehouse. We'd put a sign up for your business. I'm happy to direct them here, too. I just think it would be nice to offer my customers something to drink—and juice would be perfect. I love your business model, your energy, and I think we could be great together."

I didn't want her to think it was a one-sided situation. I wanted it to benefit both of us.

"I've wanted to tap into business by the harbor, but didn't want to rent a second location. I think this could work. Let's talk numbers and how it would work. I'd need a new machine, a small sign, ingredients, and I'd need to show you how to make the juice."

"I'm willing to learn."

She made me a tropical juice while we talked. It was amazing. When we were done, she asked, "Are you still working at the B & B?"

"You know, I'm not sure I'll be able to do it all if this takes off like I think it will. I can probably still swing the mornings, but I'd need someone to cover the afternoons and evenings."

"It's exciting when you have some success, isn't it? I started out with pop-up shops, and it took a while for me to earn enough money to make renting a space viable."

"I think this place is amazing. And once people meet you in person, they want to buy your product. You just have this energy that's contagious."

Her cheeks flushed pink. "Thank you."

I had a feeling she wasn't used to people telling her that. "I look forward to working with you."

We set a possible date to start selling her juices that gave us enough time to purchase everything we needed and set everything up.

Flying high, I headed over to Savannah's for dinner. Her shop was already closed for the evening, so I unlocked the door with my key, going up the steps to her place.

Knocking quickly before going inside, Miles looked up from the show he was watching. "Did you bring me anything?"

I placed my hands on my hips, cocking my head. "Didn't your mother buy you cookies this morning?"

Looking guilty, he said, "Yeah, but I ate them."

Savannah came into the room. "Don't let him talk you into more cookies."

Laughing, I said, "I don't have any leftovers."

Savannah beamed. "I knew you were going to have a great day."

"It was better than I expected, and I have you to thank." I hadn't advertised the booth thinking I'd have a soft opening, get my bearings, then look into marketing.

"You're always helping me at the store. It wasn't a big deal."

It was huge. Hugging her, I said, "It is."

She was such a great friend. Guilt struck me. I was sneaking around with her brother. If he was leaving soon, did I ever need to tell her?

Uneasy, I asked, "Can I help with dinner?"

She waved me away. "It's in the Crock-Pot."

I followed her to her small kitchen. "It smells good."

She lifted the lid, ladling the soup into bowls. "Beef stew."

A loaf of bread was on the counter next to a wooden cutting board and bread knife. I lifted the crusty bread, slicing it, then placing it on a plate.

Suddenly nervous I'd made a mistake, I said, "I did something a little impulsive today."

She glanced at me absentmindedly, setting the bowls on the small round table by the window. "What was that?"

"Customers wanted something to drink, so I thought about serving water bottles."

"The upsell on those is huge."

I moved the plate of bread to the center of the table. "But it didn't fit with my brand. I didn't like the idea of selling water bottles from a cooler."

"I agree." She grabbed spoons from the drawer.

Sitting in my usual spot, I continued, "There's nothing else in the marketplace to direct them to. The deli has bottled water and soda already."

"You could send them there."

"That's another line for them. I worry they'll decide to buy a sandwich instead."

"That's a possibility."

Taking a fortifying breath, I said, "I talked to Remi."

"Remi who owns the juice shop?"

"Yeah, I proposed a partnership of sorts."

Her eyes widened. "You *have* been busy today."

"Her juices fit. Her store is closer to State Circle, away from the traffic we get from the water."

"She could use a second location."

"Without the cost of a large space or another storefront."

"What did she say?"

I had Savannah's full attention. "She was interested, we

talked about what we'd need to get started, pricing, and splitting the rent of the booth."

"You'd be serving her drinks, so you should be getting a higher percentage."

"Exactly." I pulled out the paper where we'd listed the pertinent details.

"I know an attorney you can speak with to draft an agreement. Avery is helping me with the store."

"With what?"

"An agreement to buy my mother out."

I sucked in a breath. "Wow. Does she know about it?"

"Not yet. I hope to offer her enough money that she walks away, giving me control."

"Can you afford to do that?"

Her gaze slid away from mine. "I'm looking into borrowing the money."

She continued, "This deal with Remi doesn't require much in the way of costs for you. It adds to your business, not taking away from it. I think you should do it."

Pride filled me that I'd made a good business decision based on instinct. "Maybe I have what it takes to run my own business."

She rose, placing a hand on my shoulder. "You definitely do." Then she wandered to the living room. "Miles, dinner is ready."

Then she sighed. "Turn the TV off."

Looking back at me, she said, "I swear, he can't hear anything when it's on."

Chuckling, I blew on the stew, taking a tentative bite. "This is good."

Miles raced into the room, sitting next to me. "Ew, what's this?"

"It's beef stew," I said at the same time Savannah said, "Manners, Miles."

Contrite, he said, "Sorry."

"You don't like stew?"

"He's not a fan of soup."

"Oh, that's right."

She spooned out the pieces of beef, potatoes, and carrots, placing them on a plate. "See? Now it's just beef and potatoes and carrots."

He speared a piece of beef, putting it in his mouth. "Mmm, good."

I exchanged a smile with Savannah. Miles was adorable. Something warm filled my chest. I wanted a child someday. Someone to share my life with. It seemed like a far-off possibility with me spending time with Alex. He had no plans to commit.

Regret filled me. Had I been wasting my time with him, thinking he'd change his mind? Hoping he'd realize we had so much more than a short fling?

"Are you okay?" Savannah asked me.

Pushing Alex out of my mind, I said, "I had a great day."

The bakery stand did amazingly well, I had a great idea to make it even better, I'd made a new friend in Remi, and Alex delivered lunch.

"I'm so happy for you." Savannah looked a little sad.

"Things will work out for you, too. I have a good feeling." I hoped she'd get enough money to buy her mom out and take the store in the direction she wanted to go.

"I hope so. As convenient as living over the store is, I'd like to move into a home with a yard for Miles."

It was convenient being here. Close to work and within walking distance to Miles's private school.

"Do you mind if I take some stew to go?" I asked her later when I was helping her clean up.

"Of course you can." I didn't mention it was for her brother. I always had dinner waiting for him. The guilt over lying to her and keeping something so huge a secret weighed on me.

She handed me the plastic container.

My stomach churned with uncertainty. Would she understand? Would it ruin everything I'd built with her and her family over the years? Or would they be understanding?

"Are you sure everything's okay?"

"It couldn't be better." The success of the bakery was amazing. It was the rest of my life that was up in the air.

"How's Alex doing? Is he working long hours?" Savannah asked.

"This block—the one at shock trauma—has been the worst. Long hours. More stress."

Her forehead wrinkled. "I hate that for him. I know it comes with the job, but it's so tough. He told Mom his mentor offered to put in a good word for him wherever he wanted to work in New York. It's exactly what he wanted."

I knew this, but it was like the floor dropped out from under my feet, and I was free-falling with no idea when I'd come to a stop. Air rushed in my ears.

I'd buried my head in the sand, refusing to think about his inevitable return to New York. He'd be in New York through graduation in June. I'd stupidly held out hope that he'd expand his job search to Maryland.

"You'll have a free room at the B & B soon."

"He can stay as long as he likes. It's fine." It was more than fine. Having him nearby was amazing. Sleeping with him each night was a dream.

How was I going to go back to how it was before? The apartment that I used to think of as a cozy oasis was now filled with memories of him. Each time I went home at the end of the night, I'd remember what it was like having him there.

Endless nights alone piled up in front of me.

"He said you've been feeding him breakfast and dinner each day. I bet you'll be glad to be free of that."

My chest tightened. Free? I felt anything but free. I felt weighed down.

"Oh, yeah," I agreed and nodded like a puppet. I couldn't see anything in the room with clarity. Everything was blurred.

"I'd better get home."

"Of course. I can't wait for the town to start putting up the holiday decorations. I just love Annapolis this time of year."

"It's great." My words fell flat, but I smiled to cover them.

I hugged Miles so tightly, he wiggled out of my embrace. He'd adapt to seeing his uncle virtually again, but would I?

I didn't even have a reason to keep in touch. We'd never defined our relationship. We fell into bed with each other each night. We shared breakfast and whispered conversation in the middle of the night. We'd had a couple of days when we explored the town, but we were acquaintances, friends. He hadn't promised anything more.

Stepping into the cold night air, my heart felt like it was breaking. Why hadn't I kept my heart out of it? I should have known I'd fall hard and fast for the guy I'd had a crush on all these years. I should have known it wouldn't last. He'd always been up front about what he wanted. It was me who'd been lying to myself, to everyone.

I walked across town to the B & B, not seeing the lights of the boats that usually brought me joy or the beginning of holiday decorations they were hanging in some of the store windows.

I'd told myself I could date Alex without repercussions; I'd told myself I could hide it from his family. I'd lied to everyone, but mostly, I'd lied to myself.

I was in love with Alex, and he was still planning to walk away as if our time together meant nothing.

CHAPTER TWENTY-FOUR
ALEX

Elated for Ava's success, I stopped to buy flowers at a flower shop before heading home a little early. I wanted to spend the evening with her.

She opened the door, looking at me in surprise. "Alex, what are you doing home so early?"

Her greeting was a little flat, the opposite of how she'd sounded on the phone earlier today.

Moving to her, I helped her take off her coat, folding it over my arm.

"Are you hungry? I picked up takeout."

"I ate at Savannah's."

"How was it?"

"Good. It was good."

Something was wrong. She was moving around the B & B as if on autopilot. Picking things up, then putting them down.

"Did something happen?"

"Everything's great with the bakery. I even spoke to Remi about partnering with her juice shop."

"That's a great idea."

She smiled, but it was off. "Thanks. It was just an idea that came to me. Customers were asking for something to drink—and there're really not many options in the marketplace."

"You're becoming quite the businesswoman."

"I guess I am."

I moved closer to her. "What's wrong?"

"Savannah said something about how you're looking for a job in New York after you graduate. It wasn't anything I didn't already know."

"That's always been my plan—or at least it was before."

"Before what?" she asked hesitantly.

"Before you." I turned her slightly in my arms so I could capture her lips with mine. I didn't care who walked in and saw. I wanted her to know she was mine.

I caressed her cheek before pulling back.

My stomach tightened. I could tell her my view on life had changed, but it meant nothing unless I acted on those words.

"I like having someone to come home to at the end of the night, someone to wake up to."

"Is that all I am?"

"You're so much more. You're the one I want to check in with in the middle of a long shift. I want to celebrate your wins with you. I want to deliver flowers and lunch when I can't be with you."

Her breath hitched.

I pulled up my hands as if to ward her off. "Is that too much?"

She shook her head, her eyes bright with unshed tears. "No."

My heart skipped a beat. "No, what?"

Was this just a fling to her? Had I read her wrong? I ignored the ripple of pain that went through my body.

"You're not overstepping."

She moved into my body, wrapping her arms around my waist. "That's exactly what I want, too."

Once I realized she was on the same page, I relaxed into her embrace.

"I was hoping to do something special tonight since I got home early. I could take you out for dessert and drinks."

Her arms still wrapped tightly around me, she looked up. "Do you mind if we stay in?"

I dropped a kiss on her lips. "Of course not."

"I was planning on getting out the Christmas decorations."

Excitement surged through me. I hadn't decorated anything for Christmas since I lived with my parents. "Inside or outside?"

"Let's start with the back gardens. Guests love when it's all lit up. Then we can do the front porch and the inside."

"Sounds like a plan. Show me where everything is."

She led me outside to a small shed. Pointing at the stacked boxes, she said, "These are the lights for the backyard. If no animals got into these, we should have everything we need."

I checked the boxes. "Tell me where everything goes."

Glancing inside, she said, "We use these lights for the gazebo and trellis. Then we place poles around the yard to string more lights."

It was classic and simple. "Let's get to it."

We quickly established a system where she handed me the lights, and I attached them.

"Do Juliana and Nolan help you out?" I couldn't imagine her doing this by herself.

"Usually. But I think they're busy with the girls. They have their own house to decorate."

"You shouldn't be up on the ladder doing this by yourself."

"Nolan would help if I asked."

The question was, would she ask for help, or did she do most things around the B & B on her own? "You do so much around here. Now you have the bakery."

I leaned on the ladder, watching while she carefully unraveled the next string of lights.

"I like being busy."

She looked up at me, the lights in her outstretched hands and the twinkling lights we'd already hung, illuminating her face in the cool night.

"I probably shouldn't talk, but I'm worried about you. I don't want you to burn yourself out."

She sighed. "I already talked to Juliana about that. I think she has someone in mind who could start before the holidays."

"Good." I tacked on the next set of lights. "Is the B & B busy over the holidays?"

"Most people don't stay on the actual holiday. It picks up for New Year's."

I grinned down at her. "We'll have the place to ourselves?"

"We will."

Then something struck me. "We haven't told our families about us."

She looked uncertain. "Should we?"

"Isn't that what couples normally do?"

She tensed. "But we aren't a couple. If you're headed back to New York, there's probably no point in upsetting your family. Savannah already warned me away from you. Said you're not one for commitment."

I leaned my elbows on the ladder. "Were you listening to anything I said in the kitchen?"

"You said you enjoyed spending time with me."

I tipped her chin, so she was looking at me. "I want to be here with you."

The thought of moving back to New York after Christmas left a gaping hole in my chest. I couldn't promise her I'd get a job in Maryland. Most of my connections were in New York, but I could try.

Her gaze searched my face, probably for any sign of insincerity.

"I feel like I've been waiting my whole life for something. I think I've been waiting for you."

"You're saying the nicest things." Her expression was uncertain.

"I don't know how it will work, but I'm willing to try."

A flash of pain crossed her face before she carefully smoothed it over again. "I'd like that, too."

"I'm looking forward to spending Christmas with my favorite people—you and my family. Right here in this beautiful space. We have so much to celebrate this year. Me finally graduating soon—you opening your bakery."

I hope I'd reassured her. "Now hand me more lights. This tree won't decorate itself."

I was able to decorate a few of the smaller trees myself while Ava went inside to make hot chocolate.

Coming outside with two steaming mugs, Ava admired the lights we'd strung. It felt like Christmas.

I came down the ladder and took a mug from her. "Marshmallows and candy canes?"

She smiled. "Nothing but the best for the holiday decorating committee."

"Is that all I am to you?" I grabbed her hand, tugging her down to sit on the swing.

Her foot pushed off the ground, sending the swing into a gentle rocking motion while she ticked points off her fingers. "Let's see...You eat all of my food....You hog the bed...."

I held my hand over my chest. "I do not."

She looked at me pointedly. "You have to be in charge of the remote."

I smiled, loving our easy banter. "Well, yeah. Men should be."

She smacked me in the stomach.

I doubled over. "Geez. I was just kidding."

She raised her brow.

Conceding, I said, "You can choose the movie tonight. And I'll distract you."

Her gaze was on the twinkling lights we'd erected. "I like that idea."

"It looks amazing." The gazebo and trellis over the patio were finished. Several trees were wrapped in lights like a Christmas tree, and we'd managed to hang a few strands of lights from poles. It gave the yard a feeling of being alone, even though we were in the middle of town.

"You should have it lit up like this year-round."

"Guests have mentioned that, but saving it for the holidays makes it more special."

Resting my arm on the back of the swing, I asked, "Why wait for one day of the year to indulge in things that make you happy?"

She swallowed. "You're saying we should enjoy them all the time?"

I was certain she was talking about hot chocolate, candy canes, and holiday lights. I was talking about her. I didn't want to deny myself anymore. To relegate our time to stolen moments late at night and early in the morning. I wanted everything with her. I wanted her front and center when I performed. By my side at family dinner. With me when I babysat Miles. My date for hospital functions.

The thought of her wearing a red evening gown to a fancy hospital event had my heart racing in my chest.

She turned slightly to me, resting a hand on my chest. "Alex?"

I realized I hadn't answered her question. "I'm happy. I couldn't say that in the city. If indulging is the reason, then I say we should do more of it."

Her eyes softened, her head tipping slightly to the side. Unable to resist, I leaned over, kissing her softly, my hand cupping her chin.

She broke off, breathless. "We can't do this here."

"Do what? I'm having a romantic evening with my girlfriend."

She looked up at me. "Girlfriend?"

"You have any objections?"

She shook her head, her eyes full of wonder.

I wasn't questioning myself anymore. I was going with my gut—the one that was telling me I was doing the right thing and was on the right path. If I relied on my instincts, I wouldn't be led astray.

"Something that feels this right can't be wrong." I could see my breath in the air, the brisk evening doing little to cool my overheated body.

The French doors to the backyard opened with a squeak.

"Ava?" Juliana's voice rang out. "Are you back here?"

Two little blonde girls raced around her, squealing at the lights.

One stopped in the middle of the yard, twirling in a circle, her head thrown back, her hands spread wide. "Mommy, isn't it boo-ti-ful?"

The second stood staring in wonder at the lit tree.

Nolan's heavy boots stepped onto the patio. "Why did you start the lights without us?"

My heart skipped a beat. This was the moment when Ava could back down from our talk a minute ago. She could step away from me, pretending I was nothing but an old friend, a guest even.

My heart thudded in my ears while I waited for Ava to make a move…or not.

She stood, tugging me up with her. "Alex helped."

Juliana's gaze went from me to our joined hands. "Is that how it is?"

Ava smiled, slightly embarrassed, nibbling her lower lip before she raised her gaze to me, then to her sister. "That's how it is."

Juliana smiled wide before looking down at her daughter,

who was tugging at her hand. "Come see, Mommy!"

"Okay, okay." Juliana allowed her girls to walk her around the grounds.

Nolan stepped closer to us. "Thanks for helping out."

"No problem." It was fun. It was the first time I'd celebrated the holidays other than at the hospital since I had left for med school. There was no need to decorate my apartment when I only slept there. The large tree in the lobby and the smaller ones on each floor were my Christmas—but this, being here with Ava, sharing the magic with her sister and family… It was everything. It was more than I ever thought I'd have.

I wanted to hold on to it with both hands. I wasn't sure how I could make it work. All I knew was I didn't want to leave her. Whether that meant asking her to try long distance or move to New York, I wasn't sure. My chest ached with the knowledge I'd never be the same. This woman had changed me in the span of a few months.

"I can lend a hand on the front porch."

"Want to get started now?"

Nolan watched Juliana and the girls in the yard. "They wanted to come over to do the lights. We can decorate our house, but it's secluded. Not many people driving by. They love that everyone can walk by and see them here."

Nolan seemed utterly entranced with Juliana and her girls. Between Miles and these girls, I wondered if children were a possibility for me. Steve had warned me against any attachments, and I'd seen how painful his divorce was, but how could I deny myself the love that was so evident in Juliana and Nolan's family?

My job was important, but not to the point of denying myself a chance at something like this.

I squeezed Ava's hand before dropping it. "We wouldn't want to disappoint them."

Carrying the boxes from the shed through the B & B, we

made quick work of the lights on the front porch.

Ava considered the porch. "We still need to put up the greenery, but this will do for now."

Juliana nodded. "I want fresh wreaths again this year. So we don't want to put them up too early."

"Tell me what you need. I'll get it from a local tree farm I know tomorrow. If they don't last, we'll get more," I offered.

Ava wrapped a hand around my bicep, leaning in close. "Do you have time for that?"

"I'll make time." Kissing her lips briefly, a feeling filled me. It was more than love, it was this feeling of complete and utter contentment. I was right where I was supposed to be. Nothing had ever felt better.

She rested her head against my shoulder.

I looked up to find Juliana watching us. She smiled before turning her attention to her girls, who were clamoring for hot chocolate.

"I made some earlier. I might have just enough for two more mugs," Ava said.

"You do?" the one I'd come to think of as the bolder twin asked.

Ava pulled away from me, taking her hand. "Let's go see."

Nolan followed them inside, leaving me on the porch with Juliana.

I sat in one of the rockers, anticipating she'd want to talk to me.

She sat next to me, rocking softly. "Are things serious with you two? Or is this just a way to spend the time while you're here?"

I stopped the gentle rocking of my chair, planting my feet firmly on the ground. Leaning forward, I rested my elbows on my knees. "I want to be with her."

She glanced up at me in surprise. "Why is this the first we're hearing of you guys together?"

Guilt slid down my spine. "She didn't want anyone to

know in case it was temporary."

"As long as you're good to my sister. She deserves it."

"I don't intend to hurt her."

She gave me a sharp look. "Intention and reality are two different things."

I nodded. "I won't lie to you and say I went into this thinking it was serious. I didn't. I thought we could enjoy whatever this was, and I'd go back to New York when it was time."

"And now?" She fell silent, her question hung expectantly in the air between us.

I sighed, the words falling out of me in a rush. "She's everything I've ever wanted. I'd do anything for her."

"See that you do."

I knew I hadn't won Juliana over completely. I'd need to prove my intentions were good to her and to Ava. It would take time, and I wasn't even sure how to manage it.

Nolan's voice carried as the girls came out on the porch. "Sit, and I'll hand them to you."

The girls sat side by side on the top step while Nolan handed each a small mug of hot chocolate piled high with mini marshmallows.

Nolan exchanged a sweet smile with Juliana. She stood, moving to his side. He wrapped an arm around her, pulling her in close.

I almost felt like I was intruding on a private family moment.

Ava came out with a tray of mugs, setting them on the table between the rockers. "I made more for everyone."

We sat on the porch sipping hot chocolate and watching the occasional tourist or local person walking their dog go past.

I wanted more nights like this. The question was: Would it be here in Annapolis or a condo in New York? The city didn't hold quite the same appeal it used to.

CHAPTER TWENTY-FIVE
AVA

I sat in the rocking chair on the front porch of the B & B, breathing in the fresh scent of pine. As promised, Alex had purchased the greenery for the entire B & B from MacCarthy's Farm. A large wreath hung on the door, small wreaths on the windows, and garland was strung in a wave pattern from the railing on the porch. It was beautiful.

Juliana seemed happy for me. When I came out on the porch after making hot chocolate the night they stopped by, I had a feeling she'd talked to him. Whatever Alex said to her must have settled her mind.

I liked that Juliana talked to him like my mother would have done if she were here.

Alex called me his girlfriend. He'd said he wanted to work things out with me. I tried to hold on to that sentiment even as I worried the lure of New York would be too much for him.

Alex stepped onto the porch, buttoning the cuff of his blue shirt that brought out his eyes. I moved to stand in front of him, close enough to smell his aftershave as I helped him with the button.

"Are you nervous?" he asked, nodding at my shaking fingers.

I finished with his cuff. "A little."

Today was the day we were eating with Alex's family. It was the night we were supposed to tell them about us.

We'd had this same discussion many times this week. As much as I didn't want us to be kept a secret, I was worried about their reaction.

I drew in a shaky breath, looking up at him. "Do we have to tell them?"

He seemed self-assured, confident. "You're not a secret. You're the best thing that's ever happened to me. I want everyone to know."

I swayed toward him the same moment he tugged me against him, kissing me.

"We can't kiss in front of the door."

He pointed over my head at the sprig hanging from the roof of the porch. "Someone hung mistletoe."

My lips twitching, I asked, "I wonder who that could have been?"

Part of Alex's decorating plan was hanging mistletoe in random places throughout the B & B that we kept finding "by accident."

It was sweet. We hadn't really dated before falling into bed together, so his care for me and the B & B felt like one big seduction. I was melting more with each gesture.

He stroked the side of my face. "I want everyone to know how hard I've fallen for you. Especially my family."

"What if Savannah has a problem with it?" I couldn't forget how she'd said a friend hooking up with her brother was gross. Would she let go of her feelings if she could see how happy I was with him?

His eyes heated. "I care what they think, but it won't change my feelings for you."

I sighed. Things were perfect. I was dating my childhood crush, who'd become so much more than that. He'd been my safe harbor, my rock, and my biggest supporter.

The problem was, I couldn't let go of this nagging sensation that this was temporary. I never trusted when things were going well. There had to be something that could come along and derail it. I wanted to be prepared for that possibility.

"They love you. They love me. They'll be happy we're together. You'll see."

Getting into his car, I tried to repeat his words, but they didn't quite stick. If things went badly, I could lose my best friend and his parents, who'd always been there for me.

Parking in the driveway, he leaned over, giving me a sweet kiss on the lips. "We've got this."

Love bloomed in my chest.

He held my hand up the walk. The yard was filled with plastic decorations and blow-ups bobbing in the wind.

Inside, Savannah called out to us, "We're in the kitchen."

We took off our jackets and shoes, walking toward the sounds of dishes and the smell of food.

After we greeted everyone, Miles asked Alex, "Are you done working your resi—residenty?"

"Residency," Savannah prompted.

"I have a few more days there then I'm off for Christmas."

"Yay! You can help me put my Legos together on Christmas."

"Who said Santa's bringing you Legos?" Savannah teased.

"If Santa doesn't, I'm sure everyone else bought him sets," Lilliane said.

"Yeah, see?" Miles taunted his mother before running out of the room.

"I have something I wanted to talk to you about." His gaze met mine, my face heated. Savannah looked from Alex to me, a confused look on her face.

"I've found someone who's special."

"You have a girlfriend?" Savannah was still confused by his words and his constant glances at me.

"I do."

It was like time stood still as he reached for me. I went willingly to his side, my hand pressed to his chest. I needed his comfort, at the same time I cringed at the thought of their reaction to what they were seeing.

"Alex?" Savannah asked.

"Mommy, Mommy. Can you play with me?" Miles called from the family room.

"In a minute," Savannah told him absentmindedly.

It was at that moment, I realized my mistake. I should have told Savannah separately, not in front of her parents.

"I'm dating Ava."

The room fell silent.

"Are you going to kiss and get married?" Miles asked in the doorway.

Savannah laughed shakily. "Of course not. This can't be serious."

Alex cleared his throat, clearly uncomfortable with her reaction. "It's serious."

Miles's eyes widened. "Say yes, Miss Ava. My uncle is so cool. He plays video games. He lets me eat pizza as much as I want."

"Mmm. I don't know that those are good reasons for getting married," Jim said.

"They're the best reasons," Miles said seriously.

If I hadn't felt Savannah's tension, I would have laughed.

"Let's go, buddy. I think the grown-ups want to talk." Alex's dad led him into the living room.

I pulled away from Alex. "I'm sorry, Savannah. I should have talked to you in private about this."

Savannah looked from me to Alex. "You kept this from me?"

"To be fair, we kept it from everyone. We only just told her family last week. It wasn't exactly planned." Alex's voice was even.

"Are you happy?" Lilliane asked Alex.

Alex nodded, not hesitating. "I'm very happy."

Lilliane nodded. "That's all that matters."

Savannah shot her mom an incredulous look. "You're not upset they kept this from us?"

Lilliane shrugged. "He's a grown man. I'd expect him to keep who he's seeing private until it's something worth talking about."

I was desperate to talk to Savannah alone. "Can we talk?"

She nodded tightly.

We headed upstairs to Savannah's old bedroom. It still had pink walls, faded in spots where band posters hung but were long since removed. I sat on the edge of the twin bed.

Savannah leaned a shoulder against the doorframe, crossing her arms over her chest. "You were sleeping with my brother and keeping it a secret from me."

I shrugged. "I didn't think it was going to turn into anything."

She pointed at me. "I told you to stay away from him. He's said repeatedly he doesn't want a serious relationship. Not until his career is established, if ever."

How could I explain that he felt differently now? Especially when I wasn't positive he wouldn't change his mind again.

She pushed off the doorframe, moving into the room. "I'm worried about you. I don't want you to get hurt."

"I've had a crush on Alex since childhood. We spent time together since he's been staying at the B & B. We got to know each other. We realized we cared for each other. It gradually turned into something more."

She stopped in front of me, her eyes filled with pain.

Pain that I caused.

Shaking her head, she said, "I can't wrap my head around it."

With a shaky breath, I decided to tell her everything. "I was worried I'd lose your friendship. Your family became important to me when my mother left. I couldn't afford to lose any of you. That's why I told Alex we couldn't say anything to you, especially when it was just a fling."

I didn't want her to be angry at her brother when the blame lays solely with me. "He thought you'd be happy for us. I worried about what would happen when he left."

The thought of that sent pain coursing through my veins.

She tipped her head, the pain morphing to concern for me. "I wish you would have told me right away."

"I thought that if it never turned into anything, you'd never have to know. I wouldn't have to risk our friendship or your family."

Savannah sat next to me. "As your friend, I'm worried this isn't going to last."

Her words hurt because there was a ring of truth to them. "It's not just me. He loved spending more time with you and Miles."

She fell silent.

"Are we okay?"

Her face was pinched. "I just hope you don't get hurt."

I hoped so, too. Alex held all the power. He was the one with a life and contacts in New York. We could just be a pit stop for him. Just because he had a hankering to stick around didn't mean it would be forever.

I'd always been expendable, and I couldn't forget that.

CHAPTER TWENTY-SIX

ALEX

When Savannah and Ava went upstairs to talk, Dad asked for my help in the garage. Standing in the garage, Dad turned to face me.

"I assume nothing's broken?"

He waved a hand at me. "That's not why I brought you out here."

I waited for the inevitable lecture I sensed was coming.

"I hope you know what you're doing. Ava is special to us. She spent a lot of time here when her mother left."

"I know that."

"If this thing goes bad, I don't want Ava to get the short end of the stick."

"It's not going to go bad." I finally felt like my world was coming together. It was no longer this solitary path where I worked long hours. I had something, some*one* to look forward to spending my time with. It changed everything—where I was thinking of living and the kind of job I took. Quality of life meant something to me in a way it didn't before. I had Ava to thank for opening my eyes to that.

"How can you be so sure?"

"I love her."

He stilled as silence fell between us.

"I wouldn't have brought her here if it wasn't serious. If I didn't think she was my future."

His eyes narrowed on me. "You've got some things to figure out if you're in New York and she's here."

"I have to finish out my residency in New York. That's not something I can change. I can ask her to come with me to New York, or we could try long distance."

I'd been floating the idea of working here, but I wasn't ready to voice it out loud.

Dad had been largely quiet about my career over the years, telling Mom to leave me alone. "Whatever makes you happy."

"What do you think Mom will say?"

He chuckled. "She'd like to have you closer, but she understands that there's more potential for growth in New York than working here."

I'd always told my parents that. There were more prestigious hospitals there, respected doctors, and exciting research in the medical field. Baltimore had that at Johns Hopkins. For the first time, I questioned whether I needed to work at that level to do the most good. Thinking of my work on the pediatric unit and the ease with which I was able to integrate music and medicine, I wondered if working in a smaller hospital might give me more joy.

Heading back inside, Ava and Savannah were in the dining room setting the table.

I arched a brow at Savannah, wondering how she felt.

She stood, walking past me to go into the kitchen. "Just don't screw it up."

I moved over to Ava.

"I think we'll be okay." Ava smiled, but it didn't quite reach her eyes.

"Dinner is served," Dad said, placing the steaming casserole dish of lasagna in the middle of the table.

WAITING FOR YOU

I felt content being with Ava and my family. As long as I was with Ava, things would be okay.

We talked about the holidays and the parties my parents attended that I hadn't been here for in the past. The events around town, like the tree lighting ceremony, the lighting of the boats at the harbor. I was excited to be here for it this year.

After eating, I leaned back in my chair, my stomach uncomfortably full.

Then Mom served Boston cream pie. Dad's favorite.

I ate a few bites of the pie, watching Miles as he devoured it.

Ava rubbed her stomach. "Dinner was so good. Thank you."

"Even Miles ate a lot." Savannah gestured at his empty plate.

"Bribing him with pie usually encourages him to eat more of his dinner." Lilliane stood to clear the dishes.

Ava followed suit. She fit in with my family because she'd already been here for years. She knew what she was getting into with my job, but she was here anyway.

While Ava and my mom cleaned, I followed Miles into the living room to play Legos. After a few minutes, Savannah joined us.

"Miles, Grandma has something she wants to show you in the kitchen."

His eyes lit up. "Is it candy?"

Savannah shrugged. "I don't know. You'll have to go and find out."

When he was gone, I leaned back on the couch cushions. "Clever. You want to talk?"

"Please be careful with Ava. She's fragile. Her mom leaving really affected her. Then her ex did the same. Don't make promises you can't keep."

"I want to be with her. I just don't have everything figured out yet." There were too many variables. I wasn't even sure

Ava would want to try long distance. If not, I could ask her to come to New York.

Ava walked in, her body stiffening. She'd heard me. She had doubts, too. I wanted to erase those doubts tonight.

"Ready to head out?" I asked, desperate to get her home. To show her what she meant to me.

She nodded. Heading home, I interlaced my fingers with hers. "That wasn't too bad."

"Savannah was hurt, but she seemed okay after I explained everything."

I didn't mention that both my father and Savannah expressed concerns about me staying for the long term. I didn't want to worry her.

Parking at the curb in front of the B & B, we walked up the sidewalk, the lights and wreaths welcoming.

"It's so beautiful."

"Not any more beautiful than you."

She smiled softly.

Did she have any idea how much she meant to me? I hadn't told her what I'd said to my father. I didn't want to let any more time go without telling her and showing her everything.

"Your apartment?"

She nodded, unlocking the door and leading me up the steps. She kicked off her shoes. "I wanted to talk to you about moving in here. Ben Levine called to make a last-minute reservation for the holidays. I think he was a year or two ahead of me in school."

I moved closer to her. "I don't mind moving in with you if that's what you want."

"It makes the most sense. We spend most nights together."

"I'll move my stuff tomorrow."

The twinkling lights we'd hung on her ceiling reflected in her eyes. The fresh tree in the corner made the space smell like pine needles.

I pulled out my phone, setting it to play holiday music. "Dance with me?"

She moved into my outstretched hands. "I'd love to."

I loved the feel of her against me, her cheek pressed against my chest.

When the sound of strings came over the speaker, she smiled. "This is you playing, isn't it?"

I nodded. "Is that weird?"

She smiled. "I like dancing in your arms to your music."

When the first song ended, we continued dancing to the next. I lowered my head, my mouth resting against her temple. "Ava, I love you."

She tipped her head up so her gaze met mine.

"I love you," I repeated, not wanting her to miss anything.

Her hands wrapped around the back of my neck, pulling me down, kissing me deeply. We stopped swaying to the music, her body pressed against mine. I pulled her sweater over her head, her breasts spilling over her red lace bra. I sunk to my knees, kissing her navel before undoing the button on her jeans.

Her hand tangled in my hair. She tugged lightly. "I love you, too."

Emotion surged through me as I tugged her jeans down, then off, leaving her in red panties and a bra.

I stood, confidence soaring through me. She wanted me. She loved me.

I kissed her, firmer this time. I maneuvered her so that her knees pressed against the bed. She fell back, her eyes bright with desire, her legs falling out to the sides.

She was spread out on the bed for me. I unbuttoned my shirt with quick, jerky movements. I wanted nothing between us.

She moved to her knees on the bed, pushing my hands away. "Let me."

My breath was ragged and uneven as she made quick

work of my shirt, then my pants. I couldn't believe my focus had changed so much in just a few short months.

She lay back on the bed, pulling me down with her. I moved over her, kissing her, touching her everywhere. I'd never get enough of this woman in my bed, my life. Forever. She was mine.

Sharing our feelings created a new level of intensity in the bedroom. I'd never felt this way with anyone before. There was nothing between us. No secrets. Just pure love and emotion.

She pulled back to unclasp her bra, shrugging it off as I hooked my fingers in her panties, pulling them off. I placed her legs over my shoulders, devouring her pussy. This wasn't a slow seduction. It was a claiming.

I was making her mine with each pass of my tongue and each brush of my fingers. Her whimpers and the tremors in her thighs spurred me on.

When my fingers parted her folds, slipping inside, her hips arched off the bed. I moved my arm to press her down against the bed.

She was so close. I wanted her to go over. I wanted her to forget about her worries. I wanted her to let go.

Pumping inside of her, I sucked her clit into my mouth. She lifted upward, straining against my forearm as she spasmed around my fingers. I let her ride it out on my fingers while I lifted my head to watch her come undone.

"Look at me, beautiful," I said as she came down from the high.

Her eyes filled with emotion as she held her hand out to me. I settled between her legs, my cock sliding easily between her folds.

I shifted so that my cock lined up with her entrance, sliding in slowly. I wanted to savor the feeling of being inside her.

She caressed my face. "I love you."

"I love you so much." I sunk down over her so that my one hand pressed hers into the mattress. I moved with slow and easy strokes inside her, controlling the buildup. I never wanted this moment to end.

She loved me. She trusted me. It was a heady feeling. One I wouldn't take lightly. I'd made promises to her and my family that I'd keep. I wouldn't let her down. Not like she'd been let down in the past.

"Come for me," I whispered into her ear, needing to feel her come apart again.

She cried out as I ground against her clit, bottoming out. Gritting my teeth, I rallied against the sensation to join her, thrusting through her orgasm, drawing it out. Surging up, I thrust harder, deeper. She was mine.

Finally, settling deep, I let go, spilling inside her. The sensation was overwhelming. I moved so we were on our sides, facing each other. It seemed as if every part of my body was touching hers. I never wanted to untangle myself.

I pressed a kiss to her shoulder, thinking nothing would ever feel this good.

CHAPTER TWENTY-SEVEN
AVA

I woke up earlier than normal to bake what I needed for the marketplace. With Christmas approaching, ginger snaps, cut-out sugar cookies, nut rolls, and cinnamon rolls were in demand. I'd also taken on several large orders of cookies. I'd never planned on expanding the business to include special orders so soon, but it made me think a website would be necessary to take orders.

By the end of the day, I was exhausted. I took any leftovers to either Savannah and Miles or my family.

Alex was finally done with his block at shock trauma and had a week off for Christmas. He wanted to attend every holiday event he could since he wasn't working. We went to the tree lightings, walked each evening to see the lights on the boats, and went ice skating.

Both Savannah and I would be busy until Christmas, so Alex offered to help watch Miles when school let out.

We'd hired MacKenzie to help out at the B & B part time. She managed the afternoons and evenings.

I was doing something I loved—selling my baked goods and spending time with Alex—nothing could be better. I tried not to fall back into my old pattern of doubting he'd stick around. But it was hard when he was leaving for New York soon.

A couple of nights before Christmas, I stopped by Juliana and Nolan's for dinner.

"How's it going?" Juliana asked, taking the box of baked goods from me.

"This is going to sound weird, but I feel like I'm living my best life. I'm busy, and the stress from the bakery is there, but I'm doing what I love to do. I enjoy figuring out what to bake and what people will want or need for the upcoming week and then ordering the necessary ingredients."

Juliana hugged me. "I'm so happy for you. How are things with Alex?"

Pulling away, she poured a glass of wine for me.

"Good. He's taking advantage of his time off to spend more time with me and his family." He was supposed to take Miles this afternoon when school dismissed early.

I glanced at my phone to see if he'd sent me a picture of them together. There was a text from him.

Alex: Steve had a couple of doctors call out at the last minute. He needed me to help out. I'm at the airport now. I'll call you as soon as I can.

My stomach dropped.

"Is something wrong?" Juliana asked.

"I think Alex went back to New York." I didn't have any other messages or missed calls from him. "He said a couple of doctors called out. His old supervisor asked him to cover."

"That stinks."

Nolan came in the door with Laila and Charlie, bringing with them a gust of cold air. "It's coming down already."

"The forecasters are saying it's going to be a blizzard."

"What?" I hadn't checked the weather earlier, and I hadn't recovered from the shock of Alex telling me he'd left.

"Auntie Ava!" the girls cried. I crouched down to give them a hug.

"Earlier they said it was going to be south of us. I guess the system moved north."

Looking outside, fat snowflakes were coming down already.

"The roads look slick. I'd stay here tonight," Nolan said.

"Yeah, okay." Alex wasn't home anyway.

"We might be snowed in for a couple of days if we get as much as they're saying."

The girls were so excited, jumping up and down. The fact that I was here seemed to make things even better.

"It'll be fun." What did it matter if I was stuck here? Alex was on a flight to New York.

Juliana helped the girls get their jackets, mittens, and boots off. "I'm going to ask MacKenzie to cover the B & B tonight."

"Remind her where the generator is. I'm sure the power will go out," Nolan said.

"Yeah, okay." Juliana left the room to make the call.

Alex was gone, and I felt bereft. I drew in a steady breath, smiling at Charlie when she asked me to color with her. It was good I was here with my family. Otherwise, I'd fixate on what Alex's leaving meant.

We ate dinner, then I helped the girls bake cookies. It was a tradition for me to help them make the cut-out cookies they left for Santa each year. Hopefully, they wouldn't eat them before Christmas.

When the first batch was cooling and another was in the oven, my phone rang.

"Alex?" My voice shook. I wasn't sure how to feel. Since dinner, I'd felt resigned—almost numb.

"Hey. Did you get my text?" his familiar voice washed over me.

"You're in New York?" My voice sounded stiff.

"Just landed." I could hear the overhead speakers in the airport announcing it was time to board.

I nodded, even though he couldn't see me.

"Listen. I'm so sorry. Steven needs me. One of his doctors quit, and another broke his arm. I didn't have a choice."

"Of course. I understand." It sucked, and we hadn't really discussed what would happen when he left.

"I'm gonna grab my bags and get a cab. I'll call you when I get home."

He'd called New York home. "I'm at Juliana's because we're getting some snow tonight."

"I can't believe I missed it."

"Me either." It would have been fun to be stuck in the snow with him.

"Call you soon."

We hung up, and all I could think was—I was alone. He wasn't coming back for Christmas. He'd be gone until June.

I knew his schedule. He was so busy, there was no way he'd be able to travel here. Not with one day off a week.

I just started a new business. It wouldn't be a good idea to close for a few days to travel.

Getting ready for bed later that night, all I could remember was the day Juliana and I came home from school to a note on the kitchen table from Mom saying she had to leave for a little while. I couldn't process it then, and I couldn't process this now.

There was a large, gaping hole in my chest that I knew would never be filled. I climbed under the covers. Burrowing down deep, I closed my eyes. Everything hurt, my heart, my muscles, my head.

When the phone buzzed with a video call, I accepted it, resigned to whatever he was about to say. "Hey."

I tried to smile, but I couldn't. "Hey."

"This sucks."

Tears pricked my eyes. "It does."

There wasn't much to say. "I assume you'll be there for Christmas."

"I'll be working if it's any consolation. I'd rather be with you." His tone was sincere.

"You're doing a good thing." I looked away from the screen. "I just wonder what this means for us."

"I have my residency to finish, then graduation." He sucked in a breath. "What do you think about trying to date long distance?"

"Um."

"I'd ask you to come here if I thought you'd say yes."

"I just started a new business. I signed a lease for the booth."

He nodded. "That's why I can't ask you to quit and come here."

"But long distance? I don't know." I had a feeling he'd get caught up in his job and forget about me. Steve would remind him why working in New York would be better for his career.

He winced. "I meant to discuss this before I left."

"What happens in June?"

"I apply for jobs a few months before graduation. I'll take the best one that's offered."

"Will it be in New York or Maryland?" I held my breath for his answer.

"I'll apply for both areas and see what I get."

Things were still up in the air. Could I date him, knowing he could change his mind and take a job in New York? "I'll travel back and forth in the meantime?"

"I know it's not ideal. I can try and come to you sometimes."

We both knew that probably wouldn't happen.

"I don't know what to say." I loved him. But at the same time, I couldn't help but think it would hurt more if I kept this thing between us going and he decided he was more suited for New York.

"Think about it."

"I will."

"I'll call you tomorrow when I get a break."

I nodded.

We said goodbye. Laying back on the bed, I let the tears I'd been holding spill over. His leaving felt permanent, like it was the beginning of the end for us. The situation felt eerily similar to my ex getting a job in Texas and not asking me to move with him.

Nothing ever changed. I wasn't good enough for someone to stay. There was always something or someone more important than me.

I tossed and turned, unable to fall asleep. The problem was, I couldn't even find fault in what Alex had done. The hospital needed him, and he'd gone. He'd sworn an oath to help people, and it was his nature to do so.

It was what I loved about him. How kind he was. How much he thought of others.

None of it changed how I felt.

I imagined myself wrapped in a protective armor so that nothing touched me. The armor felt flimsy but hopefully, over time, it would thicken. Just thinking about the next few days without Alex was unbearable.

I needed to focus on filling the bakery orders for the holidays if we were going to be snowed in for a couple of days. My job might not be as important as Alex's, but I was bringing people joy. What I did mattered.

When I realized that, I finally fell asleep.

THE NEXT MORNING, I WAS CAUGHT UP WITH THE GIRLS, making pancakes, then playing in the snow. I tried not to think about Alex.

After the girls had drunk their hot chocolate and were sitting in front of the TV, Juliana waved me into the kitchen. I followed her, not sure what I would say if she asked about the situation with Alex.

Juliana grabbed a glass of water, taking a sip before saying, "I have something I need to tell you."

"Are you okay?" My mind leaped to some kind of physical ailment.

She nodded. "We were going to tell everyone sooner, maybe even have a party, but the girls have been arguing about it."

"Now I'm really confused."

She smiled softly. "I'm pregnant."

"Oh. That's so amazing." I moved around the counter, pulling her in for a hug, then shifted away to see her face. "Are the girls not happy about it?"

"They are, but they keep arguing over whether they want a little brother or sister. They can't agree."

I laughed, relieved to be talking about something besides my life. "As if they have a say."

"Right? Then they argue about what to name the baby. Nolan and I talked about it, and we're going to wait to find out the sex. Then when the baby's here, we'll tell them the baby's name."

"You're hoping when he or she arrives, the girls will just be happy to meet him or her."

She gave me an exasperated look. "That's the idea, but I never know with those two."

I relaxed, sitting on the stool across from her.

Juliana shifted on her feet, her expression morphing from happiness to concern. "Have you talked to him?"

I shrugged. "He's in New York. I'm here."

Her brow furrowed. "Have you talked about what your relationship is going to look like?"

I shrugged nonchalantly, even though talking about him was like a knife piercing my heart. "He wants to date long distance."

She tilted her head to the side. "Are you okay with that?"

"I mean. Not really. He's there until June. It's a long time. He could change his mind. Remember why he loved New York so much."

"It's a tough situation."

Our relationship would be missed texts and voice mails. "How will I travel when I just opened the bakery?"

"You can't worry about things that haven't happened yet."

I sighed, feeling exhausted. "It's always the same."

"You're protecting yourself. Mom left. Your ex left. Now Alex."

"I feel like I need to."

She tilted her head, softening her tone. "Just because he went to New York for a few days doesn't mean he's gone forever."

"Even if he wants to find a job in Maryland, he'll say it makes the most sense to work there until something in Maryland opens up, but by the time it does, he'll be settled in New York. He still has his apartment. He has his friends. It will be like he never left." I could picture it clearly. I'd become a distant memory—one he thought about less and less as time went on.

I looked away from the pity I saw in Juliana's eyes.

"I wish you'd give it a chance."

"I haven't given him a decision yet."

Seemingly satisfied at that, she nodded. "That's good. Take some time to think about it. You can try long distance. See how it goes."

I nodded tightly, not trusting myself to speak. Emotion had my throat tightening and tears forming, so I excused myself. I closed the door to the guest room. Was I enough? I didn't want to be the girl who was left crushed again.

I wanted to be stronger than that.

CHAPTER TWENTY-EIGHT
AVA

I was snowed in at Juliana's house for a day and a half. As soon as the roads were cleared, I headed home so I could get started on the cookie orders. I had talked to Alex several times, but I'd put off making any permanent decisions about our relationship.

Opening the door to my dad's house on Christmas Eve, I pasted a smile on my face.

"Where's your boyfriend?" Sheila asked.

"He had to work," I said as breezily as I could, stepping into the family room.

Dad sat in his oversized recliner. A holiday movie played in the background.

Laila sat in Nolan's lap, and Charlie was snuggled up next to him.

Juliana waved me into the kitchen. "You don't think you can make it work, do you?"

"Not really."

Juliana sighed. "I know you were affected differently than I was when Mom left. I got angry, and you were—"

"Hurt." That same pain that had become dull over the years throbbed to new life with Alex being called to New York.

"But it's not the same as Mom leaving. He got called away. He didn't break up with you. He wants to make it work. And you can still see him for Christmas."

I had to make her understand the utter devastation I felt when I learned about Mom's actions over the past few years. "Remember when I said we had Sam Ledger look into her whereabouts?"

"Whatever happened with that?"

"I should probably tell Dad at the same time." I called Dad into the kitchen.

His expression was guarded, his shoulders tense.

"I heard back from Sam, the guy investigating Mom. She was a drug addict, like we suspected. She had a few minor run-ins with the law, nothing that required her to go to jail or rehab." I paused, unsure how my dad would take the news.

Dad shook his head. "I don't think there's anything you can say that will surprise me at this point."

It had been so long ago, I doubted Dad harbored feelings for her. When someone let you down like she had, it was hard to maintain good will toward them.

"She got pregnant."

Juliana gasped. "Do we have a brother or sister?"

I held up my hand. "Child protective services took him because he was born addicted."

Pain crossed their faces. "I'm sorry to have to tell you this on Christmas Eve."

Juliana shook her head. "It's okay. I feel horrible for her baby."

"It was a closed adoption, so I don't have any information about the baby."

"I bet he's with someone who couldn't have kids but really wanted one. I'm sure the baby's in good hands." Dad's voice was gruff.

I liked his take on things. "I hope so. She's pregnant again. This time, she appears to be going to her prenatal appointments. She's holding down a job. Sam doesn't think she's using."

I didn't want to mention that she was in a relationship to Dad.

"Does finding this out change anything for you?" Juliana asked us.

Dad shook his head. "I let her go a long time ago. I held out hope for a few years she'd come back, but she never cleaned up her act. I wouldn't have kept her from you if she had."

I'd been so upset when Sam first talked to me, but now I saw things more clearly. "She's a nonentity in my life. I'd want to have a relationship with her children should they come looking for us, but I don't have any desire to see her. Her actions speak louder than any words ever could."

How could I explain the emotions that bubbled to the surface when I was originally told about our siblings? Honesty seemed to be the best course. "I worried her leaving made me unlovable."

"You don't still think that, do you?" Juliana asked.

"Your mother is a drug addict. She's not in control of herself when she's using. She didn't consciously leave you two. Drugs dictated her whole life as soon as she became addicted to them. This isn't the woman I married or even the woman who raised you up until that point." Dad's voice raised slightly with each word spoken.

"It doesn't mean that you're unlovable, or that Alex is destined to leave you. He loves you. He wants to work this out," Juliana said.

They fell silent for a few seconds.

Her words finally sunk in. Alex loved me. He wanted to be with me. I could fight for him. "I want to go to New York. Surprise him on Christmas."

Juliana smiled. "That's a good idea."

My mind was racing with everything I needed to do. "You don't mind if I'm not here tomorrow afternoon?"

"Of course not," Dad said.

I wasn't sure exactly what I'd say when I got there, but I wanted him to know I was all in. No matter what happened, I wanted to be with him. If I had to, I'd quit the business and move to New York.

"Don't live your life with regrets," Dad said before leaving the room.

Did he have regrets about how he handled the situation with our mom? Did he wish he'd gone after her? Would it have made a difference?

At some point over the last few days, I realized I was comparing the situation to my mom and my ex leaving. It wasn't fair to Alex. He'd been honest with me. I assumed our breakup was inevitable. I'd taken the easy way out, effectively going into my shell and refusing to deal with it.

"If you love him, you'll figure out a way to see him. Show him that you think he's important."

I wrapped my arms around my middle. I wasn't sure of anything anymore.

She picked up her phone, typing something into it. "I'll see if there's a flight."

My heart beat loudly in my ears. I wanted to see Alex. I missed him. I missed his arms around me, his voice, his unending support.

She smiled at me. "There's a flight tomorrow at three. You can spend some time with us, then head to the airport."

"This is crazy," I finally said.

"Love is a little crazy. But what better way to show him you're in this for the long haul? That you're not like your mother. That you fight for the people you care about."

It was a bit of a low blow, but she spoke the truth.

I took her phone. It was expensive because it was a last-minute flight, but I had the money. And it would be the perfect Christmas surprise.

"I'll go."

"Yay!" Juliana clasped her hands together. "It's so romantic."

"You want everyone to be happy because you are."

"I want you to be happy. Don't let Mom affect you anymore. You control your actions, not her. You decide to end a relationship or pursue it. If Alex decides he wants to live in New York, then you can discuss it. Maybe you'll want to go with him. But you won't know if you don't talk about it."

"Always the wise older sister."

"So true. Now buy that ticket."

She left the room. I quickly added the ticket to the cart, pulling out my credit card to pay. Excitement shot through me that I was going to see him. I was going to be in New York on Christmas Day. It would be a fun adventure, and hopefully, a welcome surprise.

On the plane to New York the next day, I wasn't so sure. I hadn't called Alex to say I was coming. I wanted it to be a surprise.

He'd left a message last night while I was sleeping, wishing me a Merry Christmas. He said he wished we could spend it together.

There was regret in his voice. It made me think he didn't like the space between us. But I wasn't sure he'd be okay with me showing up at his work.

He'd mentioned that he was working until eight on Christmas Day, so I planned on heading to the hospital as soon as I landed.

I'd packed light with just a carry-on. I hailed a cab outside the airport, giving the driver the name of Alex's hospital.

WAITING FOR YOU

I'd dressed casually in jeans, boots, and a thick red sweater. When we pulled up to the hospital, I drew in a shaky breath, hoping Alex would be okay with me showing up.

I paid the driver and walked inside. Beautiful string music was playing from a corner of the lobby. I wanted to go straight to the emergency room, but I had to see who was playing.

There were several groups of people standing around the room. The lobby went up several stories, with several listeners leaning on the railings, looking down. As soon as I saw the bowed head over a cello, I knew it was Alex. I placed a hand over my heart, collapsing into the nearest chair. He wore a white button-down shirt with the sleeves rolled up his thick forearms, tucked into black dress pants. His dress shoes tapped in time to the beat.

More people stopped to listen as he played several holiday songs in a row. He'd glance up quickly, but never looked directly at me. It gave me time to observe him and the sure way his fingers pinched the strings and moved the bow back and forth. The way his whole body swayed with the music as if it was part of his soul. It relaxed me. I let the music surround me, buoying me for what I needed to do.

When the last note drifted off, he looked up, his gaze traveling around the now-crowded lobby until it stopped on me. There was one heart-stopping second when he didn't react, then his lips spread into a wide smile.

"Merry Christmas, everyone. Thank you for listening to me play, but I have a very important visitor I need to see." His voice was sure and deep, echoing around the large room.

He needed to see me. His reaction, his words made me believe I'd made the right move in coming here. He wasn't annoyed. He wasn't embarrassed. He was happy to see me.

He placed his cello in his case, not bothering to close it as he crossed the room. He never hesitated or stopped to talk to anyone else. He only had eyes for me.

Managing to stand, my heart raced under my ribs. My whole body flushed with anticipation. "Alex?"

"You're here." His expression was incredulous, almost as if he couldn't believe I was standing in front of him.

He opened his arms. I moved into him, burying my head in his chest. The last few days of disappointment and worry melted away. "I missed you."

"You weren't answering your phone today. I thought the worst." His breath tickled the hair on my head.

"I wanted to surprise you." I felt warm all over, loved and cared for.

Pulling back slightly to see his face, I said, "I was upset that you left. Logically I know you had to, but I kept thinking it was the beginning of the end for us."

Now that I had some time and clarity, I knew Alex was nothing like my mother.

"I couldn't help but worry that you'd come back to New York and everything would go back to the way it was. You'd remember how happy you were here."

His face screwed up as he lowered his voice. "Ava, I wasn't happy in New York. I was merely existing. I didn't realize it until I went back home. Until I spent time with you."

Tears pricked my eyes. "Do you forgive me for doubting you and what we have?"

My heart thudded heavily in my ears. I had this vague feeling that people were watching us, but I couldn't look away from him. I had to know where he stood.

"I'm going to spend every day proving to you I'm not going anywhere."

"You're too good to be true." I couldn't believe I'd been so scared of losing him that I almost walked away from the best thing in my life.

"I planned on coming back as soon as I could. I wasn't letting you go without a fight."

"Juliana made me see that I was so afraid of everyone leaving, I was pushing you away before you could."

"You were protecting yourself." He brushed a strand of hair back from my face.

"I don't need to be protected from you."

"That's what I'm trying to tell you. I care about you. I want you to be happy. I want us to take the next step in our lives together."

"If you want to work in New York, I can move here." I wasn't so sure I'd be happy about living in such a large city. I'd never lived anywhere but Annapolis.

"I'm happy you offered, but I think there's another solution that will make both of us happy and allow us to live together.

"I really enjoyed working the PEDs unit. To switch specialties, I'd need to extend my residency. But I made some calls, and it looks like I can complete my residency at home."

Home. "In Annapolis?"

"I'd probably be in the city, but yeah, we could still live together. Just like we have been."

"And you could come home soon?"

The corners of his eyes crinkled. "Yes."

I threw my arms around him. "I love you."

He gazed down at me with so much love and affection. "I love you, Ava."

He made me feel loved and cherished. I'd never doubt him or our love again. We'd make it through anything as long as we were together.

CHAPTER TWENTY-NINE
ALEX

IT WAS SURREAL PLAYING IN THE LARGE LOBBY OF THE HOSPITAL where I'd worked for so long. The huge windows showcased the snow flurries falling during my impromptu concert. Holidays in the hospital always seemed so lonely.

When I looked up to see Ava, my heart stopped, then skipped a beat before pounding a rhythm, carrying me to her.

I was overcome with love.

"When do you get off work?" Ava asked.

"I'm done now. I brought a change of clothes with me, and offered to play when my shift was over."

"Can we go to your place?"

"Let's go." I grabbed her hand, not wanting to let her go as I packed up my cello.

Straightening, one hand in Ava's and the other clutching my case, I was intent on getting her home and showing her how I felt.

"Is this the one keeping you in Maryland?" a man wearing a white doctor's coat with a stethoscope around his neck asked, his gaze on Ava.

"Steve, this is Ava Breslin." My little sister's best friend.

My support system. The love of my life. "Ava, this is Steve Barker, my mentor."

"Nice to meet you, Ava. I didn't think anyone could draw him away from New York."

Ava smiled. "Maybe it wasn't me, but it was the right time."

"I like to think it was a little bit of both." I was happy to see that Steve wasn't upset.

Ava blushed.

"Enjoy the rest of your holiday."

"You do the same," Ava said to him.

"He seemed nice," she said as I pushed open the door to the cold night.

Snowflakes slapped our faces, the wind ruffling Ava's hair.

"He is."

"I didn't think he'd be so understanding."

"I think he hoped I wouldn't meet someone who'd take me away. I think he thinks of me like a son."

"Will it be hard to leave?"

I tugged her into my side, holding her close. "Following you will be the easiest thing I ever do."

She smiled up at me as we walked to my apartment. The snow came down, and holiday music pumped out of speakers in the stores we passed. The night was magical.

I greeted my doorman, heading into the elevator to my floor. Stepping inside my one-bedroom condo, it was like seeing it for the first time. Pristine white walls, gray kitchen cabinets, white countertops. Hardwood floors throughout. It was cold and sterile, like the hospital.

Looking around, she said, "You don't have a tree."

I wanted to take her to bed, to show her all the ways I loved her, but she was right. The ambiance was all wrong.

Feeling lighter and younger than I had in a long time, I said, "Want to go find one?"

"You think there'll be any at the lots?"

I kissed her cold lips. "I think there'll be one."

I spun her around, leaving as quickly as we'd arrived.

"How can you be so sure?" She was breathless, trying to keep up with me.

"There's always one. We just have to find it."

Everything seemed brighter. The possibilities endless. The dream bigger with her by my side. We had fun going from lot to lot until we finally found one. The short tree leaned against the fence in the back of the empty lot.

She pointed at the sign resting in the branches that read *free*. "I think it's a sign."

The tree was narrow, and there was a bare spot toward one side. "It's the perfect tree."

She nodded in agreement. "It is."

"This is the one then." I ripped off the sign, hoisting the tree over my shoulder.

"I think this is the craziest thing I've ever done."

"Flying to New York or shopping for a tree on Christmas?"

"All of it."

The craziest thing I ever did was take a chance on her, letting myself fall deeper each day into the best thing that ever happened to me.

We walked for a few blocks when she tipped her head toward a storefront decorated for Christmas. "I hope you have decorations."

I stopped abruptly on the sidewalk. "I don't."

She laughed. "This night is so ridiculous."

I shook my head, laughing with her. "It's not, though. It's the most fun I've ever had."

Her face softened, her smile widening. I'd do anything to keep her this happy.

I dropped the tree by the door of the twenty-four-hour pharmacy. Grabbing her hand to pull her inside, I said, "There has to be something in here we can use."

We walked down the decorations aisle, finding a couple boxes of leftover decorations and Christmas lights.

Checking out, Ava held a box of red bulbs to her chest. "I'll treasure these always."

I leaned down to kiss her upturned face. "Our first Christmas."

"I have a feeling it's going to be the best memory," she added.

It would be the one we'd tell our families and children about one day. I'd never forget the feeling of looking up to find her there.

At my condo, we made a makeshift tree stand out of books and boxes, setting it up in front of the large windows.

Once our lonely tree was decorated, Ava said, "It's beautiful."

I moved behind her, wrapping my arms around her. "Not as beautiful as you."

She leaned against my chest, lifting her head up for a kiss.

Our lips touched. I pulled away slightly to see her face. "I can't believe you're here. It's surreal."

She turned in my arms. "I want to be where you are."

I couldn't think of a better moment to tell her how I felt. "I love you."

"I love you."

My heart was overflowing. There were no other words to express my emotions. I needed to show her. Kissing her, I moved her with me until I fell back on the couch.

She stood between my widespread thighs, lifting her sweater over her head, leaving her in a red lace bra.

"Festive, I see."

"It is, isn't it?" She reached around, unsnapping it.

When it fell off her shoulders, my mind short-circuited. All humor disappeared. "Come here."

"Not yet." She shook her head, unbuttoning her jeans, then pushing them down, then off.

"Ava," I chided.

I needed her close.

She smiled mischievously, hooking her fingers into her thong, then pulling it slowly down her hips. She knew exactly the effect she had on me.

My cock strained against my zipper.

When she was fully naked, she kneeled between my legs.

"Ava, you don't—"

She held a finger up to my lips. "I want to."

I couldn't argue when the best Christmas present I ever had was kneeling naked at my feet. I was going to go with it. She unzipped my pants, pulling them down my hips.

I unbuttoned my shirt, throwing it to the side.

She gripped my cock, tugging it.

I lifted my hips, encouraging her to take it in her mouth.

She licked the tip, swirling her tongue like she was licking an ice cream cone.

Fuck. My head fell back as I lost myself in the feel of her tongue, her hand, and her hair brushing my thighs.

She pumped me with her hand, applying the perfect amount of pressure while alternating licking the head and sucking me deep into her throat.

After a few minutes, I pulled her into my lap. "This was supposed to be romantic."

She smiled down at me, her hair covering us like a blanket. "It's whatever we want it to be."

Nothing today had gone according to plan, but it was us. It was perfect.

I stood, her legs wrapping around my waist. "I'm taking you to bed."

She nibbled my neck, and my cock lodged in her folds. Slowly lowering her down on my bed, I couldn't think of ever feeling closer to anyone.

I brushed her hair back from her face, hovering over her on the bed. "I'm so happy you're here."

"Me, too."

I slowly entered her, never losing eye contact. I interlaced my fingers with hers, pressing her hands into the bed. It was intimate, sweet.

I lowered my head to the crook of her neck, whispering how beautiful she was, how much I loved her. Letting go of her hand, I circled her clit with my fingers, needing her to go over before I did.

"Come for me."

Whimpers escaped at my command.

When she arched up, spasming around my cock, I couldn't hold back. I emptied myself inside her, marveling that she was mine.

Resting heavily on her for a second before moving to my side, I'd never felt more peaceful. I waited until my heartbeat slowed, my breath evening out.

Her gaze stayed on me as if she was waiting for me to speak.

"I've been waiting for someone like you to come into my life and change everything—the way I thought about my life and the future. You've made me see that there are more important things than my job. There's love, family, and experiences."

"I'm not perfect. I might get scared or worried that things aren't going to work out."

"We're going to make mistakes, we're going to have doubts, but I wouldn't want to make them with anyone else."

She kissed me. "Will you play for me?"

"I'll always play for you."

CHAPTER THIRTY
ALEX

I hadn't announced anything to my family about wanting to switch specialties. I wanted to make sure it was a done deal before I told Miles.

I also had a surprise for Ava. I'd invited Ava's dad and Sheila, Juliana and Nolan, Charlie and Laila, my parents, and Savannah and Miles to meet me at the marketplace.

I talked to the owner, Brett Shear. He okayed the get-together and the big reveal I'd planned for Ava.

Ava finished up with her customers, then turned to me. "I'm so ready to get out of here. I'm starving."

I told her we'd get pizza with my family tonight.

"Hey, Dad. Sheila. What are you guys doing here?" Then her eyes widened as Nolan walked in with Charlie on one hip and Laila running ahead. Juliana walked in last with a huge smile on her face.

"I have a surprise for you."

"What are you talking about?" Ava's eyes flicked from her family to me.

I smiled, looking for Savannah. Max, the owner of the Max's Bar & Grill across the street, held the door for her and Sophie as they carried in the package.

WAITING FOR YOU

"What's this?" Ava walked around the display case, coming to stand next to me.

Savannah stopped in front of the display case. "Your bakery is doing so well, we thought you needed a sign."

Ava's friends, and the other shop owners from her business group, Shops on Main, filed in behind Max.

"We think it's *past* time you had a proper sign." Max nodded at the chalkboard that sat next to the display case, with the name Ava's Treats on the top.

Sophie helped Savannah take off the brown paper, revealing the rustic wood sign with *Ava's Treats* in blue letters.

"You didn't have to do this." Ava covered her mouth with her hands.

I wrapped an arm around her shoulders. "Yes, we did."

Max hung the sign on the hooks we'd installed with Brett's permission the night before when the marketplace was closed. Her sign swung lightly before settling in its permanent spot.

"You guys, it's so amazing."

"It looks perfect," Juliana said.

Charlie and Laila had taken one look at the sign and were eyeing the baked goods left in the display case. "Mommy, can we have a cupcake?"

"Not before dinner," Juliana said to the girls, then hugged Ava. "You deserve this. It's amazing what you've done in such a short time."

Ava worked with Remi to add her juice offerings to the menu, hiring extra help to serve customers so she could spend more time doing what she loved most—baking.

"This was your idea?" Ava asked me.

"I might have mentioned it to Savannah, and she ran with the idea."

Savannah nodded. "I had the woman who supplies the new signs in my store custom make this one. I can have another one made if you don't like the color or the font."

Ava shook her head. "I love it. Thank you."

I took photos of Ava smiling broadly in front of her new sign and display case.

Savannah waved Remi over. "Remi, you should be in here, too."

Remi stepped forward, a newspaper in her hands. "Remember when the newspaper reporter and photographer talked to us and took pictures?"

Savannah tipped her head to the side. "Yeah."

"We made the paper."

Ava had been excited when the people from the paper approached her, but they cautioned her that not every story ended up in print.

"We're famous!" Remi held up the paper for her to see the picture. "We'll be online, too."

"I can't believe it."

Max shook his head. "Believe it. Because you've made it—a shop on Main—your picture in the paper. You're the real deal."

Ava held the newspaper to her chest. "I have a shop on Main."

Ava mentioned several times she felt like an impostor at the Shops on Main meetings because she had a booth at the marketplace, not a real storefront.

Max clasped her shoulder. "You're one of us now, but I'm hungry, and I have to get back to my bar."

Everyone chuckled.

I clapped my hands together to get everyone's attention. "We reserved the second-floor room at Max's place. Let's go eat."

The crowd filed out and walked across the street. "I can't believe you and Savannah did this. I was happy with the sign I had."

I helped her clean up, putting the leftovers in boxes to take to the party. "Ava, Max is right. You needed the sign."

She glanced at the sign. "It does look good there."

"Come on. I have another surprise."

"For me?"

I chuckled, helping her carry the bakery boxes across the street. "This one is for my family."

Ava's smile widened. "It's official?"

I nodded. "I can't wait to see Miles's reaction."

We headed up the steps to the spare room Max reserved for parties. There was a bar across one wall, wood floors, and dark wood paneling on the walls.

Max had appetizers and drinks waiting for us. We ordered dinner while talking, laughing, and eating. When the kids were clamoring for dessert, I stood up. "I have one more surprise."

I looked around the room at our friends and family, knowing I'd made the right decision in moving here. "I've decided to change specialties."

Mom's brow furrowed. "Does this mean you won't graduate on time?"

I nodded. "It'll extend my residency a few more months, but it's worth it. I'm switching from the emergency room to pediatrics."

Ava smiled proudly at me.

"You'll still be in New York?" Dad asked.

I'd been in New York the last couple of weeks finalizing the details. My parents thought I was there to finish out my residency.

I exchanged a smile with Ava. "I'll be completing my residency in Annapolis."

Miles popped up from his chair. "Wait. Does this mean you're staying?"

"That's right."

Miles pumped his hand in the air. "We're going to have so many sleepovers."

Juliana reached over to say to him, "I think he'll be staying with Ava."

"Oh, man." Miles pouted.

"How do you feel about camping?" I asked him.

Miles's eyes were round. "Seriously? I'd love to."

"We have a lot of time now that I'm going to be living here."

"We're happy if you are, son," Dad said to me, his arm around Mom.

"I'm very happy," I said to them, my gaze moving to Ava.

Ava stood, wrapping her arms around my waist. I kissed her upturned face.

I heard everyone talking and laughing, but I only had eyes for her. I kissed her upturned lips softly.

"I can't remember a time when I've been this happy."

I leaned over, kissing her again. "The best is yet to come."

I was in the place I was meant to be with everyone I loved. Nothing could be better.

EPILOGUE

ALEX

One Year Later

When a hospital near Annapolis called me about a job, I talked about bringing music to the hospital as a fundraiser, as a comfort to the patients, and more importantly, as a condition of my job. I explained my need to counter the work I did at the hospital with the healing properties of music.

Thankfully, they were receptive to my ideas. Tonight was my first fundraiser to raise money to bring instruments and instruction to children with chronic health conditions. I would give a presentation on my new program and play for everyone. I was nervous yet excited. I'd invited my parents, not leaving any room for them to dissuade me from my cause. I wanted them to see how well the program was being received in the hospital and the community.

I was so happy that Ava made me see that I could meld my work with my music.

"I'm so excited for you," Ava said as she got out of the car in a sparkly red evening gown.

The event was black tie, so I wore a tux. I pulled my cello

case out of the trunk. "This never would have happened without your encouragement."

"I saw you with Braden at the hospital. I think you would have done something similar. You probably would have given them the instruments and taught them yourself."

I chuckled. "Probably."

It was Ava who saw the big picture and wanted to raise money so that every kid who wanted to learn an instrument could.

Her bakery at the marketplace had become so profitable she wasn't able to manage the B & B anymore. She still provided the baked goods, but focused mainly on selling items at her bakery and filling orders for parties. Her network of shop owners on Main Street who met frequently to discuss business had become a tight group of friends.

I left my cello case by the makeshift stage at the front of the room, then led Ava around, introducing her to the donors for the program and my colleagues. We ate dinner, and then it was time for me to make my speech. I was nervous, but my mind was already on my plans for later this evening.

I stood at the podium, pressing the button to start the PowerPoint presentation I'd created. The first picture was of me playing with my elementary school band. "I've played the cello since my fourth-grade band director convinced me to do it. He needed a cello player, and I couldn't decide which instrument to play. The first time I ran the bow over the strings, I knew I'd picked the right one. I loved the sound. I craved the way it made me feel.

"I didn't always sound good. I have to apologize to my parents. The first few years were pretty squeaky." I paused while the crowd laughed.

I moved to the next slide, which was a series of pictures of me performing.

"As I improved, I realized how powerful listening to music was for others." I met Ava's eyes. She was the first one who made me realize that. "One song can improve someone's mood. I've played in Times Square. I've played in the subways of New York. It was fun, and people enjoyed it, but nothing compared to playing for the patients and guests at the hospitals I've worked at.

"When I was working on the pediatric unit during my residency, a very special patient asked if I could teach him to play. I got him a cello, sheet music to start, and referred him to a teacher after showing him the basics. He wasn't able to run and play like other kids, but he could learn a new skill, one that would improve his mood and his mind. Maybe even heal him."

I switched to the next slide. The one that showed the kids who'd already received their instruments, practicing in the activity room of my unit.

"At times, I felt like I had to choose between music and medicine, but with the help of a very special person," I smiled at Ava, "I realized I could do both. It's important to show kids that they can love music and have other interests. They can be a doctor and a musician. They can be a teacher but still play in a band on the weekend. They don't have to choose one or the other. In fact, one helps the other." I clicked on the screen, showing the improved test scores of kids who learned how to play music at a young age.

"The benefits of music on a child's developing brain are widely known. Currently, the foundation aids kids who are undergoing long-term treatment at local hospitals, but I'd like to expand it to other hospitals through the state. I'm so thankful for those of you who've donated your old instruments, music, money, and time to make the foundation a reality."

I clicked on the final slide—the one that revealed the foundation's name—St. James Music Foundation.

Applause broke out.

When it died down, I introduced the quartet of string

musicians and their chosen piece of music for the night. "The stars of the show want to play for you tonight."

I sat down next to Ava so I could enjoy the concert with her.

She leaned over to kiss my cheek. "That was amazing."

I turned my face to kiss her lips lightly. "It's all because of you."

Dad reached over, clasping my shoulder. "I'm proud of you, son."

I turned, thanking him, then glanced at my mother, who had tears in her eyes. I was doing what I loved but it was nice to have my parents' approval.

When the concert was done, I shook hands with those coming up to offer their support and congratulate me. As soon as I could get away, I grabbed my cello case and Ava's coat, leading her outside.

I followed the lit path snaking around the building to the water.

"Alex, where are you taking me?" She tried to stop me with a hand on my elbow.

"Just a little farther." The breeze from the water was chilly.

"A little farther for what?"

I sat on a bench facing the water, pulling out my cello. "I wanted to play just for you."

I patted the bench next to me. She sat, relaxed now that she thought she knew what was going on.

I played "Pachelbel Canon" for her. When the final note was played, she said, "It's beautiful, but isn't that a wedding song?"

"It is, but it's also one of my favorites. I needed it for this." I'd recorded me playing, so I hit the button to replay it, resting my cello against the bench, and I moved to one knee.

Her breath hitched. "Alex, what are—"

I pulled the red velvet box out of my pocket, my heart threatening to pound out of my chest. "I promised I'd always play for you. But I want to make a different promise. I vow to always love you, to take care of you, to think of you first before anyone else."

Tears sparkled in her eyes as she covered her mouth with her hand.

Opening the box, the diamond reflected the lights. "Ava, will you marry me?"

My voice shook. I'd never been more nervous, not even playing my cello at the subway in front of strangers or in the middle of Times Square. Her answer meant everything to me.

She cupped my cheeks with her hands, kissing me.

Pulling away, I asked, "Is that a yes?"

I'd been so nervous leading up to today. Ava thought it was the event itself, but it was this. I didn't think she'd say no, but I wasn't positive.

"Of course, I want to marry you."

Air whooshed out of my lungs. I pulled her into my lap, infusing the kiss with everything I was feeling—love, happiness, contentment.

The lapping of the water on the shore was the only other sound.

She was worth everything I went through to make my way back to her. A small part of me knew she meant something even back when she was listening to me play on the steps as a kid. I just didn't know how special until we ran into each other again as adults. Now I saw her clearly. She was everything to me. Everything I didn't even know I wanted.

"I was stuck in New York. I thought I was on the right path but I wasn't. I'm so thankful I returned to Maryland for my residency. It led me to you. It made me realize, I'd merely been waiting for you." I brushed her hair back from her face.

Her eyes were bright with tears. "That's the most beautiful thing anyone's ever said to me."

"Well, you've just promised me a lifetime, so it won't be the last."

She smiled. "That sounds amazing."

"As long as we're together, it will be."

I kissed her, hearing the lapping of the water against the shore, ignoring the cold wind seeping through my jacket. Having her with me was the only warmth I needed.

BONUS EPILOGUE
AVA

Six Months Later

I watched in disbelief as Alex missed the turn. "You passed Juliana and Nolan's house."

He just glanced over, smiling at me. "I know."

"We're supposed to be meeting them there for Charlie and Laila's birthday party."

His smile widened. "I have a surprise for you."

My heart skipped a beat. Did he know? I'd thrown out the tests, taking the bag to the curb so he wouldn't see the results accidentally. I'd planned to tell him after the girls' party.

He reached over to pat my knee. "Relax. It's a good surprise."

I couldn't imagine what he'd be surprising me with out here. It was a quiet road, the houses spaced apart, most backing to the water.

A few minutes later, he pulled down a long drive.

"Alex—you didn't—" Why were we here?

He smiled, grabbing my hand. "Come on. I want to show you something."

He guided me around the house to the back of the property that faced the water.

"Is this someone's house?" I glanced nervously at the home.

"It is. But don't worry, we have permission to be here." He turned me to face him.

"Okay."

"How do you feel about living on the water?"

I looked out over the water. There was a long dock with a boat at the end. I imagined myself sitting at the end of the dock, dangling my feet in the water, enjoying the sunsets. Remembering my surprise, I covered my stomach with my hand. One day, we'd have a little one running and jumping off the end. "I'd love it."

Blinking back tears, I looked up at him. He was looking at me with so much love and affection. "I bought it."

"You bought it. This house?"

He gestured around us. "The house. The boat. It's ours."

"Are you serious?"

Looking uncertain for the first time, he asked, "Did you want to pick it out? Juliana helped—she said you'd love it. But if you don't, we can sell it, get something you'd like."

I threw my arms around his neck. "No! I love it. I love you."

He kissed me.

I pulled back slightly. "But I have something to tell you."

His forehead wrinkled. "What is it?"

Joy surged through me. "I'm—we're pregnant."

He stilled. "Are you—are you sure?"

We'd talked about trying as soon as we got married, but since our wedding was in a few more months, we decided to forego birth control. I nodded, tears threatening to spill over.

He lifted me, swinging me around in a circle. He slowed, lowering my feet to the ground. He dropped his forehead to rest against mine. "I'm so happy."

"I can't wait to move in, to start our life together."

"We've already started. We're making our life together."

"I like that."

"I love it. I love you." He lowered to his knees, touching my stomach. "I love our baby."

He kissed my stomach, looking up at me.

Tears spilled unchecked down my cheeks. I didn't see how life got any better than this. To think I'd marry my childhood crush. That we'd be living our dreams together. It was unthinkable a few short years ago, and now it was my reality—our reality.

He stood, wiping the tears away.

"You have keys to this place?"

He nodded.

"Show me our house." He took my hand, leading me up the steps to the deck overlooking the water and inside to the huge windows showcasing the view.

It was hard to believe it was ours. That he was mine. But he had a lifetime to show me.

I hope you loved Ava and Alex's story!

Savannah and Ethan's story is next in *Fighting Chance*.

I'm not bitter that Savannah St. James rejected me in high school. It's her cluttered storefront I have a problem with. Still, it's hard to stay mad at her when she's more beautiful than I remember and her son keeps finding new ways to sneak over to my hardware store every chance he gets. The little guy brings us together even as our pasts keep us apart.

Read *Fighting Chance*.

BOOKS BY LEA COLL

Annapolis Harbor Series

Hooked on You

Only with You

Lost without You

Perfect for You

Crazy for You

Falling for You

Waiting for You

Second Chance Harbor Series

Fighting Chance

One More Chance

Lucky Chance

Mountain Haven Series

Infamous Love

Adventurous Love

Impulsive Love

All I Want Series

Choose Me

Be with Me

Burn for Me

Trust in Me

Stay with Me

Take a Chance on Me

Download two free novellas, *Swept Away* and *Worth the Risk*, when you sign up for her newsletter.

To learn more about her books, please visit her website.

ACKNOWLEDGMENTS

I have to thank cellist, Iain Forrest for performing at my daughter's recital this past summer. His performance blew my mind. I'd never seen an electric cello before, or even heard of a looper. I got chills listening to him, and was immediately inspired to write this book.

My children love his music and frequently request that I play it for them. I was so hopeful my daughter would play the cello this year, but she chose the saxophone.

Bringing joy to others whether it's through music or words is a beautiful thing.

Iain's stage name is Eyeglasses and you can listen to his music on YouTube.

I'm so grateful to my cousin, Meredith Hill, D.O., FACEP who answered all of my questions about residency, and life as an emergency room doctor. I couldn't have written Alex's story without her help.

ABOUT THE AUTHOR

Lea Coll worked as a trial attorney for over ten years. Now she stays home with her three children, plotting stories while fetching snacks and running them back and forth to activities. She enjoys the freedom of writing romance after years of legal writing.

She currently resides in Maryland with her family.

Get two free novellas when you sign up for Lea's newsletter.

Check out Lea's books on her website.

Made in the USA
Middletown, DE
16 January 2022